Yelloweye

Devon Layne

Yelloweye

An Erotic Paranormal Romance Western Adventure

ELDER ROAD BOOKS
BELLEVUE, WA

Preface

THIS STORY is about three souls in five bodies who set out to save Mother Earth. Because it moves through both time and space, I want to point out a couple of terms that will be helpful as the story progresses.

Now-time: The twenty-first century. The now-time birth of the protagonists is in 2001 and the story ends when they are 22 years old.

Before-time: The nineteenth century. The before-time birth of the protagonists is in 1858 and they step out of time in approximately 1872 with a brief foray back into before-time in 1874.

Oxėse: Cheyenne word for elsewhere or other place. When the protagonists step out of time in 1872, they go to *Oxėse*. It is a place closely resembling nineteenth century America, if Europeans had never arrived. But time in this place is meaningless. The protagonists dwell there for as long as necessary to prepare for the great battle. In *Oxėse*, all time is the same.

I have used many other Cheyenne words, some of them correctly. Please remember that this is fiction. It is not a history and certainly not intended to either appropriate Cheyenne culture or denigrate its rich heritage. In the protagonists' before-time lives, they were members of what would become a lost tribe of the Cheyenne, the People Who Follow the Owl, referred to in my limited Cheyenne as *Méstaa'e-vo'ėstaneme*. If you are interested in the fine points of pronunciation, I suggest you check the English/Cheyenne dictionary listed below.

I couldn't always find words that directly related to the concepts that were being expressed, but still needed a word. I used several reputable sources, including the excellent English/Cheyenne dictionary of the Chief Dull Knife College in Lame Deer, MT (http://www.cdkc.edu/ cheyennedictionary/index-english/index.htm). There were times when I altered words or combined them to get the concept I wanted, like *Heove-'éxané*, the literal translation of Yelloweye.

I have also adapted some Native American myths, using languages that are taxonomically similar (Algonquian). I have, for example, adopted *gray wolf* from the Pawnee. While this story has parallels in many cultures, I found this one the easiest to blend with the characters I had created. Hence, proto-wolf is named *Manèstóhó'néhe* or Creator Wolf. I have, with greatest respect for the original stories, also referred to the legend of Sweet Medicine, the ancestor who gave the Cheyenne their laws, the four arrows, and other prophecies.

I hope you find the story enjoyable, and offer this very limited glossary of Cheyenne or near-Cheyenne words to help as you read.

Glossary of Cheyenne Words

Animals

Heove-'éxané: Yelloweye, the Owl.

Méstaa'e: Owl, harbinger of death.

Méstaa'e-vo'èstaneme: Owl Family or People Who Follow the Owl.

Mo'ohta mée'e: Blackfeather, the Raven.

Aénohe: Winter hawk, Redtail.

Hó'nehe: Wolf.

Manèstóhó'néhe: Creator Wolf.

Ma'èhóóhe: Red fox.

Mo'éhno'ha: Horse, Indian pony as opposed to wild horses.

Nàhahévo'ha: Wild horse.

Wapiti: Elk.

Ésevone: Buffalo.

Vóhpàhtse: White Mouth, the Grizzly.

Popóhpoévèsémo'éhe: Moose.

People

Ho'néené'šeohtsévá'e: Wolf Riding Woman, Caitlin's Cheyenne name.

Ho'néemé'eōhtse: Wolf Rising, Phile's Cheyenne name.

Ho'néhenótàxeo'o: Wolf Warriors, one of the names for Phile and Caitlin.

Héstahke Ho'néheo'o: Twin Wolves, a common way for the People to refer to Phile and Caitlin.

Vé'otsé'e: Warpath woman, a descriptive name sometimes applied to Caitlin.

Tsétsèhéstáhese: The People. Cheyenne.

Ho'enáséé'e: Earth Sister, Mandy's Cheyenne name.

Ho'evótse: Whiteman.

Vé'ho'e: Modern Cheyenne term for whiteman. (Whiteman is typically a single word.)

He'évánó'èstse: Wise woman.

Ma'heónèhetane: Holy man, shaman, medicine man.

Heséeotá'e: Medicine woman; herb woman.

Náhko'éehe: Mother.

Náhko'e: Mommy.

Kàsóéso: Little boy, term of endearment. Used before an official name is given.

He'éka'èškónèhéso: Little girl, term of endearment. Used before an official name is given.

Naéhame: My husband, mate.

Nàhtse'eme: My wife. Lit: my-woman

Na-mé'oo'o: Sweetheart, lover.

Hestàhkeho: Boy and Girl twins.

Tsévéhonevèstse: Chief.

Námèšeme: Grandfather.

Motsé'eóeve: Sweet Medicine Standing, Sweet Root Standing. The Cheyenne prophet commonly called Sweet Medicine. He organized the structure of Cheyenne society, their military or war societies led by prominent warriors, their system of legal justice, and the Council of Forty-four peace chiefs meeting to deliberate at regular tribal gatherings, centered around the Sun Dance. Before his death, he predicted the coming of the horse, cow, whiteman, etc. to the Cheyenne. He received the *Maahótse*, a bundle of Sacred Arrows which they carried when they waged tribal-level war.

The Earth and things sacred

Nóváhe: Sacred medicine. Archaic old term for a deity.

Ho'e: The land.

Nèške'emāne: Grandmother Earth.

Oxèse: Elsewhere; other place. A place outside time.

Nésemoo'o: Spirit guide.

Ho'e-momóonáotaovóho: Domination, dominion

Mo'xóhtse: Arrowhead.

Onéhavo'e: Drum.

Noahá-vose ("giving hill") or *Náhkóhe-vose* ("bear hill"): Cheyenne name for Bear Butte, the place where *Ma'heo'o* (God) imparted to Sweet Medicine, a Cheyenne prophet, the knowledge from which the Cheyenne derive their religious, political, social, and economic customs.

Cast:

THE STORY IS set in the 2020s, but the main characters (Phile and Caitlin) talk about living simultaneously in the 2000s (born in 2001) and in the mid-1800s.

1860s-mid70s:

Wolf Rising: Alternate identity of Phile. (1858-disappearance in 1873. Reappeared in *Oxése*.) Referred to as the Twin Wolves or sometimes the Dark Wolves.

Wolf Riding Woman: Alternate identity of Caitlin. (1858-disappearance in 1873. Reappeared in *Oxése*.) Referred to as the Twin Wolves or sometimes the Dark Wolves.

Miranda Lewis: (1849-1873) Host of the 21st century Laramie Bell when she was time traveling (*Blackfeather*). After she died in 1873 Laramie hosted her in the future (21st century).

Jason Wardlaw: (1847-1873) Host of the 21st century Kyle Bell when he was time traveling (*Blackfeather*). After he died in 1873 Kyle hosted him in the future (21st century).

Miranda and Jason are the great-great-great-great-grandparents of the 21st century Ramie, Kyle, Phile, and Caitlin.

Katie Forster: (1851-~1875) Companion to Miranda in the journey to Wyoming, Ramie's lover when she was in Miranda and third party in Miranda and Jason's marriage (*Blackfeather*).

White Horse: (~1842-1873) Jason's Cheyenne companion educated in Boston and working with him as an interpreter in the cavalry. White Horse appears in *Blackfeather* and is mentioned in *Redtail*.

Theresa Ranae Bell: (1852-1904) Miranda's stepsister and companion in Wyoming, ran off to marry White Horse. Theresa plays a prominent role in both *Redtail* and *Blackfeather*.

> *White Horse and Theresa are also the great-great-great-great-grandparents of the 21st century Ramie, Kyle, Phile, and Caitlin.*

Late 1880s

Kyle (Redtail) Wardlaw: (1873-1892) Host of Cole Bell (Pa) when he was time traveling (*Redtail*). Died young, but impregnated Both Laramie Wyoming Bell (the first) while Cole was in him, and Kat Tangeman, to whom he was engaged, just before he died. Son of Miranda and Jason.

Laramie Wyoming Bell (the first): (1873-1929) Daughter of White Horse and Theresa who fell in love with Cole when he was hosted by Kyle.

> *These two characters are also the great-great-great-grandparents of the 21st century Ramie, Kyle, Phile, and Caitlin.*

Kat Tangeman: (1871-1927) School teacher who was engaged to Kyle Wardlaw and became pregnant. When Kyle died, she married Arthur Alexander and her son "Artie" Alexander was actually Kyle Wardlaw's son.

> *Hence, Kyle and Kat became the great-great-great-grandparents of Ramie and Phile on the Alexander (Mary Beth's) side of the family.*

Katie Lynn (Caitlin) Forster: (1873-1889) Host of Genieve in *Redtail* who died young during an abortion in a Laramie brothel. She is the daughter of Jason and Katie.

> *(Three generations intervene.)*

Late 20th century

Cole Alexander Bell: (1976-) The main character/narrator of *Redtail* who traveled to before-time to inhabit Kyle Wardlaw. Known to the family as Pa.

Ashley Brewer Bell: (1975-) College classmate of Cole who married him during the Range Wars (*Redtail*). Mother of Kyle and Caitlin, by Cole. Known to the family as Mom Ash.

Mary Beth Alexander Bell: (1973-) Cole's first cousin (his mother and her father were siblings) who joined Cole and Ashley in their marriage (*Redtail*). Mother of Ramie (Laramie Wyoming Bell II) and Phile by Cole. Known to the family as Mom Mar.

Genieve Murrieta: (1976-1998) Cole's high school girlfriend who had a short duration as a time traveler hosted by Caitlin Forster (*Redtail*). Married Joe Teine.

Joe Teine: (~1970-1996) Villain in *Redtail* and time traveler who was hosted by Sheriff Cal Despain of Laramie in the 1880s.

Philemon Morgan: (~1919-2003) A time traveler hosted by prospector Bill Campbell who established a line of inheritance for Cole in the future (*Redtail*).

21st Century: The Last Generation:

Laramie "Ramie" Wyoming Bell (the second): (1997-) Daughter and oldest child of Mary Beth and Cole. Becomes a time-traveler and is hosted by Miranda (*Blackfeather*). When Miranda dies in 1873, Ramie hosts her in the 21st century. Ramie was given 'the box' by the kids on her 22nd birthday.

Kyle Redtail Bell: (1998-) Son of Cole and Ashley. Becomes a time-traveler and is hosted by Jason Wardlaw (*Blackfeather*). When Jason dies in 1873, Kyle hosts him in the 21st century.

Aubrey Diaz Bell: (1998-) Kyle and Ramie's wife (*Blackfeather*). Mother of Theresa Miranda Bell and Katherine Ranae Bell (*Yelloweye*). Theresa was born on Caitlin's 19th birthday.

Philemon "Phile" Morgan Bell: (2001-) Son of Cole and Mary Beth (*Blackfeather* and *Yelloweye*). Phile simultaneously inhabits two bodies. In before-time he is Wolf Rising (1858-disappearance in 1873). Referred to as the Twin Wolves or White Wolves. One of the principal narrators of *Yelloweye*.

Caitlin Forster Bell: (2001-) Daughter of Cole and Ashley (*Blackfeather* and *Yelloweye*). Caitlin simultaneously inhabits two bodies. In before-time she is Wolf Riding Woman. (1858-disappearance in 1873). Referred to as the Twin Wolves or White Wolves. One of the principal narrators of *Yelloweye*.

Mandy "Earth Sister" Stevens: (2001-) Girlfriend/wife to the two people and four bodies above (*Yelloweye*). Also referred to as the Voice of the Twin Wolves. Granddaughter of Merv Longsteer.

Merv Longsteer: Old Cheyenne shaman and drum maker who owns a trading post in Laramie (*Blackfeather* and *Yelloweye*). Is Mandy's grandfather. Assists in educating Caitlin and Phile in the old ways and in drum making.

John Little Elk: A Cheyenne drum maker who becomes the missionary of the White Wolves and Earth Sister.

Later on (last chapter):

Stig Wolfe: The now-time manifestation of the combined Phile/Wolf Rising.

Rita Wolfe: The now-time manifestation of the combined Caitlin/Wolf Riding Woman.

Talia Wolfe: Adopted name of Mandy Stevens as wife to Stig and Rita.

Colin Wolfe: (2023-) Oldest child of the Wolfe family. Biologically, he is the son of Wolf Rising and Caitlin.

Avis Wolfe: (2023-) Second child of the Wolfe family. Biologically, she is the daughter of Phile and Wolf Riding Woman.

Beth Ann Wolfe: (2023-) Third child of the Wolfe family. Biologically she is the daughter of Phile and Mandy.

Contents

Yelloweye

1
Birth and Confusion

The Family

SHIVERS RAN through Ramie and gooseflesh raised on her neck and arms as her hands stroked the polished wooden box. It had sat untouched for three and a half years as far as Ramie knew.

"It's not good to keep them together," Caitlin said as she handed Ramie the key to the box. *"I'll keep the box safe. You take the key."*

"It's a Schrödinger's box," Phile added. *"The cat is both dead and alive until you open the box. One day, your need to know will outweigh your fear that you'll find a dead cat."*

"When you make that decision, come and get the box," Caitlin concluded.

Her bratty brother and sister had been gone for a year now. They disappeared right after the family's celebration of their twenty-first birthday. Everyone went to bed that night just like always. In the morning, Caitlin, Phile, and their two horses were gone. Even that didn't trigger alarms. It wasn't unusual for the pair to disappear for a few weeks or even a month and then show up back at the ranch as if nothing had happened.

But when a few days stretched to a few weeks and then a few months a dark cloud seemed to settle over the ranch. The two kids had been a source of chaos on the ranch, but after their disappearance, worry and then despair had permeated the family.

IT CAST A pall over the celebration of Theresa Miranda Bell's third birthday. The elder of the third generation living on the ranch had been born on Caitlin's nineteenth birthday, a day after Phile's. The three-year-old didn't know there was a problem. She happily accepted the wagon, the dolls, and the toy horses as her due. After all, for the past few months,

1

her position as princess of the household had been usurped by baby Katherine Renee.

The family loved Aubrey's little critters. Of all of them, Miranda, riding quietly in Ramie's mind, was the most affected.

I never even got to hold my baby. Oh, my poor Kyle. How can your parents stand not having their children in their arms? How can you stand it, Ramie? How can you stand thinking you'll never have a child with our husband?

"I think about it," Ramie answered. "We'd be risking everything. But the more I look at those little ones, the more I'm willing to take the risk."

It was so sweet of Aubrey to give our daughters family names. It is like my stepsister and our lover still live in them.

"And you," Ramie added. "Our darling wife is as committed to the family as our husband. The names seem to be part of the land we dwell on."

Ashley and Mary Beth are distraught. Cole is hardly better. It is time to open the box.

"It is," Ramie sighed. Cole looked at her and opened his arms. His daughter hugged him.

"We all miss them," Cole said.

"I have something, Pa," Ramie said. "They gave it to me on my golden birthday. Caitlin kept it in her room so I wouldn't be unnecessarily tempted to open it." Ramie drew the key from beneath her shirt, held by the leather thong next to the wolf's teeth that had never been taken from around her neck.

"Tempted?" Cole asked quietly.

"It's a locked box, Pa," Ramie said. "Phile said our need to know had to outweigh the possibility that it would contain a dead cat."

"Schrödinger. Taught you kids all about that, whether you were time traveling or not."

"Are we ready, Pa?"

"Look at your moms," he said. "At me. We've aged ten years in the past year, not knowing what happened to our children. Do you think that's what is in the box?"

"Knowing the brats, they might have literally left a dead cat in it," Ramie snorted. "I think we need to know."

"Get it."

Ramie held the box in her arms almost as lovingly as Aubrey cradled their baby. They joined Moms and Pa in the ranch office. Pa was in his big chair by the fireplace and held out his arms for his granddaughter. Aubrey surprised him by plopping herself in his lap. He laughed and held both baby and daughter-in-law. Theresa ran to her grandmothers.

Kyle paused behind Ramie and put his hands on her shoulders.

"What have you got?" Ashley asked.

"Schrödinger's box," Ramie answered. "Caitlin and Phile gave it to me three and a half years ago. They said it was for when the need to know…"

"And you've been holding onto it for a year since they… left? You never once thought that we should investigate this?" Ashley demanded.

"We won't be able change anything once the box is open," Kyle said. "We always hoped there would be something we could do. The box holds the answer."

"You think," Mary Beth said.

"We decided it should be a family decision whether we open it or not," Ramie said.

"We who?" Cole asked. Baby Theresa was trying to reach his glasses and he was catching her little fingers in his lips. She giggled.

"Miranda and me. They gave it to me."

"So, open it," Ashley said. Her impatience showed.

"Mom Mar?" Ramie said. Mary Beth put her arm around her sister wife and held her, then nodded. "Pa?"

Cole sighed. He patted Aubrey on her rump and gently pushed her and the baby toward Kyle. Mary Beth handed Theresa off to Kyle and the two wives piled onto Cole in his chair.

"Open it," he said as he embraced his wives.

Ramie sat between Kyle and Aubrey and fished the key from her shirt. It was such a flimsy little lock that she could have twisted and broken it in her fingers. It was such a delicate barrier between her and the truth about Caitlin and Phile, yet there was something significant about inserting the key and turning it. The box opened and she lifted the sheaf of paper from the box. She could see the top page was in Phile's handwriting. It would take a while to read this aloud, but no member of the family wanted to be left behind in the discovery.

She took a breath and began.

Phile: Entering the World

I REMEMBER BEING born.

I was eight years old. It was summer and Caitlin and I had gone out to the pond in the north pasture. I don't remember what we were playing. We just liked to run and whoop and holler. Seemed like we always had a lot of energy. Of course, being a hot July day, we ran ourselves exhausted, dove into the pond, then plopped in the grass and went to sleep.

I thought I was dreaming, but I couldn't wake up. Then I realized that I was awake and Cait was crushing my hand in hers. She looked panicked, but I couldn't reach out to her. I had this other scene in my head that I was seeing—not just seeing. I could feel everything that was happening.

I didn't want to be born. My consciousness was telling me that it was nice and I should stay where I was, but I was being pushed and I just panicked.

I don't think babies are supposed to remember being born. They have to forget that shit in order to survive. But I remember everything about it like it happened a minute ago.

I hated my mother. She'd given me everything I needed and now she didn't want me any longer. She pushed and strained and forced me out where it was cold and light and rough and hurt. Why didn't she want me? We'd been so close. I cried.

Women I didn't know took me away from her. I couldn't understand any of the gibberish they were speaking. If they'd just speak English, I'd know what was happening. They cut my lifeline to my mother and I felt her blood cease to flow in my veins. I was alone.

Voices I couldn't understand spoke softly all around me. This was what it was like to be a baby? Hearing and thinking, but unable to understand anything? I was wrapped in a soft skin. I tried to apply the word blanket to it, but rejected the thought. Skin. It was almost like having a person wrapped around me. Then nothing. I thought they'd forgotten me.

I was scooped up in a woman's arms—the softness told me woman—and taken to another place. It was dark and I kept trying to see what kind of place I was in. I expected a hospital, but a cool breeze told me I was outside. Then back inside. My eyes didn't work right. It was like waking up in the morning with your eyes full of sleep gunk but being unable to wipe them.

And then there was real skin against me. I could feel a heart beating and I could smell nice warm milk. Instinct took over and I started sucking like mad. It tasted so good and it was like mother was taking me in her arms again. Only it wasn't *my* mother.

That's when my eyes started to clear and I looked straight into the eyes of Caitlin. I could see her in two realities. My eight-year-old sister was sitting next to me outside in front of the pond, scared and crying. My infant sister looked at me across the breast of the mother feeding us. We reached for each other and when our hands touched, I finally knew everything would be okay. As long as I had Caitlin, everything would be okay.

Caitlin: Loving

I LOVE PHILE. I've loved him since the day I was laid in a crib beside him. No. I don't remember that day. I remember the day we were born, eight years later, when I reached over and took his hand at my mother's breast. He's sweet and he keeps me from being… well, worse than I am. For a wild Indian, he gets real sentimental sometimes. I guess I take after Mom Ash. She would never talk about that emotional stuff. I know she feels it, though. And I feel it, too. I just thought that before I start my part of the story, I should make sure you know for a fact. My spirit is bound with my brother's. Our hearts beat as one.

That first week after we were born… It still seems strange to talk about something that happened when we were eight years old and we have all the memories of. Suddenly, we had Mom Mar and Mom Ash who we saw every day and had lived with for eight years, and we had another mommy who held our little infant bodies in her arms and let us suck milk out of her teats. It was impossible not to bond to her. We didn't want to not bond with her. She was our safety in the strange world we'd just been born into. She was food and warmth and comfort. And little cooing sounds and singing.

Don't know if you remember how sick we were that week. Delirious, I think Mom Mar said. From my perspective, I'd have said disoriented. Something was happening in my brain because the world I'd always known was continuing in one half while the other half was getting a whole new data stream from a different me. And it was almost like watching a DVD at 4x. You know, that fast forward thing. And neither Phile nor I could stand to be apart from each other, even when it was so disorienting that we threw up.

We'd often slept with each other. Seemed like he always knew when I was upset over something and would come padding into my room so I could hold him. Worked the other way, too, but I learned not to go wandering into his room since he shared with Kyle. If he got upset, he just came to me. It was funny that Mom Mar insisted we share a room that week so we wouldn't infect anybody else. It was what got us through the first wave of adapting.

Phile: Mommy

IT WAS REALLY confusing. Caitlin and I would lie in the bed in her room here at the ranch, and squeeze our eyes shut trying to just see one life instead of two. It was obvious that other life wasn't in the here and now. While our mommy was warm and loving, we didn't understand anything she said and conditions were kind of primitive.

"Are you sucking on a tit?" I asked Caitlin as we lay in bed. "Are we okay?"

"I think so," Cait said. "Phile, we just got born someplace else. What's happening?"

"I can… I can taste the milk in my mouth. When I look at you here in my room, I can see baby you sucking away beside me. And I know it's you, but…"

"Yeah. You don't look like your baby pictures. You're dark with black hair and brown eyes."

"So are you. Are we twins?"

"I don't think so. There was no one inside with me. I don't like to think about being born. But at least when I got out they stuck me right on Mommy's tit. I was so scared. Then you got there and I knew it would be okay," Cait said.

"Someone took me away as soon as I got out. I was wrapped in a skin kind of thing and they brought me to you. That's not like normal, is it? Caitlin? Do you think something is wrong with my mommy?"

It was the middle of the night in real time on the same day we'd been out by the pond, but it seemed like time was moving a lot faster in the… We decided to call it 'before-time' eventually, though that didn't happen right away. We were living some time and place that was long ago. But in a week or so of life in before-time, we'd still only seen Cait's mommy and not mine. I felt this deep sadness and sense of loss when I thought of my birth mother. I knew… I just knew she was gone and I'd never see her. And that kind of bled over into now-time and I was afraid I'd never see my mom here either.

"I have to go see Mom Mar!" I blurted out.

"Yeah. Let's go."

I don't reckon we'd busted in on Moms and Pa since we were little, but Cait and I crawled right into bed with them and hugged them all night. They were another anchor to what little reality we could grasp.

Moms weren't sure what to do with two thumb-sucking eight-year-olds plastered against them when they woke up. Pa mumbled something about needing a bigger bed and crawled out from the middle. Mom Ash and Mom Mar tucked us back in bed.

With the initial shock fading, we slept a lot that week. I remember a doctor came out. I don't know what he thought, but we just stayed in bed and slept most of the time. That helped because before-time was moving a lot faster than now-time and we could almost convince ourselves it was a dream if we were asleep. But we'd wake up and look at each other and still be able to see what was happening in before-time. It never stopped.

By the end of that week in bed, we were almost a year old in before-time. We could walk to the kitchen in now-time without our baby selves wanting to crawl. It was like growing a new arm or something and having to get used to it doing stuff our regular two arms didn't know about. But the physical disorientation settled down. We'd decided we were just crazy.

Caitlin: Meeting Yelloweye

MOMS WATCHED US like hawks all the time and we couldn't get any privacy so we could talk about what was going on. Seemed like things slowed up a little in before-time when we were awake in now-time. When we slept in now-time, before-time sped up. But we were learning things. Words. We had to be careful with our little before-time bodies that we didn't try to do something that our eight-year-old bodies could do. But we learned quickly that if we were really quiet, we could whisper to each other in English in before-time and people would just think we were talking baby talk. We started doing the same thing in now-time to talk in the language of the people. Moms shook their heads and said something about us talking gibberish.

We were lucky it was summer. We did our chores in the morning and lay low the rest of the day. When you look at them, you think babies don't do much but suck and shit, but these two babies were learning so much our heads hurt. All the time. We knew we were crazy, even though we didn't know the words for it. We were relearning everything while we were still trying to learn ourselves.

We figured out that we were Indians. We were in a tribe and on the move. *Náhko'éehe*, our mother, had little time to recover from childbirth before we were carried together on her back as we marched. We moved a day or two and then camped for a week or more. The first time Phile called our mother 'mama' she didn't respond at all. It took a while to figure out that the word she used was *Náhko'e*.

Being able to talk to each other in now-time and learn together helped speed things up and it started to look like we were psychic. When school started, it was almost like cheating. There was this one question on an arithmetic test that I had trouble with. The question just didn't make sense. I turned to Phile in our before-time and asked him about it. He said I missed the addition sign and to do that. In our classroom, I looked at the paper and made the correction. He didn't give me the answer, exactly, but he was always better at arithmetic than me. I did the same thing for him in spelling.

It worked the other way, too. *Náhko'e* said something to Phile that he didn't understand and was about to get smacked. We were walking out in the pasture here while we were setting up camp there and I told him what to say. He did it right away and didn't get punished.

SOMEHOW, WE MADE it through that whole first year of now-time and were relieved when school was finally out. In before-time, we were about five years old. The People—that's what our tribe called themselves—avoided us most of the time. While our *Náhko'e* continued to love and care for us, the others thought we were some kind of spirit children. An old man in the tribe we called Grandfather made sure we had food and *Náhko'e* often tended his fire. I suppose it was because we learned so damned fast. I mean, we had an eight-year head start on most babies. We had a lot to learn about life in the village, but we knew a lot already and if we didn't understand something, we could look it up on the Internet.

That first day of summer vacation, Ramie and Kyle went off riding their black horses and came back with Ramie all doubled over with cramps. She'd started her period and made like it was some kind of disaster. Not like every woman in the history of the world hadn't done it before her. But the Moms were all sympathetic and taking care of her. Pa took Kyle out for a ride and for the first time in a year, we weren't being watched.

We made a couple sandwiches and grabbed a can of soda and just walked away.

We didn't go very far. We never intended to run away or anything. We just wanted to be away from where everyone was watching us all the time. And that meant heading down to the pond, stripping off all our clothes and diving in. The water was still damn cold, but we didn't care. We were naked and excited to be out of school. We could run and be wild as we wanted and no one would ever know or care. And our before-time selves were right in sync with us. Something was going on in the village and we just wandered off to play in the creek.

And that's what brought us to Yelloweye. He scared the shit out of us when we first saw him. He was standing on a log just where the creek enters the pond. We were nine years old and barely four feet tall. That owl sitting on a log was looking us right in the eye.

And he was there in before-time, too. Talk about little! That big old owl towered over our five-year-old selves. We were terrified.

9

I grabbed Phile's hand and started tugging, but Yelloweye stopped me.

I don't mean he physically did something to block my path or anything. He just started a series of gentle hoots. I'd never heard anything with so gentle a voice. And with each little hoot I was drawn closer until Phile and me were just a couple feet away. Our other selves just plopped down on the ground in front of him.

Couldn't tell you a word of that conversation. Not because I don't remember it, but we just can't speak in that voice. Animals—even really smart animals like that great gray owl—don't talk in words. There's no one-to-one relationship that says this hoot equals that word or even that concept. They don't have the same concepts we do. They don't have the same imagery. They fly! How can someone with two feet anchored to the ground ever comprehend stretching out wings and catching an updraft to soar a mile above us?

When he'd finished talking to us, he tucked his head under a wing and ignored us. We were dismissed. We almost forgot to put our clothes on to come home, we were so excited and scared.

Yelloweye, the owl, or in the language of the people, *Heove-'éxané*, had a mission for us. For the first time since we started living a double life, things started to make sense to us. We had a gift and he would teach us how to use it.

Phile: Bullies

WE WERE LUCKY for as strange as we were. In now-time we just stuck together and we were so weird that most everyone avoided us. Grade school is like that, I guess. There were other kids who the cool kids shunned as well. I don't know why we never thought of becoming friends, but maybe we just assumed that we should avoid the weird kids, too.

The biggest problem we'd had wasn't from one of the kids, but from our teacher. She didn't like the fact that we slept in class a lot so she kept trying to trick us and humiliate us. In order to manage the inflow of experiences, one of us would stay awake in class while the other concentrated on what was happening in before-time.

"*Kásóéso*, teacher is going to call on you," my sister whispered in before-time. "She wants to know countries that touch the North Pacific."

"Thank you, *He'éka'éškónéhéso*," I said to Caitlin. We didn't have names in our tribe yet. We were just called little boy and little girl.

"Phile, would you answer the question, please?" Miss Sanders said. I know she suspected I was asleep. Well, I had been.

"All the countries of North America touch the North Pacific," I said. "Canada, the United States, and Mexico. The western edge of the North Pacific is bordered by Russia, Japan, and China."

"Very good, Phile. I was afraid you weren't paying attention."

"But where is the dividing line?" I asked. "Is it the equator that separates the North Pacific from the South Pacific? Shouldn't we include Guatemala, Honduras, Nicaragua, Panama, Colombia, Ecuador, Peru, and the Philippines?"

"Ah… In this instance, we were only discussing the major nations of the north, but… This would be some excellent research for you to conduct on behalf of the class. Monday during our geography lesson, I would like you to do a presentation on where the North Pacific is divided from the South Pacific and have a comprehensive list of all the independent nations that touch the North Pacific," Miss Sanders said.

"Yes, ma'am," I said. *Bitch.* I went back to sleep. It was Caitlin's day to pay attention.

BUT THAT DOESN'T mean there weren't bullies in before-time, too. Bent Bow was a teenager, maybe ten years older than us at the time Yelloweye appeared next to the creek. You'd think that his accomplishments as a hunter would make noticing little kids unimportant. But Bent Bow liked to torment us—all the smaller children. It wasn't unusual for him to 'accidentally' trip a toddler or to make fun of a hurt child. I'd been pushed down many times, but there was no one to complain to. *Náhko'e* was a kind and caring parent, but she did not want to hear tales. Children had to work out their own issues.

So, of course, it was Bent Bow that saw us talking to Yelloweye.

Owls, among many Native Americans, are respected but viewed as a bad omen. It seems they always show up just before someone dies. Yelloweye flitted away, knocking the two of us back as an arrow flew near our heads. Bent Bow had been determined to kill the evil omen and didn't care if we were in the way. We scrambled up and ran as he was nocking another arrow.

That wasn't the end of it, though. Bent Bow went to the village elders and told them of the owl that spoke to the 'death children'. It wasn't the first time we'd been called that. We'd long-since learned that my mother died the night I was born. *Ma'heóná'e*, our medicine woman, called us to the central fire. Cait and I held hands as we faced her and glanced around at the hardened faces around us.

"Children, have you spoken to *Heove-'éxané?*" she asked softly. We nodded. "Has he a message for us? Is death near?"

We were lucky that in now-time, we were huddled together in Caitlin's room, waiting for Yelloweye to take us somewhere that we could learn to use our gift—even though it wasn't clear what the gift was. Caitlin and I talked over what we should say. We were only five years old in before-time. So, when we spoke to the medicine woman in unison, it added a lot of weight to what we said.

"*Heove-'éxané* does not bring an omen of death to our village today," we said together. "He has come to teach us so we may help protect the village. We must learn from Yelloweye and protect his people."

Ma'heóná'e looked around the circle at the shocked elders. We had spoken clearly and together. And in adult language, not children's talk. There were some grunts from around the circle and warding signs against evil, but mostly there were nods to the old woman.

"*Hestáhkeho*," she whispered. It meant 'twins'. She took ash from the edge of the fire—to us it looked like she was just putting her hands in the fire, but the ash at the edge was cool. She drew on our faces with the ash while she chanted about the spirits guarding us and the village helping the Great Spirit teach us. Periodically, the men and other women near the fire joined the chant and circled us as she continued drawing on our chests. As little children, we didn't wear clothes unless it was cold and we had to wrap in a blanket. She painted us up front and back as the village chanted and danced. Then we were sent back to the edge of the village to our mother's tent and told to come back to see the medicine woman in the morning.

Our real education had begun.

Caitlin: Learning

WE SHIVERED TOGETHER on my bed looking out the open window, thinking about what we'd just been through in the village. It was confusing and frightening. And we still didn't know what our gift was or how we were supposed to use it.

Yelloweye had said it would be difficult, but it was important. We needed to help him save his People. Or our People. Or maybe all people. Some things just weren't clear. We couldn't figure out why he was talking to us in now-time if we needed to save the People in before-time.

Not far off we heard the hoot of the owl. It called to us. I felt like I was being tugged right out of my skin. I tried to resist, holding onto Phile and trying not to cry out with pain at the grip he had on me.

And then we weren't there in my room any longer.

We were soaring up in the night sky. Far below us, we could see every blade of grass in the pasture. Trees rushed beneath us and we felt the updraft catch under our wings and lift us so we could bank and turn again. There was a change in the direction the grasses moved and suddenly we were diving toward the earth. It was frightening and exhilarating and joyful all at once. And then we had a mouse in our claws, tearing the head from its body as we climbed into the sky again.

This is what you will learn. You will ride in the minds of the flyers, the four-leggeds, the two-leggeds. You will learn how they live and how they die. You will learn how they hunt and how they kill. You will learn the secrets of Néške'emāne, Grandmother Earth, and she will make you ready.

Yelloweye had spoken in our heads as we had ridden in his. And then we were back in our own bodies.

The Family

"MY POOR BABIES," Ashley sobbed. She and Mary Beth wept against Cole's shoulders. Tears streamed down his cheeks. Even the baby, nestled against Aubrey's bosom whimpered. Kyle rocked three-year-old Theresa in his arms. Ramie set the bundle of papers back in the box.

"I can't just keep reading this," Ramie said. "We gotta take breaks. There's children to feed and horses to care for. Pa, Alex wants to talk to you before they drive the cattle up to the summer pasture. They're late moving because the grass has been so lush down here, but they want to be moving at first light tomorrow, so you better go see him now."

"You've taken to being boss just fine, daughter," Mary Beth sniffed. She got off Cole and pulled Ashley with her. "Come on, wife," she said. "It's time to get the family settled for the night. Aubrey, may I burp the little treasure when she's done with your tit?" She needed the contact with a child as she let what she'd learned about her own youngest settle over her.

"Yes, Mom Mar," Aubrey said. "I think she's about done sucking."

"Come to Gramma, Theresa. It's time to get the birthday girl ready for beddie. Papa has to go water the horses," Ashley said holding out her arms to her granddaughter. She needed the contact as well. The child jumped to her grandma and started giggling when Ashley blew a raspberry on her tummy. The mood gradually lightened as the family went about their chores and prepared for bed.

The younger generation finally gathered the children and went across the yard to the bunkhouse. With two children and three adults, the little two-bedroom home was beginning to feel crowded. They would have to deal with that eventually.

2
Wild Indians

The Family

I HAVE A bad feeling about this, Miranda whispered in Ramie's mind as they went about their business the next day. *Jason didn't want to be there when you opened the box last night. He's been holding something back. Maybe hiding something.*

"Yeah, but don't push him. Kyle and Jason have their own demons, sweetheart. Knowing our little brother and sister were growing up in an Indian village must be hard on them. Like us remembering being kidnapped," Ramie sighed. She finished feeding the stabled horses. With the number of pleasure riders who now boarded their horses at LK Stables, they were building another horse barn and Kyle had gone to check the day's progress on the construction. The new barn would house the breeding and foaling facility so the old barn would be strictly boarding.

All day, Ramie fought the desire to simply run to the box and read the rest—or, alternatively, to burn it all so she wouldn't have to find out. But she had a business to run. She had to go to the bank to make the monthly deposits. She had to pay the loans for building and expanding the ranch. She needed to ride out on the northern trail where one of the boarders had reported a tree down across the trail. Work had to be done. Laying the cat to rest had to wait.

KYLE JOINED RAMIE on the way back to the ranch house for dinner and took her hand. They walked quietly. Aubrey met them at the door with a kiss. After they'd scrubbed up they each cuddled a baby and then sat down to a dinner of liver and onions.

"It just floors me," Cole said. "How can they live with their consciousness split between two times? It defies the laws of physics."

15

"Pa, what part of time travel doesn't defy the laws of physics?" Aubrey asked sweetly. They were all thinking the same thing, but Cole had a definite soft spot for the mother of his grandchildren.

"Well, sweetie, when it was just me traveling, and as much as I can tell the same was true of Phile and Geneive and Joe Teini, everything was one-way. We could go back in time. We affected the present by leaving treasure where we could find it in the future. We got plenty tangled up in the lives we led in that other world, but we didn't communicate with our present self while we were back in the past," Cole said. "When we were gone from here, our bodies more or less kept up appearances, but memories of those times were muted and dreamlike. Sometimes it appeared we were sick, like you were after the wolf attack, Ramie. And when our hosts died, that was it."

"Except you were trapped there for a long time, just like I was," Ramie said. "Then you went back. Twice. You went when Arthur Alexander summoned you and he gave you his body. You took me with you to meet my great great great grandmother. But for Kyle and me, our hosts communicated with us just like we do with them now. We worked as partners."

"Still, I never would have guessed that you could bring your hosts with you into our present. And Miranda and Jason, we love you and welcome you here," Cole added. "I never mean to be disrespectful to our grandparents."

"We've only ever known you as Pa," Miranda said through Ramie's voice. "I wish I could connect all those dots, but we're no older than Ramie and Kyle."

"I love learning from your experience, though," Mary Beth said. "Your pie dough is the best ever."

"Excuse me," Ashley said. "The love-fest is nice, but back to the subject at hand. I think you just captured the difference, Cole. You had Kyle Redtail as a host. Geneive had Caitlin. Ramie had Miranda and Kyle had Jason. When you were there, two consciousnesses inhabited the body and one took control. Ramie and Miranda talked about it and were companions. You just jerked control away from Kyle and made him sit quietly. But the difference is that Caitlin and Phile aren't inhabiting someone *else's* body. They've never once mentioned a host."

They sat quietly at the table as what Ashley said sank in. If it was true, Caitlin and Phile were the same people in both timeframes. They didn't have hosts. They each had two bodies.

They finished their meal and cleaned up. Ramie and Aubrey got the children bathed and ready for bed. Theresa cuddled up in Kyle's lap again while Aubrey nursed Katherine. Mary Beth and Ashley curled together in Cole's lap as Ramie extracted the pages from the box and began reading again.

Phile: The People

I HAVE TO write about growing up Cheyenne and how we found out that was what we were. Yelloweye had provided a powerful wise woman in our village to teach us, but he found someone to teach us in now-time as well.

There are certain things you never think about. Like earth. The name of our planet is Earth. We call the dirt on the ground 'earth'. Earth isn't a name for a planet. It's the same as calling it 'world'. We name the things that are other than us. Mars and Venus. They aren't Earth.

We knew we weren't Crow or Lakota. They were other than us. We wouldn't even have *looked* for a name if we didn't exist in both times. We were the People. They were Pawnee. Those others were whiteman. We didn't need to name ourselves.

It was the same with Phile and me. People in the tribe called us like they called all the kids. Little boy and little girl. Or now, they often called us *Hestáhkeho*, Twins. When we became adults, the Great Spirit, or perhaps Yelloweye, would give us a name because we were other to him.

MERV LONGSTEER CAUGHT US. We always loved that shop. It smelled like leather. We'd saved up all our birthday money and planned to get ourselves good knives. Among the people we learned how to use a knife before we were six summers. Of course, our knives weren't steel. The whole knife was made of elk bone. The handle was wrapped with rawhide and the blade shaped down to be sort of sharp. It's a lot easier to make a point than an edge, but points aren't good for slicing meat.

We got carried away in his shop and it was one of those occasions that we were talking the same both lives. In before-time, we were holding our knives in front of us while in now-time, we were looking at the knives in the case and talking about them.

"Those knives are good for skinning," Merv said as he leaned over the counter to talk to us. We were surprised, but also kind of flattered that the old medicine man would talk to us children.

"We need something like this so we can learn how to use it to make something like this," I said pointing at a longer blade. He nodded.

"What will you make it out of?"

"The first one is bone. But it's hard to get it real sharp. I want to make the next one out of flint or obsidian. I'm learning to identify the right stones," Phile said. He was enthusiastic. Merv nodded again.

"Don't use your bone knife to try to chip the obsidian," he said. He pulled the two short knives we'd been looking at out and took them out his back door. We followed. He bent down and picked up a couple stones. "First, you can make a better edge on your bone knife by using one of these stones to scrape along it." He demonstrated the proper way to scrape the stone against the steel blades, always going the same direction. "Now when you get a piece of obsidian or flint, you need to chip it by striking it lightly with a harder stone." He demonstrated again. "Many of our ancestors became experts at chipping the flint to a fine edge. But you can use the sanding stone to hone it even finer. Do that and your arrowheads and your knife will pierce the hide quickly and smoothly."

Phile and I looked at each other. When Merv said 'arrowheads' the word clicked in our minds. *Mo'xóhtse*—the Cheyenne word for arrowhead. I caught my breath and looked at Merv. All this time, we'd been speaking to him in the Cheyenne language.

"Listen to your teachers," Merv said, changing to English. "They are teaching you well. When you share these tricks with them, show them respectfully and not as though you are better than they are. Your spirit walks among the Cheyenne people. When you need more help, come and visit with me."

We thanked him and paid for our purchases. Pa examined what we'd bought and decided it was best not to tell the moms that we were running around with sharp knives. He swore that if we hurt anyone with our knives he'd use them to take the skin off our backs. We sort of believed him.

We tried not to speak Cheyenne in now-time again, but sometimes we got mixed up. Merv was the only person who didn't think we were just making up gibberish.

IN TWO MORE years of now-time, we'd aged five years in before-time. We were eleven-year-old wild Indians in now-time, doing all kinds of crazy stuff. We were trying to assimilate seven years of learning in two years. In before-time we were ten.

And in before-time, the learning was intense. The village wise woman and the elders were all teaching us. And they seemed to do it with a sense of fear—sort of like they were afraid they'd forget to teach us something vital. We soaked it all up the best we could and might not have had as much trouble except that Yelloweye was teaching us in both before-time and now-time. You all thought we were out chasing the horses when we were running along riding in their heads as they raced around the pasture.

Yelloweye explained that he couldn't open us to our gift of joining minds with other animals until we had joined our minds across time, but it was important for the children we were in before-time to grow up being recognized from infancy as touched by the owl. He taught us about natural order and that some animals were meant to be food and to supply other needs for the People. We also learned about animals who were outside our food chain and would dine on us, given the opportunity.

We could summon animals for our use, including rabbits, squirrels, some birds, and even deer, elk, and buffalo. But when we summoned them to their deaths, we needed to respect their sacrifice, be mercifully quick in our kills, and take part in the animal's… the best word we ever came up with was Karma. We did this by immediately eating the liver and letting the animal become one with our lives. After all, they sacrificed themselves for our nourishment.

Caitlin: Soldiers

WE'RE TRYING TO split up the writing, but Phile gets too emotional to write about this part, so he's working on the story of the wolves.

Among the animals that would dine on us, at least figuratively, were *ho'evòtse*, whiteman. They didn't care about food. They wanted the land to be theirs. We knew in now-time what whiteman would eventually do to the land. Farming and raising animals were understandable. But the men with rifles would kill hundreds of buffalo and leave them to rot on the prairie. Carrion birds flocked behind the white hunters who just rode on.

We were scavengers as well. When the white riders passed, we would rush to the killing field with a travois and bring a buffalo carcass or two back to the village. We would not hunt after the white killers had been through. Some in our village would not eat the meat of the buffalo killed by bullets.

We never knew our fathers. They had gone to fight the blue suits before we were born and never returned. Like the buffalo, they were left on the prairie and scavengers took their bodies. So even when we were very small, we set snares and scavenged buffalo for our mother so we would not starve or freeze in winter.

In our tenth summer, Phile and I each killed a whitetail deer. We paused over the dead bodies and thanked our brothers for giving us the food we would need and their fine skins for our clothes. We opened their bodies with our short bone knives and ate the livers fresh and warm from their guts.

We were triumphant as we loaded the carcasses on our travois and headed back to our village. The hunting men of the village had gone farther to seek prey, but we were able to call our food to us and returned long before the men would be back.

That was the last time we were ever happy. Yelloweye was sitting on our tipi.

"Children, go to the flagpole in the center of camp and stand with your mother," *Tsévéhonevèstse* Elder said. He was an old man, but he was our leader. We carried a flag of the United States with our village that was given to us by a soldier when they wrote a paper that would keep us safe. "Soldiers are coming and we must show them that we are peaceful people who abide by our word."

We stood with our mother, excited but a little frightened, too.

And the soldiers came.

We were just standing there waiting to greet them and they came over the hill with their horses galloping toward us and their long guns belching death all around us. They drew their short guns and kept firing as they closed in on us. We stared in the eyes of a yellow-haired *ho'evôtse* charging with his gun pointed at us.

"Run, children, run!" Mother cried pushing us to obey. Death stared at us and we turned to run as Mother crumpled to the ground. Our mother! Our mother was dead!

We ran. At the edge of the village where Grandfather had met us, our horses and the fresh deer stood waiting. We cut the travois loose from them and leapt to their backs to ride away. Screams. Smoke from the guns. Terrified people running away. Soldiers knocking them down with their horses. Our village was gone. Our mother was dead. And we fled. We rode our ponies as far into the mountains as they could take us before we rested. And then we collapsed together and wept.

THIS DID NOT happen while we slept in now-time. Phile and I were out near the woodlot where the old cabin was and the fireplace still stands. We were celebrating having killed our first deer. We considered catching a rabbit and roasting it, but Moms would have had a fit if they knew we started a fire in the woods. We were excited about the soldiers coming to our village in the past and stood in front of the fireplace as if we were among them.

But just as Yelloweye—our friend—sat on our tipi, he sat beside us on the old chimney.

We saw it all as we stood there and when we ran in before-time, we ran in now-time as well. We caught our horses and rode toward the mountain. We rode in panic. We rode hard, our horses understanding the urgency. We had always managed to keep some separation between the two halves of our lives, but we lost it that day. We rode and wept with our other selves, unable to differentiate which of us was which. We rode until it was dark and we were far up in the mountains.

It took us two days to separate our present selves from our past selves. We had horses with no bridles or even a lead rope. Yet they stayed near to us and came when we called them. We snared a rabbit and cooked it over a fire that we started ourselves. We had no weapons or tools other than the knives we always carried. Our before-time selves had their bows and arrows that had been left slung over their horses. In now-time, we didn't even have that. We began working to make ourselves bows and cut straight saplings to cure for arrows.

At night, we held each other for warmth.

THAT IS WHERE Yelloweye found us. We'd seen him with us in before-time and at the ranch in now-time. For the first time, we were frightened of him. He was, indeed, the harbinger of death. Our mommy was dead. Maybe our whole village. We'd seen them ride the People down and kill them.

I sorrow for you, my children.

He called us his children.

"I wish you could have learned this lesson another way," he said. No. He didn't say anything. He never said anything. We just got this wave of sadness from him. *This is what will happen to the Ho'e, the land. The ho'evòtse will kill all that is before him.*

"What do they want, Yelloweye? Why do they do this?" Phile asked.

They wish Ho'e-momóonáotaovóho, dominion, to rule over all. They wish the earth and all the creatures to bow down to them and yield their treasures, whether they will or no.

"What must we do?" I asked.

You must learn and survive. You must be who you are and talk to your brothers and sisters of the earth. The day will come when only you stand between destruction of the land and its survival.

PA LACED OUR butts with his belt when we got home. We'd been gone three days and one of the riders from the upper pasture found us and took us to camp. The next day Pa showed up at the trailhead with a trailer and loaded our horses. He wasn't going to even let us ride down to the ranch.

When he'd laid one across each of our butts, he sank down on his knees and hugged us and cried.

"We thought we'd lost you," he said. "We'd never be the same without you. Don't ever scare us like that again. You can't possibly understand how much your moms and I love you."

I think that was the first time I did understand.

Phile: Wolves

LIFE DIDN'T GET any easier. I mean this life, here in now-time. It wasn't easy in before-time, either. This gets so damned complicated. We were alone and isolated in before-time. In now-time, we isolated ourselves and were even more antisocial than we'd been.

We went wild. I know we'd been difficult ever since we first met Yelloweye. But more and more of our life in the present was in sync with the past. And we couldn't be in sync while we were around other people. When excuses failed to work, we just made it so nobody wanted to be around us.

It was easy to hate everybody.

In the wintertime, we had to go to school. Oh, we learned stuff. Sixth grade was better than our other school, mostly because we got to go to Laramie and rode the bus with Kyle and Ramie. They never said much, but we knew they were always on the lookout for us.

"MOVE, DWEEB. I wanna sit by your sister." Daniel Watson from the Bar Double-D was two years older than us. We'd had three years with him out of Centennial Elementary School and forgot what an asshat he was. I didn't want him anywhere near Caitlin and she told me in before-time that she didn't want to be near him.

"No."

"Don't ever tell me no, you little turd. I'll put your head through the back window," he said.

"Maybe you'd like to try putting my head through the back window," Kyle said. Kyle was only fifteen, but he was already six feet tall. He'd be real tall and thin like Pa. I didn't think I'd ever be that tall. I was used to thinking of myself among the People. Kyle had Daniel by the back of his neck. I thought the kid was going to swing at Kyle, but he just shrugged.

"Hey, I was just trying to be friendly," Daniel said.

"I distinctly heard you say you wanted to sit by Phile's sister," Kyle said. "She said to bring the douchebag to her. So, you come here and sit right next to Ramie while she tells you about life. I'll be right here across the aisle in case you need me."

We couldn't hear what Ramie said to Daniel Douchebag, whatever that was. We liked the sound of it. I never found out what Ramie told him, but we never heard anything from the eighth-grader again, even though the junior high was in a different building than the senior high. He avoided us. It was cool.

Ramie and Kyle were cool. I wished a lot that I could be like them. They were different than Caitlin and me. I mean, they were best friends and all that. I often heard one say to the other, 'I got your back.' But Caitlin and me… She was the only person in the whole world who mattered to me.

IF IT HADN'T been for Kyle's birthday in May, I think Caitlin and I would have run away that summer. We nearly did anyway. But we understood that in many ways, it would be harder to live alone in the wilderness in now-time than it was in before-time. There were too many people and they were always too close to us.

But on Kyle's birthday he moved to the bunkhouse and had an apartment of his own. That meant I had a room to myself for the first time in my life. Ramie moved out to the bunkhouse that summer and it was easier for Caitlin and me to slip into each other's room without being caught. We kept quiet about it, but when Moms and Pa went to bed, one of us would slip over to the other's room. Didn't seem to make any difference which. We always knew where we were going to sleep and that's where we went.

Yeah, I've been sleeping holding my sister in my arms forever. We'd never been apart from each other in the tribe. I was supposed to go to the men's tent if it hadn't been for the attack on our village. But we never rejoined what remained of our village after the attack. It was just Caitlin and me in the wilderness together. Even if we felt someone had to be watchful at night, Caitlin would sleep leaning against me or me against her. We were all we had.

I'd protect her against the world.

WE CONTINUED TO grow and learn. We didn't pay attention in school any more than it took to pass tests. There were some subjects that we liked, but they were just a little part of school. History of our people. Well that was a footnote in the chapter about winning the West. Most of the chapter was about the railroad and included a field trip to the museum in the old depot. Biology was just a couple chapters in the general science book, but we found out a lot about how animals were related to each other and how they were classified. Geography of the Rockies and the Midwest was interesting for a couple of weeks. But mostly, we still took turns sleeping and waking each other up when the teacher was about to call on us.

And out in the pastures, we continued to learn the ways of the animals. On Ramie's sixteenth birthday, Phile and I both summoned pronghorns for our hunt. We wanted to use bows for the hunt, but part of the reason we all went hunting was learning gun safety and shooting. We took our shots carefully and then rushed down to field dress our kills. Mom Mar was a little disgusted when we each ate the liver fresh from their guts. We thanked the pronghorns for helping to feed our family for the winter.

The rest of the family was really upset. It seems they watched wolves take down a small herd of elk and because of the laws, they couldn't do anything about it. Caitlin and I quested about trying to find the minds of the predators, but had no luck. The whole family developed a hatred for the 'killing machines', as Mom Ash called them.

WE GOT TO see Merv sometimes. About once a month, Caitlin and I would skip out of school at lunch and go to his trading post. Without a village, a shaman, or a wise woman, our before-time selves had to discover everything on their own. Merv was patient with our questions and helped us in both lives.

We only got caught once. It almost killed us.

Our first period after lunch in seventh grade was study hall and Mr. Adams never took attendance. Lots of kids had passes for the library or the gym. We were in his Social Studies class the period before lunch, so we'd shoulder our packs and stop long enough to use the sign-out sheet before we left. That gave us nearly two hours and we could run to Merv's in fifteen minutes.

"What's the question today?" he asked in Cheyenne when he saw that the shop was empty except for us.

"*Ma'heónehetane*, how can we honor our dead when we cannot claim their bodies from the murderers?" I asked. We'd fled from the scene of our village during the massacre. We returned in the spring and found nothing there. It was like we had never existed there at all. Merv did not ask who we wished to honor. We'd asked Yelloweye, but the concept was foreign to him.

"Ah. When we kill a buck to eat the meat and use the hide, how does the doe honor him?" he asked. "It is the same when a wolf kills a young one. How does the parent honor the child? And even if you found what remained when the spirit left, how would you honor the dead?"

"We would pray for their spirit to find comfort with the great ones," I answered.

"That is good, but it is out of your hands. We let the body replenish the earth. We let the spirit fly to the sky. Indeed, there is nothing we can do to stop this cycle. Whiteman puts potions in the body, wraps it in cloths, puts it in a box, buries it deep, and places a stone cairn over it. But even that body will eventually return to the earth."

"What should we do, then?" Caitlin asked.

"Live. The doe honors the buck by raising the young and keeping them safe. The parent honors the child by slaying the wolf so other children will be safe. We honor our dead by living a life that is worthy of them," Merv ended our lesson and sent us running back to school so we wouldn't get in trouble.

That worked except the time when there was a substitute teacher for Mr. Adams in the afternoon and she checked the library to see that those who had signed out were there. Mom Mar had to come to the school to meet with the principal about truancy and took us home after school. We got extra assignments and weren't allowed to sign out to the library again for the rest of the month.

But we weren't expecting how mad it would make Moms and Pa.

Mom Ash made us sit at the kitchen table as soon as we got home and do our homework.

"You finish that homework and then go to your rooms. There will be no running outside tonight. And I will be checking on you to see that you are in your own room. I know you don't care about anything else. You don't care that we are unhappy. You don't care that your teacher got reprimanded for letting you out of school. You don't care that even your friend could get in trouble. But you care about being together. So, you'll live tonight apart. It's the only thing I can think of that will get through to you."

It did. We'd planned to hunt in before-time, but we depended on being together in this life to stay in touch while we split up in the past. We'd already headed out separately in before-time, intending to circle our prey while talking in now-time. If we couldn't be together in now-time, we'd be apart in both lives. That had never happened before.

"No!" I screeched. Pa slid his belt out of his pants and laced me one across the back of my legs. I switched to Cheyenne and called out to Caitlin, "Go to the creek of two horses. I will go there." She was crying and screaming back, but all I caught was 'hurry'.

"And stop your gibberish!" Mom Mar yelled. Mom Ash pushed Caitlin into her room as Mom Mar came into mine. She snatched up my computer and left. I couldn't even message Cait. I was frantic. It was at least three miles to the two horses creek from where I was in my past life. But it had been the only place I could think of while my legs were stinging.

I ran.

Yes, I had a horse, but in the deep woods, I can move more quickly on foot than on a horse. I told her where I was going and knew that she'd follow as quickly as she could. It seemed to take forever. I made the mistake of a child and forgot about the gorge that lay between me and the creek. Instead of going to where I knew a path lay, I tried to descend it where I encountered it. I fell and twisted my ankle.

But I couldn't stop. I had to get to my sister. We were all we had in this world and the only thing that made it okay to go about our lives in now-time parting and coming back together was because we were always together in one life or the other. Being parted from her in both lives was like suddenly being blind and deaf. I beat at my past self, demanding that I ignore the pain in my ankle and continue up the other side of the gorge. I made so much noise that I could have been a white man stumbling through the brush. Animals that I could normally communicate with ran from me.

And then that big owl was right in front of me.

Not in the past, but in my room. While my feet still moved me forward in before-time, in now-time, Yelloweye stared me down.

His reprimand stung more than Pa's belt. I had been given a gift, but in the moment when I needed it most, I ignored it and ran like a crazy man. If I did not regain my senses, my sister and I might both be in danger. Worse. The image Yelloweye gave me was 'food'. We might be food.

I closed my eyes with Yelloweye's warning burning in my head. In before-time I stopped running and crashing through the woods. I paused to listen. In the distance, toward the setting sun, I could hear wolves. That was the only sound. My crashing through the brush caused all the nearby animals to hide. They would emerge again soon. In the air, high above, a hawk circled.

I sent my spirit questing for the bird and felt the wind lift his wings as he sought an evening meal. I greeted him and he calmly welcomed me to his flight. I looked out at the ground far below. I found the creek and gently guided Hawk along it to look for Cait. What I saw chilled me. She sat by the creek waiting, trying to calm her nervous horse that was dancing around nearby. A few hundred yards away, the wolves had stopped their howling and were stalking closer to her.

I dropped back into my body to keep it moving along the path *Aénohe* had shown me. As I moved silently along, my mind quested out for the wolves. A hunting pair. They were hungry. The male's thoughts were of gorging on warm flesh. The female thoughts were darker. Yes, she was hungry. Yes, she thought of the feast. But her brain was filled with the kill. She wanted to rip the life from her prey.

I tried to talk to them—to turn them away. But they were too filled with the scent of the prey to hear me or to care. I tried to send them fear, but this only made them more vicious. I kept trying to calm myself while wanting to scream out to Caitlin. I was closing in from one side, but the wolves were closing in from the other. My bow was ready with new flint arrowheads on my arrows. My view of Cait had shown that she did not have her bow ready to shoot as I had. She had her new long-blade knife.

After our first meeting with Merv Longsteer, we had honed our bone knives to a sharpened edge. But we had also set about making new obsidian hunting knives. Caitlin sat still, but her horse edged farther away. Its size and intelligence made it a formidable opponent for a wolf unless there was a full pack. A hunting pair would be a severe challenge for the animal who could very well die, even if it drove off the attackers.

I quested into the wolves again and saw Caitlin through their eyes. It was a strange sort of double vision as I caught glimpses of her through the trees with my human body and the pulsing meat that the wolves saw. They came into the clearing facing Caitlin, snarling at her. Caitlin was afraid, but I could tell she now sensed my approach from the other side. We were near the same size, but the wolves probably outweighed us by ten or twenty pounds each. She had tried looking through the wolves' eyes, but seeing herself the way they saw her froze her.

There was no time for great strategy. I drew my bow as I entered the clearing and moved toward them. Wolves are much happier to track moving prey than still prey. They will circle a buffalo and yip at it, diving in to nip at its feet, but not attacking while the buffalo is still. If the buffalo gets tired of their goading and attacks or attempts to run, the pack will pounce on it and bring it to the ground.

Caitlin's stillness and my action drew the attention of the wolves toward me. I was moving prey and they charged toward me as one. I loosed my arrow and caught the big male. I had drawn my second arrow, but could not track the female because Caitlin had dived for it. The male howled and continued coming for me. My second arrow stopped it, piercing its eye.

As the wolves changed direction and charged toward me, Cait snatched a handful of the bitch's fur and swung onto her back, riding her into the ground. Her obsidian knife sliced through the bitch's throat and Caitlin lay on the bloody mess.

"I knew you would get here in time," she sobbed as I lifted her from the carcass. "If I had tried to fight them, they would have attacked. Even if I killed one, I knew I could not avoid the other. It was so hard to stay still and wait. Phile, from now on we don't get separated!"

"We are a hunting pair like these," I said. "I will eat the heart of this wolf before it cools." Caitlin nodded and we fell to butchering our kills. We pulled the hearts out and held them before each other. And bit into them.

I could feel the power and fierceness of the wolf enter into me as I ate the organ. But I could also feel the lust for blood that filled me. I saw it reflected in Cait's eyes as the blood dripped from her hands and chin while she ate the meat.

Wolf is not great-tasting meat. Any animal that eats other animals or carrion tastes foul. But we burned the meat well enough over our fire that we could tear strips off and choke them down. This was our kill and we would eat it. Even the vicious predator deserved the honor of knowing his meat nourished one of greater strength.

"I will wear this she-wolf," Caitlin said. We'd skinned them and made a frame to stretch the hides as we cleaned them. "I will be *Ho'néené'šeohtsévá'e*. I am Wolf Riding Woman. I have ridden the wolf and lived."

"That's a mouthful, even in our language," I laughed. "But you are a woman. And you have ridden the wolf."

"I will save my name for when the bleeding starts. But now you know me."

"Then as I wear the skin of this warrior wolf, I will be known as *Ho'néemé'eōhtse*, Wolf Rising, for I rose to meet him in battle."

"You are my mate, Wolf Rising," she responded.

We finished our work and headed for the creek. We did not have much in the way of clothes. We'd been on our own for a year and in all that time had avoided contact with anyone else. It was easy to make a loincloth. We had buffalo robes to keep us warm when the weather turned bad. We stripped off what we wore and went into the creek to wash.

While we washed, my horse ambled into the clearing and went to where the other horse grazed. They snuffled their greetings and we sent our warm thoughts to our two friends. We emerged from the creek and turned to embrace each other. It had been a hard day.

"Wolf Rising," she giggled. "Your manhood is rising."

"Wolf Riding Woman, it is your womanhood that is causing this attention," I answered. "You know I love you. We're way too young to deal with all that sex stuff. Someday when it is more than just an uncontrolled reaction, we'll figure out what to do with it. But from this day, I never want to be parted from you again."

The Family

"I don't think I can listen to any more tonight," Mary Beth said. "I was a terrible mother. My poor babies. My poor babies."

"You weren't a terrible mother," Ashley snapped. "You aren't a terrible mother. How could we know? We were trying to raise them right."

"They were only twelve," Cole said. "Even with other time travelers in the family, none of us started that young. Twelve? Hell, eight! None of us started until we were at least sixteen. And it was always related to becoming sexually active. Even Genieve said that's how she started. If you want to be pissed at someone, yell at the old owl. He took away our children!" Cole was getting worked up and stood up to wave his arms around, nearly dumping his wives on the floor.

"I think Mom's right, though," Ramie said. "We need to take a break. My voice is getting hoarse. And I don't think this is something we're supposed to rush through. I'm exhausted. Miranda, drive."

Miranda shifted easily into control of Ramie's body and let her other self weep silently.

"I think I need to bake a pie before bed," she said. "Mary Beth, why don't we get our hands in some lard. We can make up a couple of those egg pies we read about for breakfast."

"Quiche? Yes, Grandma," Mary Beth smiled.

Evening chores got done. Kyle took the babies to the bunkhouse to put them to bed. He hadn't said anything during the reading, nor afterward. He just held his children as tears streamed down his cheeks. Aubrey sat with Ashley and Cole for a few minutes before going to join her husband.

"Something's wrong, baby," Aubrey said as she joined Kyle looking down at the babies. "What is it? You know you can tell me anything." Kyle held his love and wished Ramie would hurry up in the house.

"It was me," he croaked. "'…a yellow-haired *ho'evòtse* charging with his gun pointed at us.' I still remember it. All these years living as Kyle and living as Jason and all of both of our memories as we rode over that hill into the village believing we were riding into an ambush with our guns blazing. I killed their momma! It was me."

"You didn't know, honey. Your commander lied to you. You stopped others from being killed. You got that horrid private court-martialed. You've told us the story. You did the best you could," Aubrey said pulling Kyle to the bed and holding him.

"That didn't help my little brother and sister. We just thought they were being brats. Until the horses came. Everything changed then. But nothing could undo what I'd done."

3
Getting Grounded

The Family

THEY'D WORKED out a pattern. Everyone had work to do and no one could spend all her time reading the book left for Ramie by her younger siblings. Nor could they handle more at one time than the hour they spent in the evening holding each other as they read. Every word the kids had written cut into the hearts of their mothers, father, and siblings. Even Aubrey, the only one not related by blood, worried that the babies might be affected by hearing the story at such a young age. But more than that, she worried about her husband and wife.

Cole was late when he parked the ATV behind the ranch house. He'd driven to the upper pasture to check on the herd and his ranch hands. He was steaming when he sat at the table for supper with the family.

"They're fencing in the whole area up by the hot spring!" he shouted after they'd taken a moment to consider the land before eating. "Sons of bitches. The government sold mineral rights in the National Forest and they're exploring for oil."

"They can't fence off portions of the land that they already sold us grazing rights to," Ashley declared. "I'm going to call Arlen Logan at the Forest Service right now." She pushed back from the table. Cole put a hand on her arm.

"I called as soon as I got in range," he said. "Nobody's in the office. It's Sunday. The damned Forest Service has taken to keeping bankers' hours. Believe me, I filled up their mailbox with my complaint and we'll start again in the morning."

"After the way they stood up to the government six years ago, I had more faith in them than this," Mary Beth said.

"They got cleaned out by the administration," Ramie said. "At least they didn't just sell off the forest up there. Is it the same group that's up in

33

the Yellowstone? They've closed the whole north half of the Park because of the protests."

"It's gonna get worse before it gets better," Kyle opined. His words applied to many things.

After dinner, the family gathered again in the office to hear the next section of what the kids had written. Ramie carried the box and sat heavily on the couch. Each time she lifted it, it felt heavier. Kyle reached for her and she leaned against him.

"Laramie, honey, let me. This is too much for any one of us to take on alone," he said. "We need to share this among us." Tears sprang to Ramie's eyes as she hugged her brother/husband. She let him take the box and fuss with opening it while Moms and Pa settled into their chair.

"I'm so proud of you, Jason," Aubrey whispered. Kyle turned to look at her. "I know you couldn't take this on alone, Kyle. If Jason wasn't there to help it would be too much. I'm proud of you both. I am lucky to be loved by the two most wonderful men in the world and only have to deal with one cock."

"I love you, Aubrey," Jason said with Kyle's voice. "I love this whole family."

Ramie leaned across to Aubrey and was met by her lips. They let a long delicious kiss deepen. A tap on Ramie's knee turned her attention to the toddler, Theresa. She crawled up into Ramie's lap while Aubrey fished her breast out of her nursing bra to feed Katherine.

Kyle took a handful of papers from the box and cleared his throat.

Phile: Aliens

We were so focused on the wolves and accepting our new names in before-time as we slept in now-time that when Moms called us for breakfast and to get ready for school, we were like the walking dead. It was hard to reconcile the attack of the wolves and the time we'd spent tanning their hides and even eating their meat with the one night of sleep we'd struggled through as we were separated in our rooms. We were used to our other selves aging faster than we were but it was beginning to worry us. We wondered if in before-time we'd be old people by the time we were sixteen in now-time.

It wasn't until our hands touched at the breakfast table that we snapped into this reality again. Or both realities. I've seen Mom Mar walk around the house cleaning and cooking while the whole time she was reading some paperback book. I think we were a little like that. Only our book was a whole other life. That was why it was so hard for us to read books in school. It was like trying to keep track of a third reality at the same time as we were living two others.

We might even have gotten crazier after that incident. We concocted schemes in before-time and executed them in now-time. Even when teachers made us sit on opposite sides of the room, we'd just talk in before-time. Miss Bradley, our science teacher, was mean. Not just to us, but everybody. Especially those who were a little strange. There were a few in our class. We started playing tricks on her, like moving her books or her glasses while she wasn't looking. I know some of our classmates saw us do things. I'd ask a question about an experiment we were going to run and just as soon as she turned to look at me, Caitlin would turn to a different experiment in Miss B's book so when she turned back she was reading from the wrong formula. Some of the other kids even joined in.

We weren't invisible, but we were quiet and sneaky. A lot of the time, our classmates didn't know we'd done something until they saw the results. The day a bird flew through the open window and pooped on her desk might have been a little much. She never let us open windows again. It was Mandy Stevens that cornered us. We'd only known Mandy since we started junior high in Laramie. She was one of the 'weird ones' like us, but she'd never really spoken to us before. All the weird kids kind of kept to themselves.

"You two are aliens," she whispered after the final bell rang and we were on the way out to wait for the bus. "Can you teach me how to do that mental telepathy thing you do?"

"Huh?" when we answered with the same sound at the same time, Mandy started nodding her head.

"Like that. I won't tell anyone. Do you have, like, a hive mind so you always know what everyone is thinking, or is it more like you talk to each other in your heads? Will you take me to your ship? I want to learn how to do it. Don't worry, I'm good at keeping secrets. Oh, god! Can you read my mind?" She blushed crimson. Caitlin looked at me in our other life.

"I think she's having dirty thoughts!" she said. We were usually careful about not speaking English in before-time. But Cait just blurted it out.

"I wonder which of us she's fantasizing about," I laughed. We didn't get a chance to guess in now-time because Mandy never really shut up.

"I have to watch myself around you two. Just know that I mean you no harm. I friend." She gestured to herself. All of a sudden, she was talking like she had to explain something to foreigners who didn't speak English or something.

Mandy was a little strange, but she wasn't a bad person. Other kids sometimes made fun of her because she was a little overweight and had a blotchy complexion. We never did. Just that little bit of interaction made us like her. Besides, we felt like we could use an ally, you know? We agreed in before-time. In now-time, we both put our hands out at the same time to touch her shoulder.

"Mandy friend," we said in unison. She squealed and bounced a little.

"I knew it! I have to run right now because my mom's waiting, but I'll be ready any time." She ran to a small car that pulled up and got in the back seat. Cait and I got on the bus and went home.

Caitlin: Friends

STRANGE AS IT sounds when Phile tells that story, Mandy has been our friend ever since that day. Until you opened the box, she was the only one who ever knew the truth about us. She helped us figure out some of the stuff that was going on. And, as wonderfully crazy as she was… is, she's really smart and understands better than we could ever hope. She is a great adviser. And more.

Mandy became a kind of co-conspirator at school and we got away with things we never would have pulled without her. We just had to see Merv again after our encounter with the wolves. When Mandy saw the teacher was going down the attendance list and looking for us, she asked for a restroom pass and pulled the fire alarm. We got back to the school in time to make attendance at the rally point.

Merv had listened but had no time to respond to our experience before we had to run back to the school. He said he'd see us during the summer, but to keep learning.

"SUPPOSE YOU HAD a bucket to fill with water from the garden hose," Phile tried to explain to Mandy. "And there's a good stream of water. But then someone comes along with a firehose to help you fill the bucket and suddenly it's overflowing and you are trying to find another bucket but the water just keeps pouring in. We get now-time information just like everyone else. But we get before-time information two to five times as fast at the same time."

"This would make a great science fiction story," Mandy said as she listened. We'd started having lunch together every day and, little by little, the story came out. We weren't sure how she'd take it and were always prepared to laugh at her and tell her we really put one over on her. That made us both uncomfortable because she really was becoming a friend. "Of course, it isn't fiction, is it? What's it like to have two lives going on at the same time? How do you keep them separate? With all the input you are receiving, how do you function at all?" She believed us and she was sympathetic. The only other person we had who we could talk to was Merv Longsteer and he just wasn't available most of the time.

"It kind of drives us crazy," Phile said. "Sometimes we forget which is now and which is before. We blurt out something in Cheyenne in now-time and people think we're talking gibberish."

"I'm learning Cheyenne language!" Mandy said. "I'm a quarter Cheyenne. Maybe you are my ancestors!"

"Oh, wow! How would you like to be my great-great-great-grand-daughter?" I laughed. "That would really get confusing."

"Before-time and now-time. It sort of makes sense," Mandy said. "Do your before-time selves have a problem with that designation? I mean, to them, 'now' must be the future."

"We were separated from the rest of the People after the massacre. When we left, we didn't really have a native concept of future. The word that we'd translate to future is just the word for what is in front. Like if you walk in front of me, you are future. Even the word for tomorrow just means 'in the morning'. But that only makes a difference if we are trying to explain to someone else—which we don't. We only have one brain."

"No, that's not right," I interrupted. "It's part of the problem. We have two brains, but only one repository for all our memories. So, my before-time self is dreading the math assignment that's due Monday as much as my now-time self is. And the me that is talking to you is just as concerned about having enough meat dried for winter to survive. And skins to keep us warm."

"I'm hunting in before-time while we talk in now-time," Phile said. "What I want is to be out hunting in now-time, too, so I can bring home twice as much meat. I just can't get it to me in before-time."

Just talking about it with Mandy helped us understand who we were. In both times. And she accepted everything we said as true, even to the extent of tossing out Cheyenne words that would help. *Hétsetseha éšeēva*: today. *Nésta-hétsetseha*: before now.

WE STILL GOT confused. We could be as noisy or as quiet as we wanted in before-time. Once I let out a whoop when Phile brought down a buffalo and realized that I'd whooped in the middle of English class. We were so thankful to get out of school for the summer.

We were confined closer to the house that summer because of the reports of wolves. We never went anywhere without our rifles. But being inside was like being trapped in a cave with an angry she-bear. We stole food from the kitchen at breakfast time and didn't come in until dinner. We spent the time close to the house, but there were lots of animals we could talk to. Rabbits and squirrels were flighty and tended to have too much to do to stop and talk. That image of the White Rabbit being late is brilliant. Rabbits are always late for something and having to rush off. But they forget where they were going almost as fast as they run.

But there were some animals we just couldn't get through to at all. It was funny how we could walk down a street near school and quiet a barking dog. But there was no communicating with a wolf. We came upon a rattlesnake sunning itself on a rock and both sat about ten feet away from it and tried to reach into its mind. We couldn't tell the difference between the snake and the rock. There was just nothing there to contact.

We finally agreed that we needed snakeskin sheaths for our knives. A rattlesnake doesn't have a liver, I guess, and there was no spirit we could find there to thank. We cooked the meat and ate it anyway.

Phile: Horses

THAT WAS EMBARRASSING. If it wasn't for Mandy, though, Caitlin and I would have run away that summer. We'd started out twice and thought better of it. We'd finish our chores and go to the pond or the woodlot. We'd experiment talking with animals, but most of the animals around the ranch were dull. Squirrels, rabbits, gophers, pronghorns, and the occasional deer weren't much company. The pronghorns and deer were the best of the lot. It wasn't so much their intelligence that drew us, but their joy in freedom.

I think that's what attracted us to birds, as well. I could attach to a hawk or an eagle and fly. Their thoughts were as alien as their view on the world. They did not spend all their time hunting. Much of the time was spent flying just to be in the air.

WE WERE DOWN in the river bottom when we heard about the new arrivals. No one bothered to tell us at the house. The horses passed the word along.

Talking to a horse is more akin to talking to a human than a rabbit. Horses have very long memories. In fact, I think a horse remembers everything from the time it is foaled until it draws its last breath. It only takes a flick of the ear to communicate between them. The entire time a horse is grazing, it is listening. It pays attention to everything. When that brown gelding I sometimes rode turned his eyes to me, I knew we needed to head to the barn.

Caitlin and I could see them—sense them—long before we got to the paddock. And there was such a joy that I'd never expected. *Horses travel through time.* The two paints in the pasture knew us. They were with us in other time as well as here. It was the first time that we did something completely simultaneously in both times. We looked into our horses' eyes and they spoke to us in both times at the same time.

39

If this sounds anywhere near as strange as I think it does, it's still nowhere near as strange as it was. It was like suddenly being grounded. We were calm and happy. Neither one of us could stop talking about it when we came in for dinner. I even had to tell Ramie I loved her. She did it without even knowing what it would mean to us. She brought our horses to us.

Caitlin: Bonding

THE BOND BETWEEN our horses and us increased. Of course, Ramie didn't know the two crippled horses lived an alternate life with us. No one knew, except Mandy. Ramie and Kyle had to go to the upper pasture for two weeks, but at least Pa let them go together. It was plain as the noses on our faces that they were in love with each other. But Kyle had a girlfriend he kept sneaking into the bunkhouse thinking no one knew.

I looked at them all together and could see a bond among them that had two very strong lines. One was between Kyle and Aubrey. The other was between Kyle and Ramie. What we could see, though, was that there was already a deep bond between Ramie and Aubrey and it was getting stronger every day. We'd overheard Moms and Pa talking, trying to figure out 'what are we going to do with them?' and knowing there was nothing they could do. It was funny that they never asked that question about Phile and me. It was like they were blind to the fact that Phile was my mate, even if we hadn't had sex yet. We knew we would. We spent almost every night together in one or the other's bed. We didn't even think about wearing clothes. We never did when we slept together in before-time, so why should we in now-time.

Having Kyle and Ramie gone for two weeks was great. We were given the responsibility of caring for all the horses while they rode herd. Of course, we had to pretend to be put out about the extra work, but all we wanted to do was be with the horses. We even started picking up all the rocks in the little pasture near the barn where the two horses were the only ones allowed. The rocks hurt their tender feet and we were hoping the guy who drove them on concrete streets without shoes was having a particularly hard time in prison. We thought about sending rats to eat the soles of his feet, but we didn't know exactly where he was.

It was hot, sweaty work in the field and we welcomed showers when we came in at night.

Aside from the shower, coming into the house to sleep at night was a pain. We'd rather have stayed outside under the stars. The house was hot and muggy. We kept the windows open wide and sat on my bed to call Mandy. She answered right away and her image came up on Skype.

"Oh!" she said. "Hi. I didn't... I mean..."

"Is something wrong, Mandy?" I asked.

"No. No, of course not." She took a deep breath and stripped off her nightshirt. She had kind of floppy boobs and both Phile and me gasped when they came into view. Floppy or not, they were nice to look at.

"Mandy?" I said.

"I will always try to respect your customs, no matter what they are," she said. "If this is the way you prefer to communicate, it will be fine." I finally caught a glimpse of myself in the little window in the corner of the screen and then looked down. Neither Phile nor I had put a shirt on when we came to bed. Mandy decided that if I was topless, she should be, too!

It was a little embarrassing at first, but it was too damned hot to put clothes on to sleep. In other time, we only wore shirts when we were prowling near whites or moving with the village. We'd found a band to attach ourselves to and we were hunkered down in a valley to wait out the winter. The Wolf Twins were becoming well-known as hunters and providers for our people. Despite our ages, we often led the hunting parties.

I guess seeing Mandy naked was different, though, because Phile's manhood was paying attention. I decided right then that we'd hold all our conversations like this.

"Thank you, Mandy. It is so much more comfortable like this than in the clothes of this age," I said. Phile just nodded.

BEFORE-TIME HAD SLOWED up from the rocketing pace of the first two and ten years, but it was still moving about twice as fast as now-time. In before-time, we'd aged two years since our twelfth birthday and were nearly the same age now. That got us a little scared. We didn't want to be all grown up in before-time without being grown up in now-time, too. We wanted our now-time bodies to grow up faster, but they weren't cooperating.

We'd had a topless chat with Mandy at least once a week all summer, but it was good to get face to face with her when school started again and we were in eighth grade.

"What are you writing?" I asked.

"Um… Everything, I guess," Mandy said when she'd sat down at lunch with us and pulled out her notebook. "I'm… uh… Well, you've been an inspiration to me. I've started studying my Cheyenne heritage and how your experience fits into it. I think… You'll think this is dumb, but I think I want to become a Medicine Woman. I went up to the reservation in Lame Deer for a week this summer and talked to the teachers there."

"You didn't tell them about us, did you?" Phile asked. We were both alarmed.

"No! Of course not! I talked to them about medicine and lore. I've got books like you wouldn't believe! But I'd never betray you to anyone. Phile, you are important to me. I mean, really important, Caitlin. Like… really."

During our summer, Mandy had become really important to us, as well. We could only see Merv Longsteer occasionally. We could see Mandy every day. Even with Merv, we'd never talked about who we were. We got lessons from him when we could, but they were about the craft of being Cheyenne, not about our other lives. Mandy knew almost everything. We'd let her know who we really are.

THAT FALL, IT was even harder to get time with Merv. We'd almost been caught there when Ramie showed up and Merv started showing her how to use a knife. Like to fight with. We had a funny feeling that more things as strange as our lives were happening in our family.

Mandy asked questions that got us thinking about what we are. We couldn't begin to answer the questions she asked us. We'd never thought about which time was our 'real' time. Where did we belong? Since we were eight when we were born in before-time and could remember everything about it, we assumed that now-time was where we belonged. When a kid grows up, he normally only has a conscious memory of really big things until about the time he starts being independent. We had only fleeting memories of what our lives were like before Yelloweye gave us our other selves. Yet, we remembered every detail about growing up in before-time.

It shocked the hell out of us to imagine that our real lives—and perhaps the mission that Yelloweye had for us—was in before-time and we just needed the knowledge and experience of now-time in order to achieve the goal! Whatever it was. We did a lot of things differently in before-time than our contemporaries did, including our personal hygiene.

"So, perhaps your before-time selves are trying to slow you down in this life so they can remember more about this," Mandy suggested. "If all eight of you agree, you can synchronize your aging. It would be easier on all of you."

"All eight of us?" I asked.

"I don't think your horses would have bothered to find you in now-time if they didn't expect to be consulted about important things," she said. My mouth dropped open. "So, there's eight of you. Four in before-time and four in now-time."

"If the horses are in both times at the same time, like us, we might be causing them to age faster in before-time, too!" Phile said. "I'm getting a headache."

"Horses live a pretty long life. If they're well cared-for, they could live to be thirty or more," I said, beginning to figure out what Mandy was telling us.

"Yeah. So, if you are controlling the time and making it go faster in before-time, that means that you are moving them closer to death in before-time than they are moving here. If you are out of sync and they die at thirty in before-time, but they are only fifteen here, what's going to happen to them?" Mandy asked. Her eyes got big. "You really need to talk to the horses."

WE NEEDED TO talk to Yelloweye, too, but we hadn't seen him in either life for a long time. The only bird we ever saw around the ranch was an old one-eyed raven. I got shivers down my spine whenever I heard him caw.

I figured I'd just jump into his head and ask him if he'd seen Yelloweye.

He answered before I got that far. It startled me so much that I fell back right on my butt. Phile was on his way to the barn to get hay. He turned around and came rushing back to me. He was looking around and had his knife out like he thought someone was attacking me.

"You okay? What happened?" he whispered.

"I'm fine. Phile, we gotta sneak out tonight. We gotta meet Bells and Bows in the paddock. And the Wolf Twins need to take their horses to Medicine Rock. We're all going to meet with Yelloweye."

"Shit! How'd you know that?"

"That old raven told me," I said. Phile turned and nodded to the half-blind bird.

"Messenger bird. Thank you for your help," Phile said. The bird bobbed his head up and down like he understood English and then took off toward the mountain. "We better tell Bells and Bows."

"We did," I laughed. "This is so weird. The Wolf Twins are already with our horses and they already passed on the word."

"Yeah," Phile said. "Weird."

Phile: Getting in Sync

WE RAN TO the old cabin and got our bows from the chimney. There's a rock under the kitchen porch at the ranch house that we could lay them on so they didn't rest in the moist soil. It was mid-October and getting dang cold out at night. I knew we'd have to wear our heavy coats, but there was no way I was going outside without any weapons. We couldn't take our guns. If we were attacked by wolves—and we'd heard them howling closer and closer to the ranch—and if a bow wasn't good enough to kill one, we'd die. But if we shot one, Pa would know, and I guessed I'd rather die than have Pa find out I was out with Caitlin in the middle of the night.

It was a tense night as we waited.

"You're going to do it?" Mandy asked on Skype. We were getting used to seeing her big tits on our computer screen. I supposed she was getting used to seeing Cait's. They were growing pretty fast now. Like my cock.

"We're going out to the horses in about an hour," I said. "The raven said *méstahke* would meet us."

"You trust him?" Mandy asked. She started sorting through some notes in front of her. She kept jiggling her boobs from side to side. Even I was distracted. "You said the owl, *Méstaa'e*, was like the bogeyman. He'll get you if you go outside at night."

"Do you write down everything we say?" Cait asked.

"Mostly."

"I've never been afraid of Yelloweye. If he tricks me into a place where I die, I go willingly," I said. Caitlin nudged me in the side. Okay. I was peacocking for our friend a little!

"Ain't gonna happen," Caitlin laughed. "Don't worry, little Mandy. We'll come back for you."

"You will?"

"Neither of us has seen enough of your tits yet," she said. She kind of pushed hers out toward the camera a little. Mandy blushed. Maybe I did, too. My sister was displaying her proud breasts for our girlfriend.

"You just both be careful. Okay?"

"Yeah. See you in school Monday, Mandy," I said. We closed the window.

"Phile and Mandy, sittin' in a tree…" Caitlin sang at me.

"Hush," I said. "I just like to compare what she's got to what's sitting beside me." I reached over and tweaked her nipple a little. She gasped like a thousand volts of electricity shot through her. "And… um… you were just as turned on by her as I was."

"You better behave yourself. We aren't ready for that and you know it," Cait whispered.

"Yeah. I know. But I'm getting interested," I grinned.

We got ourselves dressed and sneaked downstairs and out the kitchen door.

BELLS AND BOWS were waiting quietly for us. We grabbed a couple brushes and started on them while we waited for Yelloweye to show up. We'd figured out how to smash a sycamore branch down so it was all bristly on the end and were combing the knots out of our horses' manes in before-time. It was cool. We were just tending our horses in both times, late at night, talking to them. I could feel the warmth of the fire in before-time, even though we had no fire in now-time.

I felt a stirring. Caitlin and I dropped our brushes and picked up our bows in both times. A man materialized from the shadows near the barn, only it wasn't a man in before-time. Yelloweye soared from the sky and lit on the branch above us. Our heads combined the two. We could see the man in Yelloweye and the owl in our visitor.

"Merv?" Cait asked, shakily. Merv Longsteer approached us and stopped near Bells.

"I expected I would see you," he said. "My granddaughter has been pushing me to help you. You quit coming to see me."

"Your schedule got kind of crowded with Ramie showing up all the time," I said.

"I see. I'll find a place where we can have lunch together occasionally."

"Who is your granddaughter?" Cait asked.

"Mmm. That would be Mandy Stevens. My daughter's daughter. She says you are Cheyenne aliens. I hope she has been helpful."

"Very. I like Mandy a lot," I said. "We didn't know she was related to you. But why are you here?"

"I'm not sure I am," Merv said thoughtfully. "I remember going to sleep. But Yelloweye said he needed my voice."

"You know *Heove-'éxané*?" I said.

"I serve whichever of the old ones have need for my voice," Merv said. "This one has trouble getting things clear. He uses my mind and my voice to tell you many things." I looked at Phile. Mandy was a little weird, but Merv wasn't quite all there. Perhaps literally.

"We want to know how to synchronize our times so we don't grow old in before-time while we stay young in now-time," I said. Might as well cut right to the chase. I figured that even though none of us had talked about living in two times, Merv was there to interpret for Yelloweye and he knew.

"Yes," Merv said. In before-time we could hear his words as though they came straight from Yelloweye. The horses shuffled around so they could face him, too. "You must forget time," he said. It didn't sound like Merv's voice. "You must be always here now. You see two times, two bodies, where I see only one. You see two humans and two horses where I see only one. You see Redtail, Blackfeather, and Yelloweye, where I see only I. Accept that you are who you are. You are one."

"I'm only thirteen. I don't understand all this," I moaned. Merv chuckled.

"It takes time," he snorted. It was definitely Merv.

"That's it?" I said. "That's all Yelloweye is going to tell us? What about trying to get ourselves in sync so one doesn't out-age the other? How do we coordinate things with the horses? What's it mean to be *one*?"

"We'll have to talk about this more. You can't expect to understand everything at once. I'll tell you what I think and you can decide what you think. I think Yelloweye has said that you are a visitor in time, not a captive. You need to accept that your before-time self is one with your now-time self. I don't think you will do this easily. It is a task that Yelloweye has set for you," Merv said. "I think that we should all go home and go to bed now." Merv turned away from us and walked toward the barn. He just faded into the shadows.

Cait and I looked at the horses and they shook their heads like they didn't understand either. We hugged them and petted them for a while, then we went back to the house. We hid our bows before we crept up the stairs and crawled into bed together.

The Family

THE FAMILY WAS exhausted when Kyle said he couldn't read any more.

"Pa!" Ramie practically shouted. "Them kids was… The kids were time traveling years before we were!" Sometimes when Ramie got excited she let herself forget good English. "They were struggling to coordinate their two halves just like we were. You stop and think about it, I'll bet their lives overlapped with Laramie Wyoming Bell's. Probably. That means with your life, too."

"They sure overlapped with our lives," Jason said. "We already know that I was the blond-haired soldier who gunned down their momma."

"Jason, honey, don't torment yourself over that anymore." Ashley said. "It was 150 years ago. If any of you knew what you know now, none of that would have happened."

"That's just it," Ramie said. "They do know. They know what happened and what is happening at the same time. They don't have moments when their before-time selves and their now-time selves are cut off from each other and have to make decisions based on partial knowledge. Whatever the old owl has planned for them, whether in before-time or now-time, what we did to protect the land will pale by comparison."

"What we've seen tonight in what they wrote is that the timeline doesn't make a difference. They'd experienced what you did before you ever started time traveling, Kyle. It was already written. You couldn't change history," Cole said.

"The box was already open," Ramie confirmed.

4
Wolf Warriors

The Family

COLE SPENT a good part of the day at the Forest Service office and on the phone to his congressman. Every member of the family made calls.

"Cole," Arlen said as the rancher sat across the desk from him, "our hands are tied. The EPA is gutted and there's been no move to replace it. The Army Corps of Engineers rubberstamps whatever they're given. They've been issued permits to explore for gas and oil in the National Forest. It's not just here. They came marching in on the first with permits for the entire Medicine Bow, the Shoshone, the Teton, the Gallatin, Lewis and Clark... They moved crews into every accessible area of the Northern Rockies. Not just crews, but heavy equipment. Ever since the samples came out of the site in Yellowstone, the permits have been flying like gnats."

"What are we going to do, Arlen? This is public land. They're fencing off areas—good grazing areas. Places where we've had the rights for generations," Cole said.

"All I can do is stand between the parties and try not to get my rangers killed in the crossfire," Arlen said. "We've got a blog up and have a campaign on Twitter and Facebook, but those became so discredited that nobody believes anything they read there unless it happens to agree with what they think. We can't get press because the press is owned by the same multinationals that own the energy companies and they're all owned by Wall Street."

"Well, we're going to keep fighting this, Arlen. We'll start with a call campaign to our representative and senators. There are too many of us who depend on the land to let them take it away from us."

"Good luck with that, Cole. I mean it. We've got one voice in the House. Montana has one. Colorado has seven. If you can get Idaho and

Utah onboard, that's six more. Fifteen out of 435. But the truth is, they're owned by the same multinationals."

NONETHELESS, THE FAMILY tried. They called their representatives and senators. They called their neighbors. Aubrey printed up some fliers and they gave them to the folks who boarded at the stables and who brought their mares in for stud service. Their campaign barely rated a footnote to the larger protest in Yellowstone National Park where the oil company had announced that the pseudo-fracking operation that would begin soon. That protest had closed the Park entirely and no traffic was allowed through the gates. Still, an estimated thousand or more Native American protesters had set up a village in the basin of the Park below the drilling site.

"I'M ALREADY EXHAUSTED," Mary Beth said as the family gathered after dinner and the news. "I was going to read tonight, but I don't think I can."

"I'll do it," Cole said. "I need to take my mind away from the local troubles. My children are more important. Maybe by reading, I can reach out to them." Cole took the box and pulled out the sheaf of papers that would make the next part of the story.

Phile: Wolves

I ALWAYS GET to tell about the wolves because Cait can't handle it. I don't mean she breaks down or is frightened, but something happened to us in before-time when we ate the raw warm hearts of the hunting pair we killed. The very idea that there were other wolves hunting in our marked territory sparked a primitive need to defend it. This is our land. I want to hunt the alpha male and gut him with my claws. Caitlin's response is even more visceral.

In before-time, Cait and I still lived apart from the village, but we were welcome there. The soldiers had killed most of the old people, women, and children when they attacked, but the warriors had been out hunting. There were enough survivors that they had to gather and protect them rather than chasing after the soldiers for revenge. The old wise woman had still been in her tipi when the soldiers came, and so she was spared. A few of the women had been gathering in the forest and ran when they heard the guns. But of a band of nearly 200, there were scarcely 75 left.

The excitement started with a fox showing up at the edge of our camp.

Bent Bow, now our chief hunter, came from his tent with an arrow already on the string. I think he would have shot right through me to kill the fox if our *He'évánó'èstse*—our wise woman—had not placed her hand on his arm. He was angry because he liked to kill animals, even when he did not need food. I suspected he was part white.

"This is a messenger, Bent Bow," the old woman said to him. "Do not let your lust to kill overwhelm you. I fear you will have much to satisfy it soon."

"The Wolf Twins are witches. We should not have them in our camp," he answered. "They should be driven away."

The old woman nodded toward the edge of our circle at the large frame where an elk hide was stretched. It had been an old bull who offered himself. Caitlin and I lowered our bows to salute his gift. Bent Bow took the shot and claimed the kill. It did not make a difference to us because it fed our village. But it added to his power in the village.

"Yet they need you to make their kills," the old woman said. "You protected them from the charging bull when they could not defend themselves, according to the way you recited the hunt. And never did they contradict you. Look in your heart, Bent Bow. Your quiver is nearly empty."

I rose from my conference with the fox and he trotted off into the woods. I turned to the wise woman and gave the message to her.

"*Ma'ėhóóhe* has seen many men on horses riding toward the sunset along the winding river. They make much noise and it disturbs his kits. He appeals to the people to make the horsemen leave."

"Do they come to hunt us?" Bent Bow asked.

"Fox does not understand the speech of the soldiers," I said. "He only appeals to us as the people of the land to protect it."

"We should kill the whites," the warrior declared.

"Wolf Twins, can you understand the whites as you understand the animals?" Wise Woman asked. I trod carefully on this path. To the People, there was no way that I could know the language.

"It may be possible," I answered. "I do not know if I can get one to hold still long enough to talk." This got some laughter from our quickly gathered council. I wasn't officially a member of the council. Cait and I were much too young to be considered part of the elders. But our status as a kind of *Ma'heónĕhetane* or shaman allowed us to speak. There was a lot of discussion among the older men and women that went long into the night. Caitlin and I were not included. We retired to our tent and took our own council.

"My wolf heart is beating hard, *Naéhame*," Caitlin said. It made me proud when she referred to me as her mate. We had not mated in the manner of man and woman, but we were recognized as a pair and no one challenged our right to be together.

"I think we need to investigate. If we can get close, we can hear what they say. It is good that our tribe does not know we understand English. They will think we read the hearts of whiteman," I said.

"More than ever, I see the wisdom of hiding this from both the tribe and the whites. The wolves must prowl."

In the morning, we emerged from our tent wearing just our loin-cloths and wolf skins. The wise woman met us at the fire circle. Meat was already roasting and my mouth watered. She tore two slabs of meat from the roasting carcass and threw them to us like we would throw scraps to a dog. When we wore the skins, we were considered part of the animal world. No one would approach us. We snatched the meat out of the air before it touched the ground. I hate eating food that's been in the dirt.

"You will hunt," she said. "Before we send braves to meet the guns of soldiers, we will know that they are a threat. If they do not hunt us, we will let them go their way and we will move on. Go."

We chewed our meat, not completely cooked, as we walked out of the village. Our horses fell in beside us as we left. We honored their presence by not mounting them where the village could see us. When we were mounted, they flew like the wind toward the soldiers.

WE RUBBED OUR horses down and they rolled in the dirt. They had worked up quite a lather and dust quickly turned to mud. If a scout happened upon them, they would look like *nähahévo'hāme*, wild horses, and not like *Mo'éhno'ha*, or what the whites called Indian ponies. There was a herd of mustangs sheltered in a nearby canyon and they ran off to join them. They would bring us even more news when we returned.

Cait and I made our way toward the soldier camp, another two miles away. We became the wolves we were dressed as and took most of the day to reach the encampment. Lying low in the brush near the river, we listened. When soldiers came near, we disappeared into the trees, but always stayed near enough to hear.

"This is the piss-poorest, god-awfulest place in the world," a soldier said to his companion.

"You didn't see Georgia when we marched to the sea," said an older grizzled man. "Everything behind us was black ash. Everything ahead of us was flying lead. Sherman didn't burn Georgia to deprive the Rebs. He did it to keep us from turning around."

"Well, ya saw real action," the younger said. "Where are these Indians we're supposed to be hunting?"

"Probably ten steps away listening to us," the older said. We crept back farther. Had he heard us? "That's the thing about Indians. They don't come out and fight like men. They'll fall out of trees on your back. They'll cut your throat in your bedroll. An arrow is silent death. You never hear it."

"Hell, you're a joy to listen to."

"Just keep your knife at your hand. You won't have a chance to draw your gun."

So, they *were* hunting Indians. That wasn't good. It didn't mean they were after our band specifically. But when we found an officer talking, that was a different thing.

"Scout says there's a band about two days' ride north of here," the captain said. "Our orders are to clear the area for settlement. I want you to take a detachment of twenty men and make sure they are no longer a threat."

"We'll leave at first light, sir," his lieutenant responded.

"We've been riding hard for a week. Give the men another day of rest before you leave. The savages won't be going anywhere."

"The men will be happy for an opportunity to kill some redskins. They've been getting itchy," the lieutenant answered.

"Make sure there is no one left to complain."

It was difficult to keep the wolf in me from attacking and killing both men. Cait and I slipped back about a mile and paced back and forth.

"We should warn the village," I said.

"We should kill them all in their sleep like that old soldier suggested," Caitlin responded.

"Cait, listen." She turned her head toward the sound we could both hear. "We've got a problem at the ranch. Wolves."

"Ma! Pa! We hear wolves down in the bottomland. It's got the horses spooked!" Caitlin yelled as we burst through the kitchen door of the ranch. "They were galloping toward the river." That's where things started getting confusing. I don't mean the craziness at the ranch with Pa and Mom Ash headed one direction and Ramie and Kyle headed another. Caitlin and I were sent to the pasture to protect the stock and took our rifles.

But things were going crazy in both timelines at the same time. In before-time, we had to stop the soldiers. In now-time, we had to stop the wolves. It was caring for the horses in now-time that gave us the idea of what to do with the soldiers. We shared all the thoughts at the same time. Bells and Bows were right there with us and met us on the run.

We didn't exactly stay in the upper pasture where we'd been told. The horses told us there was no threat from that direction. But there were two gates that held the rest of the horses in the river pasture. We opened the paddock gate and the two horses followed us, even though their feet were still tender. The boots we'd put on them helped, but they weren't used to anything on their feet and sometimes stumbled a little.

As soon as we got the lower gate open, they took off for the river. When the horses saw Kyle on his three-wheeler headed their direction, they naturally turned and headed up toward the ranch, putting him between them and the wolves. Bells and Bows met them and there was a stampede to the open gate. Cait and I got to the paddock to open the gate just as the herd came charging toward us. They were all spooked, but as soon as we got the gate closed behind them, we started shoveling hay out for them and they started to calm down.

At the same time, we were moving among the soldier horses and cutting their halters while we talked to them in their heads. We showed them a rich pasture where no one would try to make them carry heavy saddles and people. As each one left the rope corral where they were tethered, our horses guided them through the woods to meet up with the others. We had to work fast because the night patrol would be by to check on them shortly.

When they showed up, they started yelling and soldiers scurried out of their bedrolls with their weapons drawn looking for threats while they bounced around trying to get their boots on. A couple shots were fired and the last three horses broke loose. Unfortunately, they headed right for the other horses. The scout who had brought the word of our village to the troops camped outside the circle of soldiers and had his horse saddled before the shots were fired. He headed the direction the last three horses were going with intent to round them up and bring them back.

We couldn't let that happen.

Untethered horses can move fast. Much faster than a horse and rider in the darkness. And a slow horse and rider is no match for a wolf. The scout heard the snarl and pulled his gun, but he wasn't fast enough to avoid the bite of Wolf Riding Woman's knife driving into his throat. The two gunshots echoed in our ears in both timelines. Wolf Riding Woman tore at the throat of the dead scout with her teeth as I cut the tack from his horse. I finally had to kick Caitlin off him to get her moving. She started to turn on me before she came back to her senses. Blood ran from her face and down her bare chest.

It wasn't hers.

Caitlin: Sister

EVERYTHING WAS QUIET after the gunshots in now-time. I stood there feeling… tasting the blood in my mouth from before-time. I had my rifle on my shoulder looking for an enemy.

Phile laid a hand on my shoulder and I lowered the gun. The horses had bunched in a corner of the corral, but they were looking calmer.

"Let's get some hay and oats. Those rescues never get oats. They'll settle right down." We got the feed and as we scooped it into the trough Phile said, "We're missing one. Where's Lucky?"

We sent our minds questing out trying to locate the missing horse and found him hobbling up toward the pasture gate, trying to make his way to the other horses. He was bleeding. We brought him up to the barn and tied him as I hand-fed him oats and Phile tended the wounds. He called the vet and told him what we saw. The vet said he'd be out with antibiotics and sutures, and told us to keep Lucky separate.

While Phile was on the phone, I saw the ATVs racing toward the house together. Mom Mar was out the door with a phone to her ear and her hands full of bandages and medicine. Aubrey was right behind her carrying a kettle with the handle wrapped in a dishtowel. And then I saw Kyle carry Ramie into the bunkhouse.

My sister lay limp in his arms.

I AM SO sorry, Ramie, that I have never been able to tell you how much I love you. I know I was a brat, but I hope you know why now. You were kind to us kids, even when we were at our worst. You defended us on the bus to school. You brought Bells and Bows to us at the ranch. You gave us good work that we were happy doing. And you never once passed judgment on Phile and me for being in love, even when you struggled with your own relationships. But in all that time, I never told you what I felt when I saw Kyle carry you into the house. I love you, my sister.

I was frozen in place. In both before-time and now-time, I vowed to destroy every threat to our family, our tribe, our land.

Phile: Wolf Warrior

CAVALRY WITHOUT HORSES is infantry. Only infantry wears boots that are made for walking. The soldiers at the river camp wore riding boots. It would be a long time before they could pursue us. Just long enough for us to move our tribe. I picked up a couple of horseshoes that the soldiers' horses had thrown. What we didn't have among the People was iron or steel. A pair of iron horseshoes could give Cait and me what we needed most—metal knives.

When we were several miles north of where we knew the soldiers could catch us, I led Caitlin to a stream and took her wolf robe. She followed me into the cold water and I gently washed the blood from her face, hands, and chest.

Caitlin stripped off her loincloth, too. I saw blood running down her legs.

"Wolf Riding Woman, are you injured?" I asked as I bathed away the blood. It continued to flow.

"Wolf Rising, I have begun my time. I have become a woman," she said.

"You got your period?" I said in English. She laughed.

But at the same time, she doubled up next to Ramie's bed with a bad cramp. We couldn't believe it when our big sister was carried up to the house with teeth-marks on her neck. The damned wolves! We swore we'd kill every one of them. But while we were sitting with Ramie and Kyle and Aubrey, the cramps hit Caitlin and she started her menses.

She admitted to discomfort in before-time, but she was a warrior. In now-time, she was a teenage girl getting her first period. Even with Ramie lying in bed, Moms made a fuss over Caitlin. The doctor had said Ramie just needed rest and fluids with the antibiotics he gave her. In both times, I treated Caitlin/Wolf Riding Woman as the princess I thought her to be. Caitlin hugged a heating pad as she sat by Ramie in now-time. In before-time, after we had bathed, she wadded some cottonwood tree fluff into her loincloth and lay beside me to sleep. We had to keep moving so we would outpace the soldiers, if they decided to pursue us. But in now-time, I went out by myself the next day and snared two rabbits. I skinned them and presented them to Caitlin. She took them to the house and Mom Mar helped her turn them into rabbit stew. I was so proud of her. It was the first meal she cooked as a woman. I suppose Mom Mar knew what was happening, but the rabbits were to honor my woman. I don't think anyone objected, even as Caitlin spooned some of her broth into Ramie's mouth.

Merv Longsteer came out to the house and did some medicine on Ramie. Before he left, he motioned me and Cait out to the paddock.

When we were out of the sight of the house he turned to face us. He lifted a hand to touch Caitlin's cheek and turn it back and forth. She stiffened but stood upright and returned his stare.

"*Vé'otsé'e*," he said. Warpath woman. "Protect the people from danger. Do not lead them into it. Find the path that leads them to safety." He turned his gaze on me and stood back. "*Ho'néhenótáxeo'o*, Wolf Warriors, your older sister will return soon. Tread carefully. The spirits move among us and your time will come soon enough. For now, find that place where you can grow and learn. When you return, the world will have turned again."

He turned and walked away down the long drive to the ranch. A truck was parked down there and he got in the passenger side before it left.

There was a shout from the bunkhouse and we ran to find Ramie awake. She had a strange look in her eyes and I thought she'd been away a lot longer than it seemed. She looked older to me.

"Maybe that's what Merv and Yelloweye have been telling us. We need to find a place where we can live a long time in peace and learn while our bodies grow up," Caitlin said. "I think I see the way."

Trouble was waiting for us when we got back to the tribe. First was the warriors wanting to go hunt down the soldiers. That was going nowhere fast.

"The soldiers are not a threat to us. They have no horses. They will go back where they came from. Later, more soldiers will come. We have time to leave and be elsewhere before they come," Caitlin argued in the council.

"Why do we listen to an unblooded child in our council?" Bent Bow demanded.

"I am blooded!" Cait screamed. She held up her wolf robe. "The blood on my wolf teeth is from the man whose throat I ripped out with my teeth. On that same day, my woman's blood began to flow. I am Wolf Riding Woman. I will give counsel to the elders when what I have seen must be brought to their eyes. And I have seen a path we must trod."

"A full woman?" Bent Bow asked. "Then I will take you as my wife. The animal talker can find a wife when he becomes a man." The warrior made the mistake of laying a hand on Caitlin to claim her. The long blade of her obsidian knife ran up his middle causing him to jump back. A thin rivulet of blood seeped from the scratch. Cait followed it by scoring him from side to side before he could respond.

"Touch me again and I will flay the skin from your bones to make another robe," she growled. "My knife has tasted the blood of whiteman and of redman. It knows no difference."

Bent Bow howled and ran out of the council tent. We knew we would never be safe with him around.

"What is your plan, Wolf Riding Woman?" the wise woman asked.

"Honored Grandmother," Cait said. "Wolf Rising and I have been shown a path to a hunting ground of plenty. The buffalo are strong. The elk are abundant. Even trees bear food for our people. There we can dwell and whiteman will not hunt us."

"Where is this wonderful land of plenty with no whiteman?" an old man asked.

"It is on the path that Yelloweye will show us. We need only follow him," she answered.

Caitlin: Other Where

My man praises me. I sound like a swelled headed little brat.

But it was true. What I'd seen when Ramie came back was that it was possible to go someplace to live a long time and have as little or as much time go by elsewhere as was desired. Yelloweye would show us the way.

That night, the tribe gathered at the fire. We sang and beat on little drums as we danced a dance to the old owl. I believe the old men thought we would simply die. That was the meaning of the owl. To follow the owl meant that we would pass into the hereafter and be gone from this earth. Perhaps it was true. We'd go to some happy hunting ground. I thought of it more as an alternative universe. It was *Oxése*, other place—our world without the invasion of the Europeans. There was plenty of game. We could follow normal migration patterns without having to go around towns that grew up in our path.

In the morning, they were surprised to find that we were all still alive. We packed our tents and skins on travois behind our horses and walked toward the mountains. It was three days to the passage that Yelloweye showed us. It was narrow, but Wolf Rising and I held hands as the People passed us. Then our two horses and their burdens passed.

Down the trail, we could see Bent Bow tracking us, his arrow ready to fly. We were standing right in the middle of the path, but he didn't seem to see us. I pulled Phile through the passage. Yelloweye swooped through right behind us.

Bent Bow was running toward the standing stones, pulling his bow as he came. He passed between the rocks and disappeared.

"Where did he go?" Phile asked.

"I don't think he went anywhere," I said. Yelloweye landed on a branch nearby and hooted at us. "It's we who disappeared. The best Bent Bow will be able to discover is that the tracks he has been following vanished."

THE PEOPLE DID not even realize they had passed through a time change or world gate of any sort. *Oxése* was, as far as we could tell, the same as what we left. Yelloweye soothed our concerns. We were in a different version of our reality. One day, perhaps the realities would merge again and it would all be the same as if we had never left. In this reality, there were no soldiers, no whites. The people took care of the land and the land took care of the people.

We made camp at the fork of a river that looked much like the fields we knew on the ranch, but without fences or houses. When the fire was lit, we were summoned to the council. We donned our wolf skins and sat with the elders.

"Wolf Twins," the wise woman said. "We would know how far we must journey and when we will be safe."

"We are safe," I said. "We have journeyed to a place that *Heove-'éxané* prepared for us. He is here with us and has spread his wings to protect his people." Right on cue, the old owl lit next to me on the log where Phile and I sat. There was a gasp from the council. They had heard that we speak with animals and that the owl was our special totem. But there was so much superstition about owls in the tribe that it was hard to accept the bird's presence without assuming it meant my imminent death. The owl had appeared the night Phile was born, after all, and his mother died giving him life. He had sat on our tipi when the soldiers came and took my mother. Now he sat beside me.

"We are honored by your grandsire's presence," the wise woman said hesitantly. "Thank you for leading us to a place where we are safe from the white soldiers. Thank you for giving us your speakers and showing them the footsteps we should tread. Thank you for looking favorably on your people." She nodded to our chief, a man as old as she.

"Henceforth we will be *Méstaa'e-vo'éstaneme*, the People Who Follow the Owl," the old man said. "This old man shall continue his journey with the owl tonight and his spirit will watch over the people as they camp here by the laughing waters. The son of Buffalo Woman, Running Fox, will lead us where we must go in the future. He will listen to the voices of the wolf and the owl. Wolf Riding Woman and Wolf Rising, you will be welcome when you visit our people, but you must not dwell with us. There are not enough of us for frequent visits by *Heove-'éxané*."

With that, the old man retired to his tent. We knew we would never see him again.

The Family

ASHLEY HAD BOLTED from the room in the middle of the reading and they heard her throwing up in the bathroom. She returned with a wet washcloth held against her eyes and her wife cuddled her close while Cole continued to read. They all understood the necessity for Caitlin to kill the scout. They were sad that their little girl had been forced to the action at such a young age. But Ashley's daughter had done more than kill. She had ripped the man's throat out with her teeth.

When Cole finally put the papers down, Ashley curled up in his lap while he stroked her hair. Though fading, slightly, that hair was still golden enough to remind them all of Caitlin. Kyle had never seen his normally dominant mother look so small and vulnerable as Mary Beth joined her mates on the arm of the big chair.

Cole had kept reading so that the image of raiding the soldiers would not be the last thing the family remembered from the evening. Their children had led the People to a place of safety. Perhaps they were ready for a gentler chapter in their lives.

Ramie reflexively felt the faded scars on her neck. She'd been that close to having a wolf rip her own throat out. It had happened at the same time Caitlin was killing the scout. Miranda, inside her, felt the rawness of her throat from when the berserk girl she'd rescued tried to strangle her and the tongue of the great gray wolf that soothed her injury. Jason and Kyle knew the effect that losing their horses would have on the cavalry company. And what finding the scout would do to their fragile discipline.

The family crept to bed quietly, whispers of 'goodnight' sounding impossibly loud.

"This story is going to tear the family apart," Aubrey whispered as we put the babies to bed.

"What do you want us to do? Stop reading about what happened to my baby brother and sister?" Ramie snapped at her. Aubrey looked at her with tears flowing from her eyes. "Oh, my god! It started! I'm so sorry, Aubrey. Don't let me snap at you, my beloved. What will we do? What can we do?"

"Laramie Wyoming Bell, my love and my wife, love me like you have never done before. And I promise I will do the same for you."

"We should stop reading the journal."

"My love, it's too late. The cat is out of the bag. Or in this case, the box. Think. We lived with those two kids next to us for six years. They were the hardest workers on this ranch. You've had to hire four people to do what those two did. Even the horses are less settled since they left. We know what kind of people they are. They aren't the kind to do things like gutting a rapist or shooting a woman in the street," Aubrey said, reminding Ramie of what she, herself, had done when traveling back into Miranda's body.

Ramie kissed her lover passionately.

"That's exactly what we need to be reminded of! Thank you! I am going to bury my face between your legs tonight if I can nudge Kyle out of the way," Ramie said. "But first I have to go talk to Moms and Pa." Ramie went to put on her buckskins. Miranda started to object was put firmly down. "You know I got to do this, Miranda," she said.

I do, Demon Ramie. I just dread it.

Ramie strapped her Colt Navy around her hips and headed to her parents.

"Moms! Pa! We need to talk!" she shouted. Her parents came into the room, all wearing robes as they had been ready for bed. "Strap your irons on, Pa," Ramie commanded. Cole nodded and retrieved his Smith and Wessons from the study. He shared the office with Ramie now. She managed the horse ranch and he managed the cattle ranch. He was thinking maybe he should give up the cattle business. He arrived on the front porch where Ramie, Ashley, and Mary Beth were waiting. Kyle strode across the lawn carrying his Winchester. They waited for him to join them on the porch. Ramie pulled Mary Beth and Ashley in front of them.

"Look out there, Moms," Ramie said. She saw Cole pull his guns from their holsters and point to the places in the yard where, when he was time traveling, he'd killed five men. "Five men Pa killed, right out there," Ramie said. She pulled the Colt Navy from its holster and her knife from her boot. "I gutted one rapist and cut the throats of two others. I shot a woman down on the streets of Laramie with this gun."

Jason spoke through Kyle's voice.

"Old men. Women. Children. They thought they were safe because they stood beneath an American flag. But we cut them down," Jason said. "We were frightened boys who believed the Indians were lying in ambush for us and we'd surprised them."

"You don't hate me, Mom Mar. You never had anything but care and concern for Kyle, Mom Ash. You both love Pa and he never regretted saving his family that night here on the lawn," Ramie said. "You can't hate Caitlin! You can't be disappointed in her. She lived in two different worlds and did what was necessary in each of them. She protected her family. Don't turn your backs on her—or on Phile when you find out what he's done. Phile's a different kind of warrior. He was never as aggressive as Caitlin. But I guarandamntee you, we're going to find out he was a warrior. Trust your kids. Trust our family. Trust the land." Ramie was weeping and Mary Beth pulled her daughter to her as Ashley threw herself at Kyle/Jason.

"Don't ever doubt how much we love you," Ashley said. "I never time traveled, but I held a rifle at the ready to defend this piece of heaven during the range wars. I hoped it was over for us. It hurts so much to see what my daughters and my sons have suffered. I love you so much, I can't help but cry."

"And you, Ramie," Mary Beth said. "When I heard you tell about defending Miranda, I wanted to die. Not because I was ashamed of you, but because you went through what you did. Your siblings. Your mates. Your children. You are the most important things in the world to me."

"We are a family," Cole said. "We are tied to the land through generations of blood. We will stay together and defend the land and defend our own." He pulled all four of the others into his embrace and then stepped back. "Where's Aubrey?"

"Somebody had to stay with the babies," Ramie said.

"Then we need to go to them. I need to hold my other daughter and kiss my grandchildren," Cole said.

5
A Family Way

The Family

EVEN ON a holiday, ranch chores need to be done. Especially when nearly every boarder wants his horse out to go for a trail ride. Some of the boarders brought friends and rented horses from LK Stables riding stock. Ramie had purchased six gentle trail horses for just such a purpose. With the purchase of additional saddles and tack, feed, and liability insurance, she was happy to have all six rented for the day. It just meant that even with their late night previously, she and Kyle had to be in the barn at five to get horses ready.

"The trails are all in good shape," she told Deke Clark, who had brought his girlfriend and a picnic carefully packed in his saddlebags. Ramie checked to make sure the couple had adequate water. "You might want to go up to the ridge. We drove the cattle up a few days ago and the guys at the camp don't mind visitors if you want to stop there for lunch. If you want more privacy, there's a thermal spring about a mile farther on. Don't get up close to where they're putting up fence for the drilling, though."

"That stuff bugs the hell out of me," Deke said. "They shouldn't be prospecting in the National Forest."

"They've got a right to prospect as long as they don't interfere with other rights. It's not a National Park like Yellowstone." Ramie said resignedly.

"How about if we take the south trail down by the river?" Deke asked.

"You know that trail's always good," Ramie answered. "It will be hotter by about ten degrees than the mountain trail, but you'll have easy water for the horses. You'll see the herd of rescues down that direction, too."

"I think we'll go that way," Deke said. He boosted his girlfriend into her saddle and checked the stirrups. He was a good horseman and had been with LK Stables for three years. Ramie was confident in his ability to guide the less experienced girl.

"Happy birthday, Pa," Kyle said when they came into the kitchen for breakfast. After a quick hug, Kyle picked up his baby Katie from the high chair and hugged her. Ramie swung Theresa up into her arms and blew a raspberry into her neck. Theresa giggled.

"You are going to need a shower now with all that syrup she just smeared on your face," Aubrey laughed at Ramie. "Now sit down and eat."

"Gonna need a shower anyway as sweaty as we got already."

"Stinky!" Theresa giggled, holding her nose.

"That's the smell of money, honey," Ramie said. "Unlike when you get stinky. Let's finish up your pancakes. Did you save me some?"

"Mom Au cooked."

"Well, I better kiss the cook, hadn't I?" Ramie kissed her wife and sat with the rest of the family to eat.

"Anything special planned for your birthday, Pa?" Aubrey asked.

"Nothing special. Thinking I'll take my beautiful wives for a trail ride, too. We'll sit in the saddle and solve the problems of the world. When we get back it will all be better."

"We all wish," Ashley said. "And pray."

Like all trail rides on Cole's Independence Day birthday, the three seemed naturally to end at the family burial plot. The family tradition since long before Cole's birth had been to place a plain white slab at the head of each grave. The stones were unmarked, but there was a row for each generation.

During Cole's time travel days and after Miranda and Jason had shown up in his children, they had added several stones. Looking at the burial plots—some, like Katie Lynn's, empty because the body was buried elsewhere or lost completely—was like looking at a genealogy chart without the names. Beside Theresa Ranae Bell and White Horse's

Yelloweye

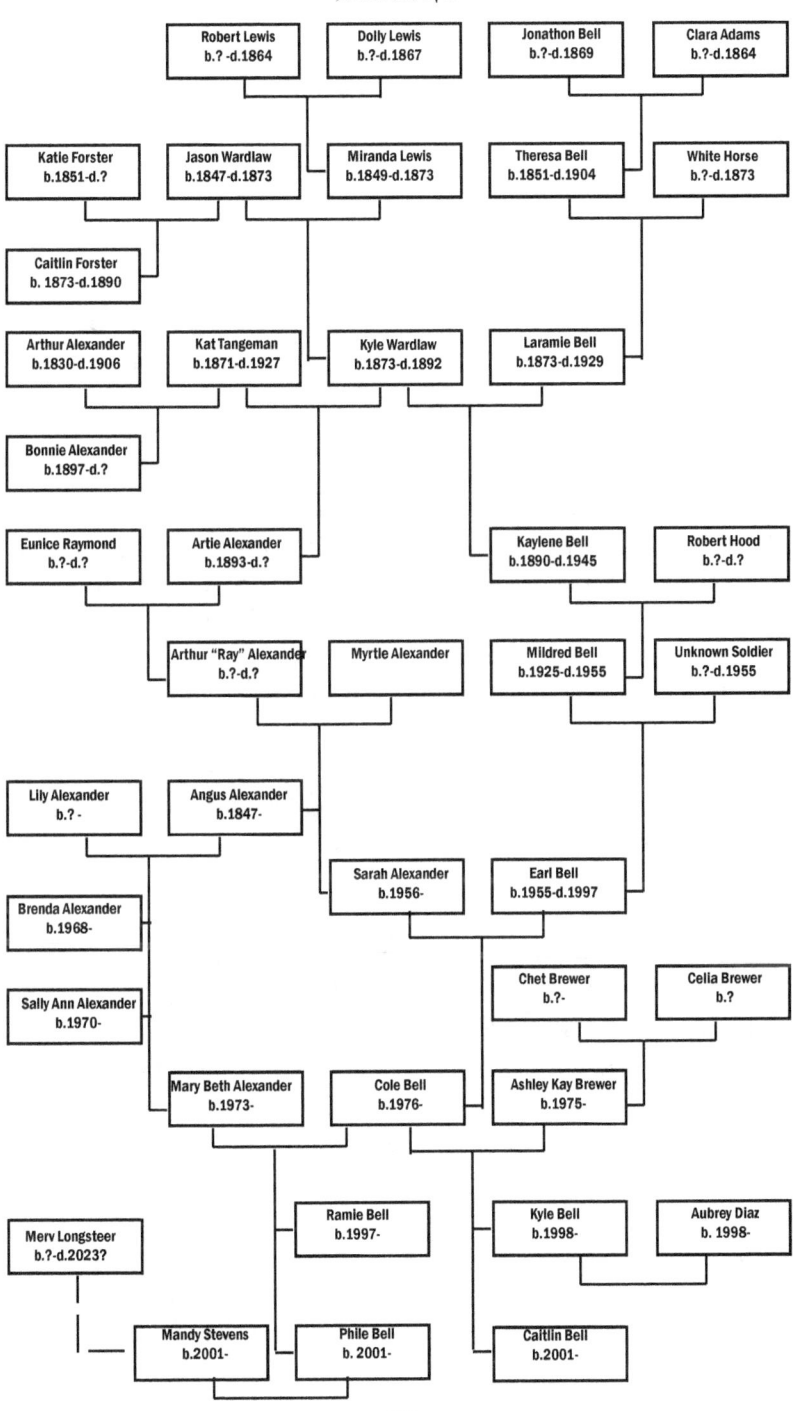

stones were markers for Miranda Lewis, Jason Wardlaw, and Kathryn Forster. Laramie Bell, Kyle Redtail Wardlaw, and Katherine Alexander were in the next row. Kyle, while possessed by Cole, had fathered Kaylene Redtail Bell while Kyle had fathered Arthur Alexander on Katherine just before he died. The Alexander line diverged from the Bells, though they homesteaded next door.

Cole's father had married his distant cousin, Sarah Alexander, bringing the lines together again. Sarah's brother's daughter Mary Beth had become the wife of Cole and Ashley and was the mother of Ramie and Phile. Ashley was the mother of Kyle and Caitlin.

Cole could recite every generation, the names and dates of each one. He had expanded all the listings in the old Bell family Bible to include every member of the family he could trace. Even back to White Horse and Theresa, this land had been in his family. Maybe further back, though there was no evidence that in their before-time selves, Caitlin and Phile were ancestors. Still, this had been a sacred place for them as well.

The family was tied to the land. The land was tied to the family.

Ashley took her husband's hand and led him to their wife, Mary Beth. The three held each other and sank to the ground. In an act that would have appalled their children—what child wants to think of his or her parents having sex?—the three managed a birthday blow job and a promise of more to come.

"Why don't you kids plan to stay in the big house tonight," Mary Beth said. "Let's put the babies down to sleep before we read. I can't help but think this is stressful for Theresa and Katherine, even if they don't understand the words."

The family agreed and after the babies were asleep, they gathered together.

"I'll read," Ashley said. "I have to read. Please, let me read tonight." Ramie handed the box to her and Ashley settled in the middle of the sofa with Cole and Mary Beth on either side. Cole motioned for Kyle to take the big chair with Ramie and Aubrey cuddled close to him.

Caitlin: Probing the Mind

THE BIG DIFFERENCE between now-time and *Oxése* was school. We had to be back in school for three more weeks after Ramie got attacked. And in school there was Mandy. By the end of the first week of December, she'd convinced her grandfather to move her horse, Wildfire, to LK Stables for boarding.

Nobody thought a thing about us spending time with her when she visited her horse. And the fact that we were sometimes out on the trail when she rode was never noticed. We often patrolled since there were wolves hunting in the hills. Phile and I had eaten the hearts of wolves in before-time. Ramie wore the teeth of the wolves who attacked her in this time. It seemed that wolves were binding us closer and closer together, both across time and within our family.

"PERHAPS IT IS because you operate on a different wavelength than those animals who are strictly predators," Mandy suggested. Even when we couldn't get together, we talked online every night. We were all getting comfortable with seeing each other's hard nipples. Mandy was thinning down some, too. That made her breasts even more impressive. We'd been talking about not being able to link with rattlesnakes and how we only got the surface thoughts of wolves when we tried. "I think I would call it an affinity," she continued. "We'll put all the animals you can communicate with readily on the left side of a T-chart and all the animals you know you cannot communicate with on the right side. Then we will list other animals that you have not had the opportunity to try. As you encounter each one we will move it to either the left or right side of the chart."

Mandy expected that we would be able to look at the list of animals and simply check off the ones that would go on each side. It wasn't that easy. She kept coming up with other tests. She wanted to know if the Chihuahuas have a different language than the German Shepherds? Did some animals carry on more intelligent conversations? Could we order insects around?

We couldn't carry out all her tests in now-time, but we'd gotten pretty good at jumping into most creatures in before-time.

And we got to look at Mandy while she put together her experiments.

Phile: Wapiti

WE LEFT OUR tribe in the morning after we had blessed the tent of our dead chief. The tribe parted before us as we led our horses, dragging their travois, and headed toward the prairie.

We had no idea what we were doing, but Yelloweye was in complete agreement with Mandy that we needed to learn more about other animals and to listen to how they talk. It was a concept that was beyond us, but our lives slowed down. It seemed that with the beginning of Cait's period, we were finally in sync with before-time. A day was a day and not two or five or whatever. We were still learning with double input but, with the synchronization, we were no longer feeling exhausted all the time. We progressed and learned at the same rate.

As WE HEADED toward our fifteenth birthday, Mandy was changing. She'd thinned up some and her complexion was clearing. In fact, Mandy was turning out to be really pretty. She'd grown about six inches in the past eighteen months and it was like her body had caught up with her personality. I know Caitlin already mentioned this, but I was about to turn fifteen and Mandy was the only person other than Cait that I'd ever seen naked. Except Wolf Riding Woman.

That was the thing, though. Caitlin and Wolf Riding Woman were the same person inside, but they were very different outside. Cait and I went to bed with no shirt on and sometimes she slept partly on top of me or curled up in front of me or with me curled up in front of her. We were used to each other's bodies. I could touch her breasts and she sometimes wiggled against my prick. Well, we touched. But I had all the sensory input of those same positions and feelings with Wolf Riding Woman.

And her responses were different.

You'd think that if kissing Caitlin behind the ear would make her shiver and reach for me, it would do the same for Wolf Riding Woman.

But it didn't. She had different physical responses to different stimuli. As Wolf Rising, I had to learn a whole different set of ways to turn my twin on. I guess that's why I wanted to know if it would be different to touch Wolf Riding Woman with my now-time body. And I thought, if I touched Mandy, I'd know if my senses were different. Than Wolf Rising. You know?

Oh well.

"No WAY! I can watch?" Mandy said. I wasn't saying too much because I was looking at Mandy in front of me and Cait beside me. My mouth was kind of dry.

"Haven't you ever seen it before?" Caitlin asked.

"No! How could I? It's all old stuff to you, but I live in the city and have never had an opportunity."

We were sitting out at the old cabin ruins having a conference. Everyone had been warned to travel in groups and Moms were threatening Caitlin and me with being separated again if we went wandering out into the mountains by ourselves. I was really surprised, though, when we got out to where it was private and tied the horses. Mandy turned toward us like she was expecting something and then just popped all the snaps on her shirt open and took it off. She stripped off her bra and sat on the ground Indian-style.

I caught my breath. I saw her like this on Skype, but this was… real.

"Don't you always meet like this?" she asked. Rather than argue with her, Caitlin popped her snaps open and gave me a nudge. I took off my shirt, too, and we sat in a little circle. "You don't, like, go completely naked, do you?" she asked a little uncertainly.

"Not outside," Caitlin reassured her. "When you talk to us on Skype, we don't usually have anything on. But we're on a nice comfy bed then."

I found it a little distracting. I was becoming more and more aware of both Caitlin and Mandy as women and had discovered how to relieve myself before we went to bed at night. It wasn't that unusual, though to wake up with my hand caressing Caitlin's breasts or even with her hand on my hard-on. We'd both had orgasms by this time and knew what they were like. We'd even helped each other out, but something kept us from just having sex.

Mom Ash had taken Caitlin to the doctor soon after her first period and the doctor gave her a shot that she said had to be renewed every three months. When she told Mandy about it, our friend decided she needed to be protected as well. Since, you never know. Right?

I think Moms and Pa just assumed that we were having sex. They knew we'd been sleeping together since forever. I guess that's part of why we didn't feel any pressure one way or another. Yelloweye explained it as knowing when our season came.

Part of our education was learning the cycle of life from the animals. Yelloweye had told us that we needed to connect with our horses when their time came to deliver the foals this spring. We finally told Mandy she could watch, too.

Our meeting in the woods came to an end and we stood to get dressed again. Mandy almost knocked me off my feet when she slammed into me and kissed me. Her bare chest against mine felt different than Cait's. I didn't have time to say anything before Mandy left me and slammed into Cait with just as much force and a kiss every bit as intense. Seeing those four tits smashed together made me a little dizzy and a lot hard. Mandy pushed Caitlin into my arms and to humor her we kissed as well. I figured just a little light kiss. But it was so exciting, neither of us wanted to let go. Feeling Cait against my chest as our tongues played with each other for the first time was something I knew I wanted to have happen again, real soon.

"Now we all know. We're like blood brothers and sisters," Mandy said. "Only with saliva instead of blood. I'll do anything for you two."

"Mandy, we'll do anything in our power for you as well. We're all kids, but we feel strongly about each other," Caitlin said. "Thank you for this."

"I'm a kid," Mandy smiled as she snapped up her shirt. "You two are aliens."

It was funny. Somehow in that kiss, I felt like we'd created an anchor in now-time that we didn't have in before-time or *Oxése*. We could always get back here.

PARTICIPATING IN THE birth of the two foals was more than I could stand. Men aren't supposed to feel their whole insides opening up to let a humongous big beast out into the world. I was sure not going to ever put Caitlin or Mandy through that! I don't know exactly what Cait felt, but she was panting and sweating as much as me. It felt like I passed a bowling ball out my penis.

And we went through it twice. Bells foaled in the middle of the night, so Mandy wasn't there to watch. She was out first thing in the morning though and held Cait and me together as Bows pushed her big boy out. There was one thing for damned sure and that was that we weren't going to get any use out of our genitals for a month. Even peeing reminded me of giving birth.

I was going to be too sore to ride.

THE EXPERIENCE TRANSCENDED our two separate times. Wolf Riding Woman and Wolf Rising were just as shaken as Caitlin and Phile. But old Yelloweye wasn't done with us yet.

We were being sent to talk to other animals. And the two of us were alone in *Oxėse*. We wandered far and wide. Sometimes we saw other villages of the People, but we didn't disturb them. We didn't know what tribes would welcome us and which might attack us. Just because there was no whiteman anywhere we wandered, didn't mean everyone was at peace. It was still common for one tribe to raid another for food, horses, or mates. I wasn't enthused about getting killed so some badass like Bent Bow could have Wolf Riding Woman. Since our little experience with Mandy, we'd discovered we liked kissing each other. More and more, I liked feeling her breasts against my chest while we slept.

I'm getting distracted. That was one of the problems and it almost got me gored by a big bull elk. I was glancing over at Wolf Riding Woman and thinking about how her exposed breasts were different than Caitlin's. Our people were built smaller. I was thinking—I guess daydreaming—when we stumbled into a small clearing where there was a bull with three cows and two calves. We were startled. The bull was startled. He shook his head at us and started pawing at the ground before he lifted his head with such a shrill bugle it hurt our ears. Let's just say that you do not want to be fifteen feet from a huge bull elk when he bugles his territorial challenge.

The fact that he was surprised made him angry and with him angry it was hard to talk to him.

"Cousin *Wapiti*," I tried. I felt Caitlin add her efforts to mine. We stepped back between two trees, but he kept shaking his head and pawing.

"I will not be prey!" he declared boldly. Cait and I shed our wolf robes on the ground behind us. They were like a second skin to us these days. We dropped our bows as well and stood before the big elk in just our loincloths and moccasins.

"We come not as predators, but as calves seeking your wisdom," Cait said. Cait and I couldn't communicate directly with each other in our minds, but we could hear each other when we talked to the animals. It was another of the things we were learning. The elk backed a step and I was afraid he was going to charge. I put a hand on Caitlin's shoulder, ready to push her away.

"What would you learn, two-legged?"

"We would learn the way of *Wapiti*," I said. "We would learn how to live in the same world without fear."

"You would have the wolf lie down with the calf?" he demanded.

When we were hunting, in before-time or in now-time, we knew our relationship with what we stalked. Maybe that is one of the things most people don't understand. The prey resists. The predator insists. Usually, the prey submits. The predator thanks the prey for providing food. In our now-time, death is thrown at the prey from a distance and the prey seldom participates in the hunt. But the prey's role is as important as the predator.

Cousin *Wapiti* knew that we would, in a different time, take him or one of his for food and clothing. But he knew this was not that time. And, for a while, he let us ride in his mind.

That ride was a wild one. Having heard the territorial challenge of the old bull, another answered. The cows and calves continued to ruminate while the bull strode out to meet the new bull. He appeared over a rise about a hundred yards away. After a dozen bugled challenges, the two animals met in a clash. Feeling the ground shake as the eight hundred pound bulls thundered at each other caused our hearts to race. But the jolt as the two met shook acorns out of the trees.

There was a fierceness in the old bull that was not unlike that of the wolf. The elk, however, were focused on their territory rather than prey. Included in his territory was his harem, the cows and calves he had attracted. The challenging male had only one cow following him and hoped to attract others by defeating the old man.

His hopes were dashed. Experience and brute strength drove the challenger from the clearing. His cow started to trot after him, but the old bull stretched his neck out and tilted his antlers back as he circled the cow. He explained to her that she was his now and herded her back to his harem. She made a couple attempts to escape and rejoin her former mate, but soon acquiesced and joined his harem.

The bull paced around the harem, looking up and away to detect if any other challenges needed to be met. He looked toward us once or twice, but let us continue to ride in his mind. His pacing became more agitated as he strutted before his cows and Cait and I could both feel our hearts racing again. The bull was becoming aroused as he paced around the new cow and she was swishing her tail up in the air at him. Cait and I were becoming aroused as well.

Without apparent warning, the bull spun around and mounted the new cow. His penis was close to a foot and a half long. He made several jabs at her and we could feel the tension building in him. She hunched her back a little, raising her opening and the tip of his penis lodged in her. They both froze in position for a few seconds as he stood on his hind legs with just the first inch or two in her as she pushed back to welcome him. Then he lunged forward and the entire length drove into her. She started to move forward, but now his bulk came down on her to hold her in place while he made three full thrusts and emptied his seed into her. Then she lunged forward and he dropped to the ground.

Cait and I fell backward where we'd been watching, our connection to the old bull suddenly broken. Both of us were panting and our loincloths were soaked with our emissions. The bull paced out and around his harem again, stretching his neck out and tilting his antlers back. We slipped away, dragging our wolf skins and bows with us.

When we reached our camp, we stripped out of our clothes and took them with us into the stream to wash. Then we washed ourselves. And each other. For the first time, I reached between Wolf Riding Woman's legs and felt the hot cleft that awaited my fingers. She wrapped her hand around my renewed erection and we explored each other thoroughly until we both climaxed again.

"Is it always like that for a male?" she asked. "I could feel it building in him. The heat of her opening on his hardness. Building and building until he could do nothing but lunge. And the explosion as he sank into her. I could feel the balls rising and the long path of intense release as his semen was unleashed. Wolf Rising, will it be like that for you when you take me as your mate?"

"You are my mate, Wolf Riding Woman. We will enter our season soon. Until then, we will not know what it is truly like. I know that even though the bull's explosion was more intense than anything I have felt, having your hand on my manhood when I climaxed was a far more pleasurable experience," I said.

"Then expect that you will feel it often," Cait said in my ear in now-time. I was thankful that we were nearing the pasture when our before-time experience overtook us. We would both still have to shower and clean our clothes when we returned to the ranch.

Caitlin: My Baby

I've let Phile do too much of the hard stuff. I might cry all over the page, but I've got to say this.

They killed my baby.

You didn't understand when Phile carried me screaming into the house on Christmas Day. How could you understand? Bells' foal was dead. The damned wolves got her and I was going to kill every moth-er-fucking one of them.

It wasn't *just* a foal! *I'd* given birth to her! I was in Bells' head when that baby was born. She was *my* baby. They killed my baby.

Ramie and Kyle went to the mountains to put an end to the problem. I had my own solution. We'd kill all the fuckers in before-time and they wouldn't be here do damage in now-time. Wolf Rising and I had been on the plains talking to buffalo, but we mounted our ponies and headed north to the mountains to hunt and kill wolves.

Phile: Riding the Wolf

THE ONLY WAY I kept Caitlin at the ranch was because in *Oxėse* we were riding toward here as hard as our ponies could go. Yes, toward here. We got Mandy involved via computer that night before Kyle and Ramie rode off into the mountains to hunt wolves. She's a whiz on the electronics stuff. When we were transferred into *Oxėse*, we figured it was a sort of parallel to our world and time didn't really mean the same thing. There was no whiteman chasing around our world. That meant that none of the major landmarks that we knew of as our home in now-time existed.

Mandy downloaded some astronomy software that would let her enter our coordinates and play the stars backward and forward from the present to other times. As Mandy showed us the star charts in now-time, we watched the sky in *Oxėse*. We finally got a picture that matched what we were seeing. Then we could navigate. We were headed toward the Rockies from Western Nebraska. The place was a desert with sand dunes blowing across the path. We made our way toward Laramie. Mandy got a better fix on our location when we started describing mountains. It took three days of hard riding to come to what we decided was our world's equivalent of the Little Laramie River, not far from where our village was camped.

We had heavy buffalo robes that we wore as our horses plowed through the snow up to the ridge. We'd been planning to move farther south with the buffalo, but wrapped ourselves up and just kept going. Things were quiet. The game had mostly moved down into the basin, but we saw sign of the heartier animals like the bighorn sheep and the bears. And the wolves.

We thanked the horses and told them to go back down to lower levels. I knew we could call them when we were done, but they were no longer helpful in plowing through the deep snow. We tunneled into a snow bank and lined it with the buffalo hide. Then the two of us huddled together wrapped in our skins and furs to stay warm. We began to regret our hasty drive up into the snow and cold.

But we heard them that night. It sounded like a thousand wolves howling in the forest. They seemed to echo, not just through the mountains, but through time. We held each other, removing all our clothes to pile them on top of us and hold our heat together.

We did the same in now-time. It was the first time that Caitlin and I had taken off all our clothes and held each other through the night. For some reason, we'd always kept underwear on. We touched each other. Touched each other in now-time and *Oxèse* and came together so powerfully that we passed out.

We awoke to the howling in the morning. Caitlin and I dressed and grabbed our rifles to go check on the horses, hearing the wolves up on the mountain where Ramie and Kyle were hunting. Wolf Riding Woman and Wolf Rising pulled on our elk hide boots, britches and shirts. Then we pulled the wolf skins over us, took our bows and burrowed out of our snow cave.

Wolves. A dozen, snarling, pacing wolves waiting for us to emerge. We held our horseshoe hatchets in our draw hand as we put arrows on the gut of the bow. But before we could loose the arrows, Yelloweye swooped in. Where he passed, another wolf took shape in front of us, facing the others.

Ride!

We heard the command deep in our hearts and our minds leapt into the brain of the huge wolf before us. The other wolves backed away a few steps, still snarling and snapping.

We had been unable to reach into the mind of a wolf before this, and to find both of us riding in this giant was a shock. When we had attempted to find the mind of wolves before this, we had only found hunger, lust for blood, and anger. But these paled next to the overwhelming power and anger of the giant in which we rode. The pack shrank behind its alpha and the two wolves met in a leap that had claws and teeth bared and seeking a quick kill.

It wasn't quick. The big wolf we rode fought hard to put the pack alpha on his back and tear its throat out. I felt the blood rush to my head and my heart swell. I could feel Caitlin goading the big wolf on to take the two younger wolves that leapt at him. One shortly dragged himself away from the fight with his haunches bleeding. The other, thinking the big wolf was vulnerable, launched himself at its back. But in a quick roll, the big wolf raked the belly of the attacker and opened it so that the guts fell out. The alpha female paced back and forth before the big wolf. We waited to see if she would challenge him or accept him. The rest of the pack hung back, unwilling to interfere in this showdown. She lay down and crawled toward Wolf. He snarled at her and placed his jaws around her neck, piercing the flesh, but she did not move. He backed away.

Wolf swung his head toward where we still stood, holding our bows at the ready. He looked back at the pack and howled out a challenge that rang with only one word that we could understand.

MINE!

The rest of the pack, eight in all, crept forward on their bellies. One by one, Wolf placed a paw on the back of his new pack's necks. He turned back toward us and we were thrust out of his mind and back into our own bodies facing him. The powerful thrusting of us from his mind echoed again with the word.

MINE!

The Family

"Not sure I should be listening to this," Cole rasped. "Doesn't seem right to read about my children discovering their sexuality and getting all…"

"Turned on?" Ashley said. She took the box from Cole and set it aside. Then wiggled herself into Cole's lap. She felt the bulge of his cock against her ass and kissed him. Mary Beth had already stripped her shirt off and pressed an ample breast at Cole's lips.

"I've always wondered how it felt to a male," she sighed. "I would do anything to ride in the head of a bull during mating. Or even Ramie's stallion."

The mention of her name caused Ramie to pull away from the lips of her lovers. Kyle had a hand under her shirt, lightly grazing across her nipple as she kissed Aubrey. The three looked at the parents in Cole's big chair.

"I don't think we should be here to watch this," Ramie said as Ashley stripped off her shirt.

"If you two don't get me naked and start sucking my tits, I'm going to explode," Aubrey gasped. The three younger generation stood shakily and left the study where Cole, Ashley, and Mary Beth scarcely noted their absence.

6
Running with the Herd

The Family

A RANCH IS work. Work kept the Bell Family sane. Cole drove by way of the Forest Road to the upper pasture to meet with the Forest Service and the oil company. Ashley went to the Wyoming Cattlewomen's Association meeting she presided over and encouraged the members to call their congressman and senators. Trail riders were checked in, their horses saddled, and sent out on the trail. Kyle and Ramie rounded up the eighty rescues and drove them to the corral with the assistance of their four hired hands. Two were paid by the rescue foundation and two by LK Stables. It took all six of them for a job Caitlin and Phile could have done by themselves. The vet checked the general health of each horse and put his white chalk checkmark on the left flank. Aubrey and Mary Beth cooked, cleaned, and tended the babies—the next generation born to the land.

"I love being a mommy and a ranch wife," Aubrey sighed. "It would be nice, though, if one of my four lovers had a few minutes for a little afternoon nookie," she giggled.

"Wait till winter," Mary Beth laughed.

"Oh, yes. I better see the doc next week and get protected or you'll have another grandchild next summer. I don't mind walking bowlegged but I hate waddling. Teach me how you make that roast so tender, Mom Mar."

"I'm so glad I got one daughter who loves the kitchen as much as I do," Mary Beth answered. "Of course, between your tortillas and Ramie's piecrust, I could get an inferiority complex."

"If it weren't for Miranda, Ramie wouldn't know how to bake a pie," Aubrey said. "She could burn water in a Teflon pan." The two women worked companionably in the kitchen and taking care of the children all day.

"I CAN'T BELIEVE they're telling us we have to move our cattle for them so they can get their survey crews in," Cole complained as they sat for the late-night supper in the summer. "Let us pause to consider the land," he intoned and the family bowed in silence for a moment before resuming. "It's like they are afraid of a couple cows." He ladled shredded roast beef, rice, and gravy onto his tortilla and rolled it up. Their dinners had become a fusion of Aubrey's Mexican heritage and Mary Beth's ranch cooking.

"Probably just scared of stepping in a cow pie with their fancy city shoes," Kyle joked.

"At least Arlen was polite about it. He worked hard to negotiate where they would work and when the cattle needed to be moved," Ashley said. "I don't think the Forest Service is any happier about the companies prospecting for oil up there than we are."

"Damned government. Sold off the mineral rights without ever thinking about how it would affect the natural course of things. The court wouldn't even stop the pseudo-fracking of Yellowstone. I thought after Standing Rock, things would get better," Cole said. They all bowed their heads for a moment to remember the lives lost defending the water.

Pseudo-fracking was a technique based on the old system of forcing sand and water deep into crevices of the earth's mantle to allow oil to flow more freely. The new method focused on releasing the synthetic oils from shale, a reservoir of which had been discovered in the Yellowstone.

"So many protesters have converged on Yellowstone that they closed the gates," Kyle said.

"That's illegal, isn't it?" Mary Beth asked. "Three U.S. Highways run through Yellowstone."

"Not right now. All traffic has been rerouted to 90 and 15. We're even seeing traffic increases down here on 80," Cole said. "I wish we were still in the days where they wanted wolves in the mountains. Now they want oil corporations."

"World's gone to hell in a handbasket," Ashley said.

First Live Report

"THE GOVERNMENT IS a trustee of the land, not its owner," the stately young woman said as she faced the camera. The Bell family sat in front of the television in the family room to watch the news. One of the boarders who had been out to ride mentioned that it appeared the Yellowstone standoff was taking a nasty turn, so they'd taken their dinner to the family room to watch. It was a rare occurrence in the Bell household.

The ribbon at the bottom of the screen identified the woman as 'Earth Sister (*Ho'enáséé'e*) of the Northern Cheyenne'. Her dress was not typically native. Her left shoulder was bare and the right shoulder of her blouse was pulled low. The reason was obvious. She had what appeared to be a full torso tattoo that ran down her arm as well. The cameraman was fascinated enough by the tattoo that he got several angles of it. The back of the wolf's body ran out of sight from her left shoulder blade. The wolf's face looked out from her collar bone. Her left arm was a full sleeve of the wolf's shoulder and foreleg all the way to the claws on her left hand. From beneath the blouse on her right, a second wolf peeked out.

The family sat riveted to the television.

"That's not… It couldn't be Caitlin, could it?" Ramie asked. The woman on television had black hair and Ramie was certain she was smaller busted than her sister. But most striking was that beneath the wolf's snarling mouth was the face of a woman.

"Not unless her nineteenth century body was transferred to this time," Ashley said. "That's not my daughter. That's her spokeswoman."

"This protest village that sprang up over the winter," reporter Sarah d'Angelo interrupted the speaker. "Can you tell us how what is now known as Yellowstone Grizzly Village came to be?" Earth Sister ignored her.

"Grandmother Earth will not allow the destruction of her body to continue. The People stand in witness," she declared, sweeping her hand toward the line of natives standing on the village earthworks behind her. There was a flicker over the faces and the cameraman jerked back to the ranks of protesters. But there were only people there. "Mother will bring her children to totally destroy what you have built. And to you who stand with the corporations raping mother earth, flee. Flee before it is too late and you are trampled beneath the hooves of her army."

All through the confrontation at Standing Rock years before, no aggressive words had been spoken by the water protectors. As a result, they were sprayed with water cannons in freezing weather, shot with rubber bullets, and devastated by shock grenades. They stood fast until the bulldozers moved forward and proceeded to simply bury those who held the line. No one thought the Native Americans would return to protest yet another destruction of habitat and resources, but during the late winter, the village had materialized in Yellowstone. The official word was that they had trekked in from the North unobserved. No one could figure out how they moved with such speed and stealth. The interview proceeded with a final pan across the protesters to Earth Sister and the prairie beyond her. Bison browsed, but as the camera held on her, the bison began to group together and face the construction site.

Drums began a low rumble in the protest village. As they took on a distinct rhythm that echoed through the basin, more bison came over the rise beyond to join those already in the meadow.

"Are you threatening the workers on the jobsite?" asked the newscaster.

"Look beyond me," said Earth Sister. "*Ésevone*, the buffalo are the first to arrive. This is their home. It is not we feeble two-legged people who come to oppose you, but the legions of Mother Earth. Next will come *mo'éhe*, the elk. *Ho'néené'šeohtsévá'e* and *Ho'néemé'eōhtse*, the White Wolf Twins, will come to lead them. But every one of the old ones will join them. Owl, Raven, and Hawk will lead the feathered. But even those who are too small to be seen will infect you. They will enter you through the water. They will eat you from the inside. Your walls will be trampled to dust and the mountain lions will feast on the bones. The rats will chew through your power lines while goats consume your food. No trace of this abomination will remain." Below her the buffalo began to move forward at a measured pace, not stampeding, but moving like they were intelligent beings on a mission, then stopping to face the drilling site. "Flee," Earth sister said. "It is your only hope."

The Family

"She called them by name. The Wolf Twins," Aubrey said into the silence after the news had changed to the latest baseball scores.

"The White Wolf Twins. That has to refer to now-time Caitlin and Phile," Ramie said.

"There's only one person that could be."

"Call Merv Longsteer," Mary Beth said.

"Mom Mar, Merv is gone," Ramie said. "He left soon after Phile and Caitlin disappeared. I went down to see him and ask him what he knew. You know Merv. He said we had all the answers in our hands. Then he said that his time was near and he was going to the reservation to join his ancestors."

"And I'll bet he took his granddaughter Mandy Stevens with him," Ashley said. "That has to be her. Who else would tattoo herself with the images of our children in their wolf robes? You could almost see them moving. We need to be up there, Cole."

"They wouldn't let us close," Kyle said. "They blamed the problems at Standing Rock on the outsiders. No one who doesn't live there is allowed west of Cody."

"I'll read tonight," Mary Beth said. "I feel that reading will lend my strength to Caitlin and Phile. Be safe, my babies."

Caitlin: The Belly of the Wolf

We weren't finished with the wolves. I still hated them, but somehow, I was now one of them. This massive silver ancestor that we could only call by the name he gave us: *Manèstóhó'néhe*, Creator Wolf, demanded our obedience, our submission, just as he did that of his pack. We lay down on our bellies with our wolf robes covering us so that we must have looked almost like the wolves in front of us. And he placed a paw on our necks.

I am your Nésemoo'o, your spirit guide. I will teach you the way of the wolf and you will lead my pack to the great battle.

WE RAN WITH the pack that day. We chased down three deer and when *Manèstóhó'néhe* had his fill, we tore into the kill and ate with our pack. Of course, we did not have the tearing canine teeth of the wolves, but we had the sharpened iron horseshoe axes that we hacked at the carcass with and tore the raw meat. We journeyed in the belly of the wolf for many miles that day. The wolf knows its pack. The wolf knows its hunger. The wolf knows its territory. This territory—this land, was ours. Communicating with the wolves had to be done on the level of base desires.

We slept with the pack. Our dreams were wolf dreams. The hunt. The kill. The gorge.

Our *Nésemoo'o* led us back to our snow cave in the morning after all the wolves had stuck their noses up our butts. Oddly, when I sniffed at the alpha female, I could tell her scent from the younger females. The males had a stronger scent than the females. But none of us were in season, so the males ignored us.

You, like me, dwell in many ages. We will find each other many times. You will guard my territory and keep it against all others. I will help you call the wolves when it is time to hunt.

With Creator Wolf's words ringing in our heads, we packed our limited gear—our buffalo robes and bows. We returned to the valley and called our horses. We needed to follow the buffalo south.

WHEN RAMIE AND Kyle came down from the mountain, they said the wolf problem was solved. But they didn't bring any pelts or teeth. Ramie wouldn't say they were dead. All she would say was that we wouldn't have any more problems with wolves.

I didn't trust her.

Or maybe I didn't trust myself. Even having traveled in the belly of the wolf, even having *Manèstóhó'néhe* as my spirit guide, I hated the wolves.

OF COURSE, WE called Mandy. She came out to visit her horse the day before school started. It was a quiet day after the excitement of the hunt.

We talked in the stable as she brushed Wildfire and we rubbed down Bells and Bows and the one remaining colt. I cried over the horses.

"Is there somewhere we can have a powwow?" Mandy asked. "A talk like we conference." I looked at Phile. He was wide-eyed.

When Ramie and Kyle moved into the other side of the bunkhouse with Aubrey, Moms and Pa finally let us move out to the two singles they used to have. First thing Phile did when we were home alone was cut a door between the two apartments. Mom Ash came out to visit me when we were all moved in and Phile was painting the trim. She shook her head.

"We need to have you checked at the doctor to be sure your birth control is up to date," she said. "I don't want you pregnant while you are in high school. I figure it will come soon enough as it is."

"Mom, I wouldn't be much of a woman if I couldn't control when I got pregnant," I laughed. I'd learned all about that from the village wise woman when I became a woman in before-time. It had been a busy time and we'd had to travel to *Oxèse* and it gave the wise woman and several other older women a chance to give me the whole instruction on being a woman. It wasn't hard if you paid attention to your body. Mom Ash just shook her head.

I looked at Mandy and just knew what Phile was thinking.

"Scout and make sure the way is clear," I said. Phile took off and I led Mandy as he signaled it was clear. She was awestruck when she saw our apartment. Not that there was much to it. Two rooms with a big bed in each, thanks to Kyle and Ramie sharing Aubrey as a lover. A chair and bathroom and mini-fridge. I offered Mandy a water and turned to see her stripping. Phile wasn't much behind her. Mandy had her shirt and bra off before I could get my shirt unbuttoned. She hesitated as she looked at the bed and Phile unbuckling his belt.

"We're inside and going to meet on the bed, right?" she asked. I nodded. She unfastened her jeans and shoved them, panties and all, down to her ankles. She had to sit on the bed to pull them off her feet. "I've never been naked with anyone," she said. "Except… Well, when you told me you were naked on your bed when we conferenced, I started getting naked, too. Except we never pointed the cameras down to see that," she giggled. "Now. Oh fuck! Here I am."

"And here we both are," I said as I pulled my socks off. My room was warmest. Ramie told me she always was too hot in the room but Kyle was always too cold in his. With the door open between the two, it mostly balanced out. I was certain that, based on my own reaction, Mandy's hard nipples weren't the result of a cold draft.

We all got on the bed and poor Phile was the most embarrassed because his arousal was so obvious. I was sure both Mandy and I were wet, but you couldn't see that unless you were doing a personal investigation. Nonetheless, Mandy got us focused on business. We told her all about our wolf hunt in before-time and about Creator Wolf. I just couldn't let go, though. Those damned wolves killed Bells' foal. My baby. I still wanted to kill them all.

"You've got white-itis," Mandy said. I looked at her like she'd just told me I was an alien. Again. "Whites believe that what happens to them is unique. It's more important than it is for anyone else."

"Wait. You're white," Phile said.

"I'm less white than you are," Mandy said. "I just never paid any attention to my heritage. Once I started hanging around with you two, Grandfather Longsteer started teaching me about my heritage. I'm a quarter Cheyenne, just based on his blood. But his wife was half Arapaho. It was my mother—three-quarters Indian—who married a white cowboy. I figured out the percentages and I think that makes me three-eighths Native American. Next summer, I'm going up to Montana to the reservation to study my cultural heritage."

"Wow! We're only like a sixty-fourth or a hundred and twenty-eighth, or something. Not enough to be considered of the blood," Phile said. "It's in before-time that we are full Cheyenne. Now what about white-itis?"

"We are the People. *Tsétséhéstáhese*, what we call ourselves, just means people. But we also think of the whites as people and the blacks as people, they're just people who are other than us. When you think about before-time, I'll bet that you even think of the elk and bison as people. I'm absolutely sure you think of your horses as people. But whites... They think they are the only people. Some of them don't even include all whites. It's only the ones who are in their church or in their social club that are really people," Mandy said. I had to agree with that. I knew good people and bad people, but they were all people.

"So, if a white baby gets killed, that's a tragedy. Call out the police and the National Guard and hunt down the murderer," Mandy continued. "But if a black baby gets killed, well it's a shame really, but what do you expect?"

"What's that got to do with this?"

"When you kill a deer for food, you honor it. You thank it for its sacrifice that you can live. You praise its bravery. Because the deer is people. What you forget is that every one of the people of every species that die to feed you is somebody's baby. But you've got white-itis. It's a shame, but what do you expect?"

"I understand," Phile said. "But it's part of the cycle of life. There's predators and prey. It takes us all."

"But in the case of one little foal, a beautiful little horse that you gave birth to, she has more value than the people who needed food and killed her. White-itis."

I looked at Mandy and burst into tears. She and Phile both moved at the same time to wrap me in their arms as I wept for my baby and tried... I really tried to forgive the wolf.

"You hunted with the wolves. You killed. You ate. You slept with the pups in their den. You were there," Mandy said. "You know that even if you don't understand their hearts, they are people. What's more, you are wolves."

We fell back on the bed with Mandy and Phile both sort of on top of me. It wasn't uncomfortable. I kind of liked their weight pressing into me. I kissed one, then the other. Then they kissed each other. I felt the roundness of Mandy's ass in my hand and I liked it. I felt her caress my breast and I liked that, too. I felt her hand join mine to stroke Phile. Mandy rolled off the bed.

"I don't think we're ready to do everything yet," she said. She looked kind of longingly at Phile's erect cock. Then I realized she was looking between my open legs, too.

"Yelloweye says our season hasn't come," Phile said. "I mean... Mandy, Caitlin and I are mates. We're going to be together all our lives. We're going to make love and probably have babies one day. But we haven't done anything yet and we both really like you. You are our healer. And you're pretty. And..." he looked at me and I nodded.

"Tell her," I whispered in before-time.

"And we love you," he finished. Mandy came back and gave us a hug, then started putting on her jeans.

"In old times, it was common for braves to have more than one wife," she whispered.

Phile: Calling the Herd

AFTER OUR ADVENTURE with the wolves, Wolf Riding Woman and Wolf Rising followed the buffalo as they made their way south across the Great Plains. I've heard there are about a million bison scattered across the North American Continent in now-time. There was no way we could count what we saw. There were bison as far as the eye could see across the plains.

Like cattle, bison don't clump together like you see on a TV western. They come together for protection and migration, but they scatter for grazing. If they were all close together, there wouldn't be enough food nearby to eat. The prairie grasses grew as tall as the buffalo, so unless we found a rise to look down on them, it was almost impossible to see individuals. We just saw brown shadows as the grass moved.

Mandy continued to track our movements using her astronomy and geological software. She was very smart and we learned from three sources—the animals of before-time, the school, and Mandy. We managed to get together almost every day at school. Other kids just referred to us as the weird ones who ate lunch together. We got to hang around after school together on days that Ramie and Kyle had late classes. That made it possible to go to Merv Longsteer's place, though we avoided the days that Ramie was there. Merv taught us the lore of the people. Mandy was soaking that up like a sponge. Cait and I spoke to animals. Mandy could speak to people.

She still referred to us as her alien lovers, and we were getting a lot closer to *being* lovers. Whenever we could find a place to be alone, we'd kiss and pet. We slipped her into the bunkhouse on a couple of her visits to see her horse. We got naked under the pretense that we were having a meeting and then we'd just make out. The first time Mandy made me come was a shock to all of us, but she was lost in the orgasm Cait was fingering her to. We all knew we were coming into our season.

Cait and I missed Mandy when we went to bed at night and we did a lot more kissing and petting, moving together and getting each other off at night.

IN *OXÉSE*, WE were learning more about the herd mind. When we entered the mind of any of the big beasts, it was like we entered them all. Ten million minds with one thought—to graze. Even when a big bull mated with a cow, the others rubbed against each other.

It was different with the horses. Every horse is an individual. They have complex communication and social organization. Out here on the plains, where other horses were available, our two mares acted differently than when we had been in the mountains or isolated. When they came into estrus, we tried to calm them down, but ended up linked to them when the herd stallion covered them.

We ended up naked on a buffalo robe in our tent, rolling and pawing at each other. If I had been riding in the stallion instead of the mare, we would probably have had sex. But I felt the opening and receptivity of the mare, lying there with Cait longing to be filled, even though I didn't have a vagina to fill. And 'longing' is an inadequate word. It was all-consuming, like I would die if a stallion didn't mount me. And when he mounted our mare and we felt his shaft entering it was like the world's purpose had been fulfilled. I don't think a human orgasm is even comparable to what the mare felt when she was covered.

It would be soon. We knew it would be soon.

IN SPRING, THE scent of new grass turned the herd of bison northward. It was a new experience for us. Always in our mind-riding with animals, we initiated contact and asked to talk or to ride with them. When the herd turned, we felt the pull from them. We found our minds to be part of the full herd, bent on spring grasses. We ran among the animals as they picked up speed. Soon the sound of hooves was like thunder. When these big animals started moving, we could easily be trampled.

Yelloweye swooped in over the top of us with a sharp command. *Ride!*

The picture he gave us was not of melding minds, but of riding on top of the buffalo. Cait and I both grabbed the wooly shoulder of a passing bull and swung ourselves up on his back. Our consciousness sank further into his with the contact and we were caught in the thrill of migration. It was as intense as the sexual thrill of the mustangs.

We rode for three days before the animals slowed and began to spread out again around the lush prairies of Kansas. We slipped from the big bull giving him our thanks as he found a dusty spot and rolled.

We moved through the herd toward the mountains and when there were only scattered animals around us, our horses rejoined us. We went into the hills and set up a camp near the hot spring above our village. We would stay there for the summer while we replenished our supplies that had been scattered across the plains. It's funny how this little bit of land where our family homestead is called to us, even in *Oxèse*.

Caitlin: Riding a Woman

MANDY SPENT THE night with us the last weekend of April. It wasn't hard to arrange. She'd been at the ranch all day with a dozen other riders who wanted to take advantage of the open trails—even though there was still some snow on the ground. We'd been busy with all the riders and we received three mares that day for breeding to the big Standardbred, Harley. Ramie and Kyle were riding fences because they'd just brought in some more rescues.

When Mandy came in from her ride, she suggested we have a burger at the Bear Claw. It didn't take much to convince Moms that Phile and I wanted to go without ever mentioning that Mandy would be there. I think they were concerned that all we ever did was work on the ranch and go to school. They were pleased that we wanted to go out somewhere, even if it was just the two of us and only a mile away.

We took a four-wheeler and buzzed up to the restaurant. We met out back for some serious kissing before we went in. Rachel, the waitress, had worked at the Bear Claw for as long as we'd been alive. She smiled and seated us well away from the door to the bar.

"A new generation of chili burger connoisseurs," she laughed. She brought us Cokes and a platter of fries long before the burgers were ready.

"Now you three listen up to the rules. Don't try to sneak into the bar or get anyone to bring you a drink. Frank will ban you from ever coming in again. You are just three high school friends on a date. I put you back here so no one would pay attention to who was sitting by whom. Don't get loud and don't get demonstrative. And if your girlfriend needs to leave her car here overnight, pull it around next to my white truck out back. It'll be safe enough. Your business is your business as long as you don't make it everybody else's. You understand what I'm saying?"

We looked at her with our mouths hanging open and just nodded.

"What was that about?" Mandy whispered. We sandwiched her between us in the booth.

"I guess we're kind of a weird family," I said. "But I don't think we're the only ones. Grandma Bell lives with Gram and Grandpa Alexander. They're all retired and go to Arizona in the winter, but they're *very* close. Pa and Mom Ash are married, but Mom Mar wears a wedding ring, too. You might not know our family as well as some folks. Like Rachel said, it's our business. But you are our girlfriend. You should know these things. Mom Mar and Pa are cousins."

"So that's how you keep your secret powers in the family," Mandy said. We laughed. Quietly.

"You ain't heard nothin' yet," Phile said. "Our brother and sister, Ramie and Kyle, share a girlfriend, Aubrey."

"Like you two share me?" Mandy asked.

"No. Ramie and Kyle are stupid. They're afraid that if they were boyfriend and girlfriend, they'd end up with two-headed babies. They both love Aubrey, though. And Aubrey's been around for a couple years now, so I think it's gonna stick."

"Why isn't that like us?" Mandy asked. She cast her eyes down and Phile and I held a hurried conversation in *Oxèse* before I answered her.

"Honey," I said, "Phile and I both love you. Not only that, you've been our only friend for the past four years. I think, our only friend ever."

"I love both of you, too," Mandy said. There was a sparkle in her eye.

"The difference is that Phile and I love each other, too. Mandy, honey, if you make love to us, you have to know that we're going to be making love to each other, too. In now-time and before-time. Phile is my mate. I plan to have his baby someday. Nothing would make me happier than to raise him with your baby. So, these are just some of the things you need to know about our family before you take any last steps."

"Have you already made love to each other?" she asked.

"We haven't done anything more with each other than we have with you," Phile said. "We just have the opportunity to do it more often."

We ate our burgers and conversation lightened up. We talked about how we were ever going to get through the last month of school. Mandy was already sixteen, but we were still two months from our birthdays. She was planning to leave right after school got out to go study with the old women and medicine men on the Northern Cheyenne reservation at Lame Deer, Montana.

"I'd like to have a conference," Mandy said. We looked at her. We'd been talking non-stop for two hours. "In your 'conference room' at the ranch," she concluded. *Oh!* The last couple conferences we'd managed on my bed hadn't involved much talking. They had involved a lot of bare skin touching each other. We nodded. "All night," she added. We grinned, paid the bill, and left. Mandy moved her car around back next to Rachel's truck and climbed into the four-wheeler. Phile swung around back of the bunkhouse to let Mandy and me off at our door and then went to park the four-wheeler and let the parents know we were back and going to our rooms.

MANDY AND I went into my room while we waited for Phile to park the four-wheeler. Mandy looked at the map on my wall. Ramie had started the map. She and Kyle were always studying history and once told me that it was filled with information about where our ancestors had come from. As soon as I moved into the room, I began filling in our own movements as best as I could tell where things happened. We didn't have a good feeling for dates, so I wasn't sure how our marks related to theirs. I did recognize one place as a starting point. Ramie had found the massacre that took our mother and pinpointed it on the map. From there, we plotted the various journeys.

"I think this is as far south as you journeyed," she said. "The Red River of the South divides Oklahoma from Texas. It matches the description of where you said the buffalo went to drink and some crossed farther south."

"We were farther north when the herd turned and headed toward the spring grasses," I said. "We were here in northern Nebraska when they bedded down and we walked west."

"Yes. And you ended up here again. Have you ever noticed, Caitlin, how you are always drawn back here? I believe you are tied to the land, my alien lover," she said turning and taking me in her arms.

"Are we going to make love tonight, fair one?" I asked. I had nothing against the idea. I was ready. Ready for her and ready for Phile. He joined our embrace, kissing each of us softly.

"Yes. No. Not exactly," she said. "I'm as wet as you are just thinking about it. Phile is hard and I… I want to take him in my mouth. With you. I want to feel his… and your tongue between my legs. I want to taste you and share your nectar on his tongue. But there is something more that I want, my lovers. I want you to ride me."

"Um… That sounds like you want us to make love," Phile said. I could feel his hardness pressed against my side and I was ready. We started undressing each other, taking turns removing an article of clothing from one of the others. That had intent that we'd never experienced before. We'd been naked together several times, but we always removed our own clothing. Somehow, removing the others' clothing for them made it different.

"Yes. Someday I want you to ride me like that," Mandy said. "But we have to deal with something else."

"Mmm. Even Wolf Riding Woman is wet and Wolf Rising is sniffing around," I said. I could feel the hands of my lovers on both my bodies.

"That's what we need to include. When we make love in now-time, you'll experience it in before-time as well. I want to, too."

"I don't think we can take you there," I said.

"How many animals have you ridden the mind of?" she asked. *Wow!* I had to think about that one.

"Um… Elk, deer, goats, buffalo," Phile said.

"Wolves, bears, mountain lions, coyotes, foxes," I continued. Riding a mountain lion had been an unbelievable experience. When we asked to ride along, it was like the lion said, 'Yeah. Whatever,' and ignored us.

"Horses, antelope, marmots, squirrels, rabbits," Phile continued.

"Hawks, owls, ravens, eagles, sparrows," I concluded. I was sure there were more. We hadn't been successful with reptiles. We'd tried snakes and lizards, but it was like there was nothing there.

"Human?" Mandy asked.

"We can't even communicate mentally with each other unless we're both riding the same animal," Phile said. "It looks like we do because we can talk to each other in before-time and answer in now-time without talking it over, but that's different. We are always completely aware of both times."

"Like right now, we are talking over the same ideas in before-time while we sit in our tent naked, touching and kissing," I said.

"But other people?"

"Um… Never really tried, I guess," Phile said. "People have big barriers around their heads. I think language does it. Words separate our thoughts from reality."

"I'm dropping all barriers," Mandy said. "I'm inviting you into my mind. Both of you. Like you rode the herd of buffalo. I'm inviting you in." She leaned forward to kiss us and I could feel her invitation. She was inviting us to touch her as she touched us. And what I never considered before was that Wolf Riding Woman and Wolf Rising were touching her through us.

You're so beautiful, Mandy. I was startled to hear what I knew was Phile's voice, yet there was no sound in my ear as we continued to kiss.

I love you both in both your incarnations. Mandy's eyes were closed and her lips were sealed against mine. It wasn't words I heard. I could feel her love deep in my heart—in both my hearts. Wolf Riding Woman and Wolf Rising were weeping. I felt my tears in now-time splash against Mandy's cheek. I just wanted to flood her with my love.

And joined with my love as Caitlin was my love as Wolf Riding Woman and Phile's love and Wolf Rising's love. There has never been anything more intimate. We marveled at tastes, touches, sounds of each other across the time, joined all together in Mandy's mind. We kissed and licked and sucked each other, experiencing every thought, emotion, and discovery in each of our minds and in each of our bodies. The mental feedback of our orgasms tripled in intensity.

All five of us passed out and slept until morning.

The Family

"WHY DID WE never know or meet this Mandy girl?" Ashley demanded. "They started sneaking her into their room six years ago? Seven? How could we have never seen her?"

"I met her a few times," Ramie said. Kyle nodded his head. "She was a boarder. In fact, she was one of our first boarders. About three years ago—a year after the kids graduated from high school—she took her horse and left. Said she was moving to Montana."

"Our poor babies," Mary Beth cried. "I can't bear the thought that the story will be of their broken hearts."

"I broke all our hearts," Aubrey said. "That first night we were all together and I found out my lovers were time travelers and hadn't told me." She turned to growl a little at the two she was cuddled with. "They were the most miserable months of my life."

"It gave Kyle a chance to court me," Ramie said. "But it was a miserable time for us, too."

"We got the barn painted," Kyle laughed. Both women poked him.

"And the reunion brought us back here with you," Miranda said through Ramie. "If you hadn't all three got together, we'd still be homeless spirits."

"Well, that's one mistake it doesn't look like the younger kids made," Cole said. "It doesn't sound like Mandy had any trouble believing they were living in two timelines, and it sounds like she helped them. I'm sorry they couldn't trust us with what was going on in their lives, but I'm glad they could talk to her."

The family got up and went off to their beds after closing the box and leaving it on the mantel.

7
The Human Mind

The Family

COLE SPENT most of the morning in the Forest Service office again. Arlen was sympathetic, but felt his hands were tied. Next, Cole picked up Mary Beth and Ashley and they drove to Cheyenne. It might seem unlikely that a rancher could walk in and visit the governor, but Wyoming was a state of only 600,000 citizens, ranked tenth in total area for states, but 50th in total population. The elected officials knew who the influential ranchers were in their state.

"Cole, I know you didn't support me in the election, but that doesn't make a difference to me. I know and you know that you were responsible for saving my daddy's ranch back during the range wars with that bastard Joe Teine. Don't bother to deny it. I know it's buried too deep to ever prove, but you were the one. I just know it. Frankly, I wish Harry Harrison had won the damned election. Then I wouldn't be presiding over a state that is becoming the target of every angry environmentalist in the country," Governor Meade said.

"George, there has to be something we can do about this," Ashley said. As president of the Cattlewomen's Association of Wyoming, she carried influence in her own right.

"I wish," the Governor replied. "I can't even send state troopers up there. It's Federal land. I know we've had a policy of encouraging energy exploration, but none of these licenses that Shale Oil is using come from the State of Wyoming. They are issued straight from the U.S. Department of Agriculture. The very people who are supposed to be looking out for your interests. The Forest Service is part of the USDA. After the Department of the Interior rolled over on the Yellowstone site, USDA just followed along. Whoever had the bright idea of putting National Parks and National Forests under two different departments was loco."

"What about pressure on Richard and Elaine?" Cole asked. Wyoming's two U.S. Senators had been quiet on the whole affair.

"They don't even return *my* phone calls," George said. "I'd guess the money that paid for their elections came from Shale Oil and other big energy companies. Aside from the fact that they're ugly, we could put a hundred windmills down by the Laramie River and power the entire State. The only reason we need oil is for money. How many barrels of oil is a fat steer worth? Believe me, the projections for output from those new wells is a lot more than that. But do you think the state will see any of it? It's not ours. It's Federal."

"You can't eat oil," Mary Beth said.

"I'd like to try force feeding a few of those bastards," George grumbled. "What I *am* going to do is talk to my National Guard liaison to see what we can do to protect the village up there. I don't want private militias deciding to take action by themselves like at Standing Rock." The Governor looked intently at Cole. The message was for him, as well.

Second Live Report

"This is Sarah d'Angelo coming to you from the Yellowstone Grizzly Village where tensions are mounting after yesterday's surprising appearance of buffalo—excuse me, bison—approaching over the far ridge to stand looking at the Shale Oil drilling site. The Park Service has estimated that there were more animals in the herd than had ever been counted in Yellowstone. As you can see, the spokesperson called Earth Sister is just cresting the earthworks to approach our cameras."

Drums picked up a rhythm from the village, perhaps louder than the day before, though it was difficult to tell on the television. The echo reverberated throughout the basin.

"Earth Sister, thank you for taking time…" the announcer began.

"Today the elk come," Earth Sister interrupted the reporter. "This is not a protest of one human economic class against another. It is not between the corporation and the People. This is Grandmother Earth rebelling against the way you have treated her. She has been passive and you have ignored her. Now, she becomes active." The spokesperson swept her hand toward the horizon and elk poured from the tree line. With the elk, however, were also whitetail deer, pronghorn antelope, mule deer, moose, and bighorn sheep. The fact that well over a thousand animals appeared on the horizon was almost overshadowed by the number of species represented together.

"These are her representatives to warn you. Depart. The wolves are near," Earth Sister concluded. She handed her microphone back to the technician standing by even as Sarah d'Angelo was trying to ask a question and turned to go back to the village. As silently as they had appeared, the animals moved back into the trees. The news cameras panned over the encampment.

IT WAS ASSUMED the People had moved into the park via over-snow vehicles during the winter. By the time regular roads opened in April, over a thousand people had taken up residence. Few people knew that Park Rangers who had been granted admittance to the village found the settlement had the appearance of having been there a hundred years. The village even included an earthworks fortification so that anyone coming across the meadow could not see into the village but could be seen from the ridge. From the position of the television crew, people could be seen going about their everyday business in the village close to a mile away.

Satellite imagery was ordered, tracking the site for the past several months. The results were classified as top secret. One day in March, the scene was a tranquil winter basin. The next day, a village occupied the space. Officials were baffled, but were not letting the sudden appearance be known. The civilization represented by the primitives in this village had not been encountered before.

When tourists began to show up in May, they found the northwestern part of the Park closed. The Grand Loop Road was blocked from the Fishing Bridge to Old Faithful. The north and west entrances were barricaded by the park service with only access being granted to the drilling site from the north. Yet the protesters' village survived without resupply.

Unlike Standing Rock, the protest occurred on Federal land, so local law enforcement had no authority to even assist Park Rangers attempting to keep the protesters away from the construction sites. But they found themselves in a non-confrontational situation. The protesters welcomed the Rangers, fed them, and thanked them for their care of the land entrusted to them. They insisted that they were witnesses only, and that stopping the construction and pseudo-fracking was Earth Mother's task and she would take care of it.

Even as Earth Sister finished her daily warning in front of the news cameras, huge drums changed tempo. It was the same every evening. The natives danced and summoned the power of Earth Mother.

The Family

"I DID SOME research," Aubrey said. "While you were all out taking care of business today and I had a baby on my tit, I looked up information about Earth Sister. She's been seen at many tribal gatherings for different tribes all over the country. She is known by her tattoo and as the Voice of Twin Wolves. Some drum maker has been talking up the need to resist the rape of Mother Earth among all the different Native American Nations and he frequently cites the words of Earth Sister. That absolutely has to be Merv Longsteer's granddaughter, Mandy Stevens."

"They are there, aren't they?" Mary Beth whispered. "Who else could talk to the animals and lead them into valley? Into the valley of the shadow of death. Who else could move supplies and people in and out without using the roads? Our children are going to lead the attack."

The family cleaned up the meal and put Theresa and Katherine to bed. Then they returned to the office. Ramie got the box off the mantel and turned to see who would read. She faced her own dear wife, Aubrey, who held out her hands.

"I'll read tonight," Aubrey said. "I'm the only one here who isn't blood related. And I'm a third, like Mandy. I'll read their story."

Caitlin: Mapping the Future

WE WERE OUT early and took Bells and Bows out for a little ride before breakfast. I don't think anyone noticed that Mandy rode double with me as we trotted down the road and let her off at the Bear Claw to get her car. She came back later in the day to go for a ride, but we didn't have a conference. We were busy with all the boarders and pleasure riders who came out.

Phile and I rode scout along the trails to make sure they were safe and no wolves were prowling the area. We hadn't heard anything from them since Christmas, but I didn't trust them. Pa was still debating whether to drive the cattle up to the leased pastures, but we all figured that's what we'd be doing the day school got out.

"See if you can do it while I'm out riding," Mandy said. "Only don't go having any orgasms. I might fall out of my saddle."

She took off and we linked easily so we could ride with her. Of course, we had work to do. It's never a holiday on the ranch. When we had to concentrate on a task, like driving the tractor load of hay down to the bottomlands for the rescues, we found we could easily transfer the link to Wolf Riding Woman and Wolf Rising. They were used to our time as well as their own. We really weren't four people. We were two people with four bodies. Regardless, it was a thrill to Mandy to be directly in touch with us in our other lives. She had a million questions and assured Wolf Rising that she wanted to make love to him as much as to Phile.

It surprised me that she spoke Cheyenne to us, even though the dialect was a little strange. Turned out that Merv had been teaching her so she'd be able to understand us better.

"No secrets from you, are there, woman!" I shot at her.

"Never have been," she answered. "Even before I knew the language, I recognized things you were saying. That's why it finally occurred to me that you could get into my head. Oh! Look at that beautiful doe and fawn!"

Of course, we saw them through her eyes. We didn't control her; we were just along for the ride.

We decided to see how long we could keep the link open. Mandy went home and we had no difficulty staying connected as she drove to her house, nor reconnecting after dinner. We all pleasured ourselves that night, one at a time so the other four could all experience what we felt. The feedback loop was once again intense, even though we were miles apart and only one at a time entered the circuit.

"*NA-MÉ'OO'O*," I WHISPERED gently. "*Na-mé'oo'o*, awake and hear me."

"What? Who?" Mandy sat upright in bed.

"It is Wolf Riding Woman, my beloved." I'd concocted this experiment myself and I was surprised that it was working.

"You're… Is Caitlin…?"

"My other self is sleeping. But I wanted to reach out to you from here in the *Oxése*."

"Why? I mean, this is fantastic! You contacted me across centuries! From a different world. I knew you were present with us when we joined, but that you could reach me like this is amazing," Mandy spluttered. "Why? Are you okay?"

"Yes. But it was more than an experiment. I wanted to tell you, my sweetheart, that I love you. I don't know why it is important. I am the same person as Caitlin, but if she were here with me, I would make love to her. Perhaps one day we will be united. It is important that you know that I love you across all ages, *na-mé'oo'o*. Even if my hand never touches your face, you are my beloved and Wolf Rising's. We love you across his chasm, just as Caitlin and Phile love you in their bed."

"Oh, *Ho'néené'šeohtsévá'e*, I love you."

In the morning, I would tell my others about what I had done.

Phile: Night of the Wolves

The three weeks that followed our first ride on Mandy were exciting, exhausting, and filled with adrenalin rushes. And lots of orgasms. We were linked together while we took our final Social Studies exam. Wolf Rising thought it would be fun to masturbate and the three of us in the exam room let out a gasp and sigh right in the middle of the exam. Mr. Hanratty made us empty our pockets on the table to make sure we weren't receiving messages through an electronic device. He always seated Caitlin and me on opposite sides of the class, but now he looked strangely at Mandy, too.

Of course, it wasn't all having orgasms and fun. But there was a lot of that. A subtle change had come over our school in the past two years. Guys were getting bolder and it seemed like they were caring less about women. We'd all heard rumors about rapes, but there were never any court cases. I'd been in the bathroom between classes and Mandy wanted to find out if she could feel me pee. She said it was different than a girl. I had to work a little at getting things tucked back into my jeans with the things she was thinking. I walked out of the bathroom and saw Mandy at her locker about twenty feet away. I looked past her and some big oaf had Caitlin pinned against her locker with a hand on her breast. She was pushing at him.

"Mandy!" I screamed in her head. "Caitlin needs help to your left." I was rushing toward them, but Mandy was fast. She spun and reached between the guy's legs and grabbed. I could feel her squeeze and gave her a little boost of my own anger to make it harder. The guy threw back his head and screamed. In front of him, Caitlin, suddenly free from his attack, reached out and grabbed both his nipples and twisted as hard as she could. He screamed again.

"You grabbed my balls!" he screamed at Mandy, jerking away and putting both hands over his nipples.

"Oh. Sorry," Mandy said. "I wanted to feel your cock, but I couldn't find it. You sure you've got one?" I was willing to bet that if he did, it was all shriveled up in horror.

"And you!" he screamed rounding on Cait. "My nipples!"

"You were pinching mine," Cait said. "What did you expect? I just wanted to see what it felt like."

"That's assault!"

"The Attorney General says grabbing someone's genitals is not sexual assault," I said. "Want to take it to court?"

"You freaks aren't human. Fuck you!" he said as he backed away, then turned and fled. I leaned against a locker and casually slipped my knife back into my boot. We'd long since found that our bone knives didn't show up in the metal detectors at school. I was glad in a way that he ran away. I was sure Mom Mar would beat my ass if I put a knife in him.

It was too bad that Mandy couldn't initiate the link. At the same time, it was probably a good thing or we'd have fallen off horses, swerved off the road, or hurt ourselves pitching hay when she showed up. She had a bit of a headache after I'd screamed in her head. We walked her over to her grandfather's and Merv nodded at us as we went out back. Nobody could see us out there and we fell together in a hot make-out session for about ten minutes.

We were all linked together and could feel the growing pressure.

"Tonight," Mandy whispered. "Just link me in when you start to make love. I want to be with you."

"We should all be together," I protested.

"Two of my lovers will be in a different time zone," Mandy whispered. "It's our season. I will feel everything you do if you bring me along."

"Mandy, you know how much we love you, don't you?" Caitlin said. "How much I love you."

"I sure do. And you, too, Wolf Riding Woman and Wolf Rising. I think I'll have you tattooed on my chest so I can carry you with me all the time." I touched the chest in question and she pushed herself into my hands. We heard Ramie's voice in the store and Mandy slipped home while we went inside.

SEEMED LIKE IT took forever to get the family celebration over with. Nothing against Kyle's birthday, but we really had more important things to do. I had a feeling my other siblings wanted to get to their apartment, too. Caitlin and I stripped down and collapsed onto the bed together. I kissed her hard in both timelines. Wolf Riding Woman and Wolf Rising were as ready for this in *Oxése* as we were in now-time. We'd gone to the trouble of building our own special wigwam next to a hot spring on the ridge overlooking what I knew would eventually become our homestead. We'd piled it thick with furs we'd collected over the winter and were naked and waiting.

We all sat facing each other. That sounds strange, but when I looked out of my eyes I could see both Caitlin and Wolf Riding Woman. She could see both Phile and Wolf Rising. We took hold of each other's hands and concentrated our thoughts. In a second, Mandy was in our minds and we were in hers. And it wasn't that she shared with one of us. I could feel her disorientation as she experienced seeing all four of us through the others' eyes. And then we were in her head as well and I could see myself looking at Caitlin.

"Mandy, I can feel you and talk to you, but I can't see you," I said. "I want to see your pretty eyes and sweet breasts. Don't you have a mirror?"

"Oh, wow! That's kinky!" she said. She turned on her bed and faced her closet mirror. Not only could we see her breasts and eyes, but as she sat on her bed, we could see between her legs, too. I ached with desire for her. I wanted so much to touch her and she raised her hand to her own breast. I felt her caress herself as I caressed Caitlin. I looked at all three of my women and just poured out my love to them. They were so beautiful!

"I love you," I said and they knew I meant all of them.

"Is that really how you see me, Phile?" Mandy asked. "I seem so much prettier in your eyes than when I look at myself."

Caitlin leaned forward and kissed me. It was more than me that she was kissing. Mandy gasped.

"I love you," Caitlin said to all of us.

It took us a while to sort things out and relax. It was true that Mandy was with us in our minds, but we couldn't touch her. It was frustrating. No matter how intent we were on each other, we were missing something.

"I wish we could all five be physically in the same space," Caitlin moaned. "I want to come. I want to feel you in me. I want my lovers to all be touching me."

And then the wolf howled.

We could hear him outside both the bunkhouse and the wigwam. We could hear him inside our heads.

Wolf Rising and Wolf Riding Woman didn't bother dressing. They grabbed their horseshoe hatchets and rushed outside to face the silver wolf. Caitlin and I pulled our underwear on and slammed our feet into boots at the door as we grabbed our rifles and went outside. Ramie, in just her t-shirt and panties, was face to face with the huge wolf.

"Wolf! I'll kill it," Caitlin screamed as we came around the bunkhouse. Wolf Riding Woman raised her hatchet.

"Caitlin, rest your gun. He won't hurt us," Ramie commanded.

"They killed my baby," Cait cried.

"Not this wolf!" Ramie said.

We knew. Since our night among the wolves in December, we hadn't heard from our spirit guide. We still hated that he was Creator Wolf. I'd rather have had a prairie dog as a spirit guide. But he owned us. Owned our souls.

105

"*Nésemoo'o*," Mandy said. I'd forgotten she was riding with us, in all our heads. "Listen to the spirit."

Caitlin was only wearing panties and it was damn cold out. Of course, I wasn't wearing much more, but Pa handed Caitlin his shirt.

"Here, baby. You're freezing your tits."

She gave him her gun so she could pull the shirt on and he wouldn't give it back. We all gathered behind Ramie in now-time and a pack of wolves gathered behind *Manèstóhó'néhe*, Creator Wolf. In *Oxése*, the pack we'd bonded with gathered behind the spirit as Wolf Rising and Wolf Riding Woman faced him.

In now-time, Wolf was licking at Ramie's scars. I never realized she'd formed a bond with him, probably because of the bite she'd received and the teeth she wore around her neck. We could all hear Ramie declare Wolf's blessing.

"This land is forever ours. Even our spirits will protect you, our pack, and our hunting. We will never rest. And we are deadly when we hunt."

But the five of us linked together heard more. Creator Wolf leapt into our heads to deliver the rest of the message.

You *are our spirits.* You *are our pack.* You *must never rest.* You *must be deadly when you hunt.* You *will call the packs, the herds, the flocks, the lone beasts to the aid of Néške'emāne, Grandmother Earth, and they will listen. And you, Ho'enáséé'e, Earth Sister, will be the voice of the Twin Wolves to the people. Your time comes soon and you will be brought together.*

The wolves at the ranch disappeared when a raven swooped in and grabbed them. In *Oxése*, Yelloweye landed and Creator Wolf loped away with the pack. We went back to our room. No one else seemed to have heard what we heard. Everyone just turned and went to bed. We were still linked together with Mandy and she joined us as we sat to listen to Yelloweye. The idea of having sex was put on the shelf.

Caitlin: The Journey of Earth Sister

WHEN YOU'RE DEALING with spirits that are thousands of years old, soon is a relative term. I was so pissed at Creator Wolf and Yelloweye that I could hardly focus on what we'd been told. I was about to make love and they had to go and interrupt everything. It was so unfair!

Phile and I got under the covers to get warm, but we held Mandy with us. Wolf Rising and Wolf Riding Woman retreated to their bed skins in the wigwam and the old owl walked right in with us.

I try to put what we got from the two mystical creatures in words, but even when Phile wrote down what Creator Wolf said, it wasn't like he literally spoke the words. So, when I write what Yelloweye said, I'm just making up the words and trying to sort of interpret them. Sometimes, I didn't quite understand him, but Mandy helped me write this down. Like *Manèstóhó'néhe* said, she was the voice of *Héstahke Ho'néheo'o*, the Twin Wolves. Here's the way she wrote of our time with Yelloweye.

Mandy: Voice of Twin Wolves

The Twin Wolves came to me to make me their woman and gladly I went to their furs. Their hearts entwined with my own and I loved them. But as we sat naked on the earth, *Heove-'éxané* called hoo-hoo and sat before us. He fastened his eye upon us and delved into our hearts. Coming to rest upon my eye, he commanded, "Ask!" And I knew that I must seek the questions that would reveal his purpose.

"*Heove-'éxané*, the people know you come to collect the spirits of the dead. Have you come to collect us, your servants?" I asked.

"No." He declined to add any details—just that we would not die tonight.

"*Heove-'éxané*, your wings span time, just as the hearts of Twin Wolves are in two places at all times. Whose death do you portend? Tell us that we may offer comfort and prepare Mother to receive her child." I said.

"I have seen Our Mother die," Yelloweye said sadly. We sat in silence and wept, for if Mother Earth died, the People would also die.

"Is this written?" I asked. We all knew that once the history was written, the story was told. But we did not know if the future was bound to our visions.

"It is a vision," the Owl said. "I have seen a great scorpion stinging Mother repeatedly, filling her with his poison and bleeding her of life. I went to the spirits of the two-leggeds. I cried to them that we must battle the scorpion. But when I told them of the scorpion, they responded, 'The scorpion is god! We will worship the scorpion. No other could cause the Mother to submit.' I wept.

"I went to the spirits of the four-leggeds. I cried to them that we must battle the scorpion. 'Lead us,' said Creator Wolf. 'We will do battle.' But when I flew to the heavens, they could not follow. Creator Wolf howled his frustration for he was lusting for the blood of the scorpion. 'Bring us a leader we can follow!' he howled.

"I went to the spirits of the winged ones. I cried to them that we must battle the scorpion. And the winged ones took council. 'The two-leggeds will not hear us. The four-leggeds cannot follow us,' said Eagle. We must bring forward a champion who will count coup on the enemies of Mother Earth. 'I will find a champion among the two-leggeds,' cried Redtail and he flew to a man to become a champion. The man counted much coup on his enemies, but he did not kill the scorpion. 'I will find two that will fight the scorpion,' Blackfeather boasted. 'They will cause the four-leggeds to follow.' Blackfeather found two who could bridge the gap in time, but they could only make peace between the two-leggeds and four-leggeds. They could not lead.'

"At last I was sent. I would find a champion. 'One did not work. Two did not work. I will find five that will be as the fingers of the two-leggeds' hands. They will close together into a fist and all the people will follow. The four-leggeds will answer their call. The two-leggeds will turn from their ways. The fliers will blanket the sky. And the fist will hammer the scorpion to his death.' And I searched through all time to find the spirits that would be one hand."

Understanding that Yelloweye spoke of us, we wept because we were children and the task was too great.

"I have chosen you," Yelloweye proclaimed. "No task is too great. I have given you three spirits that you may stand firmly on the ground and not waver. I have given you five bodies that you might span time and summon all the People to follow. I have given you teachers among all creatures that all would understand and follow you. And your task is soon to come."

"What must we do?" I asked our mentor. "You have made us and you will rule us."

"You have not yet learned all that you must. Your bodies drive you forward to mate and become one flesh. But you are still in different realities. You must bring all five fingers together in order to make the fist. Only as the fist can you battle the scorpion. Use the lust of your flesh to bring the fingers together and you will be sated beyond your imaginings," Yelloweye said. We blushed our shame, for if Creator Wolf and Yelloweye had not interrupted us, we would have sated ourselves this night. Yet each of us knew that would not have been enough.

"What must we learn?" I repeated. "And from whom?"

"You must learn to make the mountains echo with thunder," Yelloweye said. "You must forge a bond so deep that it transcends realities. You must learn to open the door between the People and the worshipers of the scorpion that they may be defeated. To learn these things, you must visit *Vóhpáhtse*, White Mouth. He will teach you to roar."

"Where will we find *Vóhpáhtse*?" I asked. Tears ran down my cheeks for the great grizzly bear struck fear into the hearts of braves with just his roar.

"The Twin Wolves will follow the pack. They will lead you to the place. There you must make peace with White Mouth and learn to bridge the worlds," Yelloweye said. He gazed again into each of our eyes and screeched a hunting cry. Then I found myself in my own bed, sitting naked before my mirror, looking into the eyes of Earth Sister—she who would speak for the Twin Wolves.

Caitlin: The Way to White Mouth

I WAS BITCHY the rest of the weekend. The family all assumed it was because of the wolves and that I didn't get to kill one. Well, it was in a way. It was because they interrupted us making love and now we had to wait again. I did apologize to Ramie, but it didn't do much good. Her girlfriend broke up with her and Kyle. I felt bad for them and blamed the wolves for that, too. I didn't know what I'd do if we lost Mandy.

Wolf Riding Woman and Wolf Rising were running with the wolves in *Oxése*. We took only our knives and hatchets, dressed warmly, and wore our wolf skins over the top. The wolves were leading us north through the mountains, stopping long enough to hunt along the way. We didn't cook our food, but cut a haunch from our kill and ate it raw.

We made the first kill and the pack waited until we ate the liver and tore into the meat before they fell to gorging.

The pack changed day after day. Wolves are territorial and our first pack fell back as we crossed into the territory of the second. There was a lot of sniffing around, but even the alpha didn't growl at us. I saw him look up and in the distance caught sight of the silver wolf moving on. This pack escorted us farther north. I figured we covered about thirty miles a day, and we traveled for the better part of three weeks.

In the meantime, we had work to do on the ranch and school to finish. We got out of our junior year about the same time that the pack—the fifth one since we started the journey—all lay down at once. Out ahead of us was a huge herd of buffalo. More than I'd seen anyplace but in the southern plains. It was still early in the summer and I didn't think these guys had migrated. Still, there were thousands of them. At first, I thought we were going to hunt and gorge, but after we'd rested a few minutes, the pack all slunk away. There were no others joining us. We waited there for a day and decided we needed to hunt or we'd starve. We were apparently where we were supposed to meet White Mouth.

I wasn't enthused.

I'd never tried to communicate with a grizzly. I never wanted to hunt one. It took a whole hunting party to take down a full-grown grizzly, and even then, it wasn't unusual for one or more to get hurt or killed. There was smaller game to be had. Game that didn't have three-inch claws and teeth. Even smaller black bears if we wanted tallow and a good hide. We set snares and caught a couple rabbits, found some edible roots, and built a fire.

In now-time, Mandy came to the ranch on Saturday after school let out. She pulled a trailer behind her truck. We found time to lead her out to the woodlot where we'd had our first face-to-face conference. It didn't take long for the three of us to get naked.

"You're leaving," I cried as I held her to me. Phile was holding her from the other side and I knew it would only take a couple good twitches to have him inside her. She held him back.

"I have to go to the res for the summer," she said. "After I load Wildfire, I'll pick up Grandfather and he'll go with me. Whatever it is that we have to do, I'll need all the *Nóváhe* medicine I can get in order to accomplish it."

"We've seen you almost every day in school and out here when you ride. Mandy, I'll miss you."

"Sweet loves. My lovers. Learn what White Mouth has to teach and call me to you. You can always link and ride my mind. I am always happy to be joined with you. I know the time is coming," she said. "Mmm. And if you keep twitching right there, I'm coming, too!" We enjoyed our love, but we didn't take the last step. Deep inside, I knew Yelloweye was right. We needed to all five be together when we made love. I just didn't know before that it was possible.

The Family

"I DIDN'T EVER want to remember that horrid night and morning when I left you," Aubrey sobbed as she put the pages back in the box. "I'm so thankful you took me back!"

"Hush, you silly goose. You'll sour your milk and Katherine will be upset," Ramie said as she hugged her wife. "If you hadn't given us that jolt, Kyle and I might never have had the courage to be with each other. You have to admit that when we got back together it was twice as good."

"Three times," Aubrey laughed.

"Five times," Jason's voice said through Kyle.

"Do you realize that according to Yelloweye, we were all an experiment?" Cole asked. The younger generation looked at him expectantly. "Yelloweye's story, according to Mandy—or Earth Sister—was that Redtail and Blackfeather both tried to find the champion in our family and only got part way there. They sent me back. They pushed it and even sent me back without a host. They sent you two back and then brought Miranda and Jason forward. Then they sent Caitlin and Phile back, but they didn't give them a host. They gave them two bodies. I think there was more than that, too. Ramie loosened Wolf from his time trap and brought him forward. I wish I knew what was going to happen next. It makes me want to stay up all night and read the rest, but somehow, I believe we are supposed to be reading this now at the pace we are reading. It's something important."

"I think it's something about the box," Ramie said. "I think we have to open it slowly. Things that are in the box haven't been set yet. I'm scared."

Kyle and Aubrey hugged their wife as Mary Beth and Ashley hugged Cole. Out there somewhere, three souls in five bodies were planning something important.

8
Echoing Thunder

The Family

COLE AND Ashley had taken a four-wheeler to the upper pasture and returned upset. This had the potential to turn into another range war. The Forest Service had cancelled their lease.

"Those fuckers can't do that," Ashley stormed. "We've leased that land for forty years. We've cared for it. Now they want us off so the cattle don't interfere with the oil company. How many people do they think they'll feed with oil?"

"Doesn't make a damn bit of difference," Cole said. "Kids, we're going to have cattle coming back down next week. Rafe and the boys will be rounding them up this weekend to start the drive. We'll have to share the pasturelands. What do you think we can sustain?"

"The horses don't graze the land down as badly as cattle do. We've never had to supplement in summer before. We put four hundred head of cattle out there with the hundred rescues and we'd have that pasture so bare it won't be fit for grazing for two years."

"I don't want to risk your operation," Cole said. "Yours is the future. We'll drive the cattle to the Alexander pens and I'll ship them to the auction house."

"Don't do that, Pa," Kyle said. "We've got an option on the Calhoun ranch. We've been dickering over terms for near a year. If we go in with a cash offer, we could own 2,000 more acres next week. We can sustain the cattle for two weeks without doing any damage."

"So, you want cash?" Cole said.

"Pa, you aren't fifty yet," Ramie said. "It was never our intention to put you out of business. We want your cattle to thrive. The Calhouns haven't run anything on their range in the two years since Obert died. It's a good move for the cattle and it's good for the land."

"You're right, as usual," Cole responded.

"Cole, you know you've wanted that piece of land forever. Your kids got an option on it. Bankroll them."

"Let me make a couple calls. How soon is dinner?"

Third Live Report

"Earth Sister, you've threatened the oil company with buffalo and with elk. Yet they disappear after a brief appearance. Ron Grisholm, the president of Shale Oil Inc., says that you are dealing in illusions," said reporter Sarah d'Angelo as she interviewed Earth Sister.

"He is avoiding the inevitable," Earth Sister said. "This site will be returned to Earth Mother. He needs to salvage what he can and retreat. And not only from this site. The Rocky Mountains are Earth Mother's backbone. She will shake herself and rid the mountains of this abomination like a dog shaking water off her back."

"The Park Service has indicated that their investigation revealed no tracks to match herds the size we have seen on the rise over there," the reporter insisted. Earth Sister turned to face the camera and pulled the right sleeve of her blouse down her arm. The faces of both wolves were revealed. The exposure of her skin was only barely within the limits of broadcast television.

"Today, the wolves," Earth Sister announced. On cue, the drums in the village began.

Buffalo and herds of elk, deer, and sheep had made no sound in the past. But the howl of wolves on the hunt preceded the appearance of the first heads over the rise. Nearly a hundred wolves were known to inhabit the greater Yellowstone area. Three times that many came over the rise. Nor were they alone. Foxes, coyotes, bobcats, and cougars came with them. And behind them came bears. Black bears loped on all fours as grizzlies rose on their hind legs and bellowed. In the lead came a massive silver gray wolf.

"It's Wolf!" Ramie exclaimed. "She's called Creator Wolf!"

"I don't think she's doing the calling," Mary Beth said. "She's the voice of the Twin Wolves. Our children are out there somewhere."

The animals stopped after they had crossed the rise, just as the herds of buffalo and elk had done. They continued to howl and snarl, however, as the silver wolf loped toward Earth Sister and the frightened reporter. From nearly twenty feet away, the wolf sprang. The cameraman was backing up steadily, but kept the camera focused on Earth Sister and the frozen reporter.

The wolf landed lightly with massive paws on the reporter's shoulders as she screamed. She dropped to her knees in front of the wolf.

"Don't kill me. Please, don't kill me!" the reporter cried out.

The wolf paced around her, glancing at the cameraman, who backed away farther. Then, in complete disdain, the wolf raised a leg and pissed on the reporter. He loped away and the wolves, foxes, coyotes, bob cats, cougars, and bears retreated over the rise.

"Explain that illusion to the president of Shale Oil Company," Earth Sister said to the reporter, still on the ground in front of her. "I am sad for the men and women who stand between The People and the scorpion," she continued, pointing at a distant line of security guards surrounding the fenced in site of the pseudo-fracking machinery. "Tomorrow we darken the sky."

The Family

"WE BACKED YOUR offer and the Calhouns accepted it." Cole said as the family settled into office to read. "I don't know what's coming, but Mandy—Earth Sister—said every site would be destroyed. I don't know how they'll do it, but I know the Yellowstone site is only one of twenty-three sites that have they've surveyed in the mountains. I just pray that our children have not been trapped by the ancients."

AFTER VERIFYING THERE had been no more developments at the Yellowstone standoff, the family gathered again to read. Ramie claimed the polished box and plopped herself in her father's chair. Then getting up so Kyle could sit down, she settled in his lap with Aubrey cuddling the babies next to her.

"I think I need a bigger chair," Cole laughed as he settled on the sofa with Ashley and Mary Beth cuddled against him.

"Sometimes I just need to be closer to my family than others," Ramie said. "I need to read. I'm getting too fidgety to listen."

"Go ahead, daughter," Mary Beth said.

Caitlin: Making Thunder

FOR A LONG time, Wolf Riding Woman and Wolf Rising waited, looking at the herd of buffalo. It was a rich valley that supported thousands. We made camp and built a hut of sticks and mud. We set to work taking a cow from the herd and smoking the meat. We stripped the hide and cleaned it. An old doe from a herd of whitetail approached our camp. I leapt into her mind and she offered herself. We took her and thanked her spirit for this gift. I searched for roots, berries, and wild grain that we gathered into our camp, preparing for a long winter, even though it was still the long days of summer.

The alpha female of the pack was sitting by our fire when I came out in the morning. I'd almost become used to seeing the wolves, but I still fingered my hatchet. I hacked a piece of buffalo from the meat we were roasting and tossed it to the bitch. Phile and I sat to eat our roast and berries for breakfast. I seldom tried to touch the mind of a wolf, but I could feel her reaching out to me.

"It is time," she said. "White Mouth awaits."

She led and we followed. It was unusual to be led by the wolves without having the whole pack with us. Having just one made me nervous. I reached out to Mandy in Lame Deer in now-time and she gladly came into my head.

"This is it?" she asked. "I will be quiet and watch. Tread with care, my loves."

The wolf led us to a small clearing high on the mountain. Above us, I could see an indent in the rocks and was certain there was a cave entrance on the far side. The wolf approached us and in an unusual gesture, licked our faces. She bade us farewell. No one fronts a bear in his cave.

We sat at the edge of the clearing and stilled our hearts. In now-time, Phile and I hid in the barn so we could focus all our attention on *Oxése*.

We waited.

We cast out our minds and felt the grizzly deep in the cave. And then he began to growl. He was deep in the cave when the sounds began, but we could hear them clearly, both in our minds and in our ears. He lumbered forward until his bulk filled the cave entrance. We sat as small and as still as we could. This was no ordinary grizzly bear, though even an ordinary one would have frightened me. This boar was Grandfather White Mouth. He weighed a ton and stood twelve feet tall when he walked on his hinds.

And when he roared, the thunder echoed from the mountain.

When we touched his mind, he let us glide around the edges. What we got was that he was a bit of a showoff. He liked being the biggest animal on the mountain. He was one of the few who could stand a buffalo charge and hold his own. He normally ate small things—fruit, berries, grubs, and an occasional mole or rabbit. He traveled down to the river to fish. He had frozen a small elk with his roar and killed it with a single swat of his massive paw. He feasted on that flesh just before hibernating.

He loved to hear his own voice echoing through the mountains.

"HOW CAN WE make that sound?" Phile asked. We'd been to the clearing to observe the great bear three days in a row. I tapped on the deer hide we had stretched at our camp to dry. It thudded.

"Have you ever used a drum?" Wolf Riding Woman asked.

"Sweet Medicine gave our people small drums so we could dance and celebrate," Wolf Rising answered.

"Drums," I whispered in now-time. Phile squeezed me in our bed.

"*Onéhavo'e*. We need big drums," he said.

DRUMS WERE NOT unknown to our people. But we were migratory. We followed herds and moved across the prairies and into the mountains. We did not collect a lot of things that were hard to move. Wolf Rising and I had made and discarded countless bows, clothes, and dwellings. When we rode north on the buffalo herd and when we ran with the wolves, we took nothing with us but the clothes we wore, our hatchets, and our wolf skin robes. We had abandoned our tent in Oklahoma, our wigwam in Wyoming, and sleeping skins whenever we had to move. Even our horses roamed wild until we called them with our minds. Drums were small things among our people. We held them in one hand while we beat on them with the other.

Drum-making is hard work. We studied in now-time and practiced in *Oxése*. It would be days before we could experiment. We had a deer hide stretched, but not tanned. We cut branches and wove them into a hoop and then stretched a circle of rawhide across the hoop. We wet the hide to shrink it and let it dry in the sun.

Merv had left his trading post in the hands of a cousin and we visited to buy a pair of small drums. He explained that they were Ute drums, but made a pleasant sound. He didn't treat us seriously when we said we were interested in Cheyenne drums. I scowled at him and we bought the pair of little drums for a price that Merv never would have charged.

These were hollow log drums. They had skins stretched across both ends of a cylinder. We could beat them with our hands or with a wrapped stick. For little drums, they had a pretty big sound.

Wolf Rising located a hollow log and cut a length to fasten a skin to for a drumhead. He broke the first one by swinging his hatchet too hard. We learned from that to make tiny light strokes.

After weeks of work, we took our little drums to the cave of White Mouth. When we heard him start his morning grumblings, we answered with beats of our drums. He came lumbering out of the cave on all fours and stood before us to roar. I thought we had offended him. It was hard to read the mind of this primitive and egotistical creature. He grabbed my hoop drum out of my hand with his teeth and lumbered back to the cave. He dropped it on the ground and turned to roar again—a roar that echoed throughout the valley.

I heeded his call. Wolf Rising and I approached the cave mouth. We had never come fully into the clearing before. This was the home of the great spirit bear. I picked up the drum from where he dropped it. He stood on his hind legs in the mouth of the cave and roared. Then I could feel it. The massive sound was echoing from inside the cave and out the mouth as an amplifier. I thumped my drum and it was ten times louder echoing from inside the cave. Wolf Rising joined me on the log drum he had created and with White Mouth leading us, we duplicated the subtle changes of his mighty voice. As we beat our drums in concert with the great bear, I could see reality waver and the great valley beneath us was filled with animals that disappeared when I stopped beating the drum.

And for just a moment, I saw my other self.

WOLF RISING AND I had to hunt to have food for the winter. It appeared we would be in this location for a long time. But hunting gave us rawhide for drums. And in now-time, we found the meaning.

Phile and I went to Lame Deer under the pretense of checking on a couple new horses. Kyle and Ramie had thrown themselves into the upkeep of the ranch so thoroughly that I don't think they noticed we were gone. It was nearly five hundred miles, but we drove it on Friday, expecting to return on Sunday. By Friday evening, Mandy was in our arms.

"My darlings, I've missed you so much," she panted. "Not that there is anything wrong with mental orgasms, but I want my arms around you as we make love."

"Mandy, my love," Phile said. "You might get your arms around all of us."

"How?!"

"We think we've learned how to make thunder echo from the mountains. At the moment, it's just a little thunder, but it might be enough," I said.

"What happened?"

"We made drums in *Oxèse*. We don't have time to make drums in now-time, but we've bought some. When we experimented a few days ago, we actually saw each other," Phile said excitedly.

"Saw? You mean you saw Wolf Riding Woman and Wolf Rising? Could you touch?" she asked.

"Almost," I said. "Mandy, my Earth Sister and my voice, I think we need you as our catalyst. I don't think we can cross between times without you."

Mandy hustled us to her cabin and we spent the night in each other's arms as we explained what we believed was happening. We wanted to try it immediately, of course, but Mandy suggested we wait until Saturday night.

"There will be a powwow with dancing, singing, and drumming," she said. "Let's use the group music to augment our own. Please, please, let this work!"

119

It was mid-August. The nights were warm and the skies were clear. Over a hundred tribal members gathered to celebrate first harvest. The drumming and dancing started in the middle of the afternoon. At first it was just the old men who gathered. Younger people started to arrive at dinner time and the tables were spread with tons of food. We joined and were welcomed. We made a show of drumming and learning some of the traditional dances. Mandy, of course, had been practicing all summer. But after dark, we slipped away to her cabin with the various drums we had brought.

We stripped ourselves in both timelines and sat with our drums, three of us in Mandy's cabin and two in front of the bear cave. We started tentatively, but the strong rhythm set by the drummers in the circle outside filtered into our hands and we all five started to play on our drums. I was lost in the rhythms and seemed to float on the drumbeats. And then I felt lips on mine. Soft and sensuous. I thought Mandy had moved to kiss me, but when I opened my eyes, I saw myself looking back at me. My lips sought the lips of Wolf Riding Woman and she touched my soul. Beside me I saw Phile in a very unexpected embrace with Wolf Rising. Then all four of us turned to Mandy, who stared at us in disbelief. Our drums were forgotten as we embraced our dear love.

"It's real. You are all here with me," she gasped as Wolf Rising kissed her deeply. "I am beloved by all four and I love you equally. Take me. Make me your lover and your woman."

There was remarkably little confusion as we celebrated our love physically for the first time. I don't know if it was Phile or Wolf Rising that penetrated me for the first time. I don't know if it was Phile's come or Wolf Rising's come that I licked out of Mandy and Wolf Riding Woman. I know that I felt every rise and every release of each of my lovers.

I was sixteen years old. I'd had my share of orgasms, diddling my clit with my fingers. I'd had a good share of orgasms with either Phile or Wolf Rising doing the diddling. I'd joined with Mandy as we pleasured each other. But having five souls wrapped together, all experiencing not only their own orgasm with the other four, but experiencing the other four as well…

There has never been a woman—nor a man—who had more joy in her first sexual experience than I had. Unless it was Wolf Riding Woman or Mandy. Or Phile or Wolf Rising, for that matter. It was our season and we made love as often, as hard, and as long as we could last. Somewhere in the back of my mind, I felt the drums of the tribe beginning to slack off. I knew our time together was coming to an end, as did my mates.

I kissed myself—Wolf Riding Woman—again. I kissed Wolf Rising as I stroked his hardened manhood and pointed it at my other self. I held fast as Phile penetrated Mandy again and kissed them as the drumming finally faded to a stop and we found ourselves again in Mandy's cabin, still making love. Wolf Riding Woman and Wolf Rising left their drums at the cave entrance as they returned to their hut to make love again and again. Mandy and Phile made love to me all night long and we kept our link together. Now, no matter what, we would not hesitate to couple in any combination.

WE PURCHASED TWO quarter horse mares that weekend and brought Mandy's Wildfire home with us. We knew now. Not only could we reunite with our other selves, but we could make love with our sweet Earth Sister whenever we wanted. And we wanted often.

Our junior year in high school was a different experience. I was happy when Aubrey got together with Ramie and Kyle again. They got married on Christmas. All three of them together. It seemed there was a lot of moaning next door that fall. But maybe that was just me moaning. I loved Phile so much that I welcomed him into my body at every opportunity we had. Mandy continued to come to the ranch to tend to her horse and get screwed senseless as soon as we could get her alone. It looked like it would be a wonderful year.

Phile: Lovers

I GUESS ONE of the advantages of having been such pains in the butt for so long was that no one noticed how often we were sneaking out. Moms had assumed that Caitlin and I had sex when we were twelve or something. So, when we actually started, no one even batted an eye. Except Caitlin and me. We were stunned.

First of all, it was almost impossible for Wolf Riding Woman and Wolf Rising to make love without Caitlin and I being at least aware of it and most of the time participating. The same was true in reverse. Second, we had Mandy riding with us almost all the time. Sometimes literally. It was so easy to slip up to the Bear Claw in a four-wheeler and bring her back to our room. We could be up before the cowboys and zip right past the Alexander place in the morning to get her back to her car.

The best, though, was all those weekends we went camping, even in the snow. On those weekends, we'd tap on our drums up on the ridge and feel Wolf Riding Woman and Wolf Rising join us. Then we'd all five be together. Some of those weekends, we never got out of our sleeping furs, it seemed. How ideal is it for a teenager to have a place to go make love that literally no one knows about? Absolutely no chance of discovery.

It was becoming so easy to move between now-time and *Oxèse* that we could move Mandy with us even when she wasn't physically in the same location. We didn't have to worry about her driving up to the Bear Claw in winter for us to pick her up. We'd all drum, link our minds together, and bring her to us.

And that's what it seemed that Yelloweye wanted us working on. We had an anchor in two worlds and could move freely between them.

Caitlin: Two Sticks

I WISH IT was all as rosy as Phile says. Well, dipping his wick in three hot girls is kind of a fantasy, isn't it? Even if two of the hot girls shared one mind. All the stories I'd heard about that were similar were a girl in one body who had two different personalities. I had pretty much the same personality but two bodies.

You just can't imagine what it was like to receive two different sensory experiences. Yeah, one mind, but the input from the two bodies was completely different. To start with, Phile and I were about six inches taller than Wolf Rising and Wolf Riding Woman. So, it was a completely different sensation when I lay beneath Wolf Rising than when I jumped Phile's bones. And my now-time body reacted differently—chemically—to Phile and Wolf Rising.

It's really no wonder that we spent every opportunity in bed. But add in Mandy. She changed the dynamic all the way around and it was all for the better. I think she had the strongest orgasms of the five of us and when we were linked together it wasn't unusual for us all to pass out when she came.

But it wasn't all fun and games. We had school in now-time. Junior year was different than lower grades. We had a lot more independent study and small groups. Teachers seemed to give up on trying to separate us—or else they just didn't care. We learned a lot and actually got some use out of things that other kids swore they'd never use.

For instance, if you want a round drum that is eight inches across, how long a piece of wood do you need to bend into the body? $C=2\pi r$.

And that was what we had to figure out. White Mouth told us so.

It was nearing time for his long winter's nap and he was grouchy as... um... a bear. We'd noticed, after we'd drummed the five of us together, that White Mouth was joining less and less in our thunder making. We were preparing hides for drums, and had made one that was a little larger, but the thump seemed dead. We decided the body was too thick and we weren't getting enough echo inside. We brought the drum to the cave mouth to see if that improved it.

Not only did it not improve it, White Mouth got angry.

He roared from deep within the cave and the sound knocked us off our feet and into the clearing. Even when he was showing off it hadn't been like this. He lumbered out of the cave and looked at our drum. Then he stuck his claws through the two log drums and shredded the skins, hurling the heavy logs past us as if they were pebbles.

In the time of Sweet Medicine, I taught Tsétsèhéstàhese to make drums. You must go to the sacred mountain of the people and learn there how to bend the tree to your will and make the skin echo the thunder.

We didn't have enough drum power left to call Mandy to us to speak for us, but she was listening and prompting our questions.

"*Vóhpàhtse*, where is the mountain and how shall we get there?"

We will go to the time of the People. Ride!

Usually, we reach out and make a jump into the mind of an animal, but this was more like having our minds dragged out of us and into White Mouth. He was not content to have just our minds, though.

He made our hands grab the thick fur at the hump of his back and he lurched forward. Only Wolf Riding Woman and Wolf Rising made the physical leap, but Phile, Caitlin, and Mandy were all physically knocked out as we made the mental ride with White Mouth. The fact that we were meeting with Merv after school at the time was the only thing that kept us from discovery. We rode with the bear across time and across the mountains. And when the bear slowed to a stop, Wolf Riding Woman and Wolf Rising were in before-time facing *Náhkòhe-vose*, called Bear Butte, in the Black Hills.

Go in! Here you will learn to make the People's drums.

Wolf Riding Woman and Wolf Rising entered the mountain.

IN NOW-TIME, PHILE and I woke up next to Mandy. Merv was kneeling beside us, chanting softly. The journey had been breathtaking and we weren't entirely back in now-time as we journeyed into the mountain with Wolf Riding Woman and Wolf Rising. At the same time, we rode with Mandy as she spoke to Merv.

"Grandfather, it was amazing. We rode on the back of White Mouth. He has left us at the gate to the holy mountain and we have found the passage inside," she gasped.

"The passage? At *Náhkòhe-vose*?" Merv asked incredulously. "Why are you there?"

"We must learn to make drums," Phile said. "We must learn to make Cheyenne drums."

Merv looked at us for a long time—at least it seemed like a long time. Then he stood to leave us.

"I must think on this," he said. "Making sacred drums is a secret. My granddaughter, you are not permitted this knowledge because you are a woman. Women work a different kind of medicine. And you two… you would be considered hobbyists—white people who try to take the ways of the People and make them your own. Yet if *Vóhpàhtse* has taken the Wolf Twins to learn to make drums, I cannot deny them. I must sleep. Perhaps the old ones will come to me in a dream."

He left us and we turned our thoughts back to our other selves, carrying Mandy with us in our heads.

WE JOURNEYED INTO the mountain, not knowing where we were going. There was some powerful magic going on. We knew that we were inside the mountain—underground—yet we could see perfectly well, as if it were daylight. Yet there was no sun and no fire. Wolf Riding Woman and Wolf Rising had only what was with us when White Mouth commanded us to ride—our hatchets, knives, and ever-present wolf robes.

Deep within the mountain, we heard a single drum beat reverberate for many seconds. Then there was a second, but of a different timbre. Minutes later, there was a third beat and we entered a vast chamber where a man walked among a dozen drums, picking each up and striking it with a padded stick. When he had struck the drumhead, he paused to listen to it echo through the chamber. Two drums he took to his work area and began taking them apart.

"Come," he said. "I will speak the legends and you will learn to make the sacred drums of *Tsétséhéstáhese*."

Thus began our apprenticeship to Two Sticks.

"LONG AGO, THERE lived a man of the People named *Motsé'eóeve*, Sweet Medicine. He was touched by the ancient spirits. I will not recite all the things that Sweet Medicine did in his life. You should know that he brought order to our society, rules to live by, ways to judge truth and people. He was given four arrows that dwell yet among the People. Two were for war and two for hunting. As long as these arrows are with us, we have good hunting and victories. He also prophesied that the *ho'evótse* would come with horses and with guns and the People would change. These things are known to all the People and we see the coming of the white man and how he throws death from far away—farther than the best bow," Two Sticks said.

A long trough filled with water ran through the center of the cavern. Into this trough, Two Sticks placed poplar saplings that had been flattened and smoothed on one side. He moved to a stack of logs and selected one. This he held with his knees as he scraped it with his knife. As he scraped to flatten one side, he continued his story.

"But in addition to rules and strength, Sweet Medicine returned to the people with many other arts and skills. He showed us how to make the earth house, the tipi, and the smokehouse. And he taught us to dance and to drum our thanks to the spirits. In order to dance, we had to learn to make the thunder drums. This is what I do in the mountain even today."

THROUGH THE WINTER, we worked with Two Sticks to learn how to bend the saplings into a perfect circle, glue the ends together, wet and stretch the hide over its frame, and to lace it and tighten it until it rang clearly. When completed and struck, the sound of the drum would fill the chamber and echo from the walls.

No matter how it was when Sweet Medicine came to the mountain, neither Two Sticks nor we were confined to the mountain. We needed to hunt. We needed to trade with others for food that we could not grow. And as we traded, we learned a bit about the world we now lived in.

Even though Bear Butte was sacred to the Cheyenne, most of the People had been pushed farther west by both whiteman and other tribes. The nearest villages to the mountain were Lakota. When we took skins and meat to trade for vegetables and fruit, we learned much about what was happening in the world.

Red Cloud had signed a treaty, but Crazy Horse was gathering bands to oppose the white eyes. We knew how that worked out. I was ready to go find him and help wipe out the blue coats. Mandy and Caitlin convinced me otherwise. This was not the battle we were being prepared for. Still, I seethed and I could tell Wolf Rising was barely constrained. They spoke of a yellow-haired general who was gathering an army to oppose them. I knew at once, from school history, that they were talking about General George Armstrong Custer. And I remembered standing together under a flag while the blonde soldier and his companions screamed into our camp shooting at us—killing our mother. The anger and pain in my heart threatened to spill out into the mountain.

Inside the mountain, though, Two Sticks showed us the construction of drums and talked long into the night about how to awaken the drum spirit. Each step had a prayer, from bending the frame to smudging it with the sacred smoke to using the yellow mud to bind the skin to the frame. He taught us that it was not only the tension of the drumhead that determined the timbre of the drum, but also the thickness of the hide. Hides of different animals gave different sounds. He even traded for the hides of cows that were now being herded by some of the People.

We stayed with Two Sticks for the entire winter and we listened. Prior to this time, the only human mind we had entered was Mandy's. But while listening to Two Sticks, we found ourselves looking out his eyes. He seemed unaware that we were there. But riding silently, we learned much more than the making of drums.

Two Sticks' mind was a constant narrative of the lore of the People and their history from long before Sweet Medicine to the present. And this he shared with us.

And on those nights when we journeyed away from the mountain, we beat our little prayer drums and joined our five fingers together in love.

The Family

"How could making drums be so important?" Mom Mar asked.

"I traveled with John Hamm, White Horse, for many years. I think we've all figured out that he was Theresa Ranae Bell's husband and the father of the first Laramie Wyoming Bell," Jason said. "John and I had a dream that we'd be able to bring true peace between the People and the whites. He always said that true peace would never be possible until the white man's heart beat in time with the Cheyenne prayer drums."

"The drums were that important?" Cole asked.

"The drums were given to the People along with the rules—what we'd call the law. They were small, only about a foot across and a couple inches deep. But they were said to speak with the voice of the old ones," Jason said. "I heard them a couple times when John and I visited a tribe. But I never got to witness one of the sacred dances."

"I think I'd have shit my pants if I'd have grabbed a twelve-foot grizzly's hump fur," Ashley said. "I wish I had known how incredibly brave my children were."

"Remember when they came up that morning and said there was a mare in distress among the rescues and they were going to go get her? They said to call the vet and they'd have her up in the paddock in an hour," Ramie said. "The vet got there and that horse had an inflammation in her uterus that none of us would have guessed at until she was dead. There's no question in my mind anymore that those kids talked to the animals."

"And the animals answered," Kyle affirmed.

"Still, wolves? Elk? Grizzly bears?" Mom Mar said. "I just wanted them to be my babies. Even when they were older."

The family wandered off to their beds. There was no longer any question about the younger generation going back to the bunkhouse. For the duration, the babies were in Kyle's old room and Ramie, Kyle, and Aubrey were in Ramie's old room. Without saying anything, they all hoped Caitlin would bring Phile back to her old room.

9
The Hunger

The Family

SATURDAY, THERE were chores to do and riders at the stable. Cole and Ashley took the Forest Service road up to the trailhead and hiked in to the base camp for their hired hands. The situation was tense.

The oil company had hired 'security' people, supposedly to guard their equipment. In reality, they had spent the night in ATVs racing in circles around the site, spooking the cattle off in all directions. All Cole's cowboys were on their horses attempting to round up cattle that had scattered as much as a mile away. There was a small meadow half a mile north that was sufficiently far from the continued noise that they could gather the herd to get ready to drive them back to the ranch. It would take all weekend.

Cole was storming when he returned to the ranch.

"Blake, this is Gold Watch Cattle Company," he said into the phone. Ramie looked up at her father from across the desk they shared. She'd never heard of Gold Watch Cattle Company. "Well, we hoped we were out of the business. I know it's been a long time.— No, the wolves haven't been a problem for five years now. You guys did good work protecting the cattle without calling attention to yourselves.— You don't have people working on the Shale Oil team, do you?" Ramie listened as her father spoke to the unknown person about a company she didn't know about. "Just wanted to make sure. I need your help, but I didn't want to risk a conflict of interest.— Yeah, they're spooking our cattle and stampeding them up on the ridge faster than we can round them up to drive down the mountain.— How long?— We're looking for no casualties. I think Mother Earth will take care of that. Let's roll." Cole hung up the phone and stared up at his daughter and wives. "Gold Watch Cattle Company is back in business."

THERE WASN'T TIME to explain with the number of people out riding on a sunny Saturday. Ramie and Kyle had warned everyone off the trails up to the ridge and had their hired hands go out to block those trails with yellow tape. As riders returned in the afternoon, the four hired hands and two owners assisted with saddles and trailer loading for those who had just come in for the day. It seemed like there were an awful lot of them, but people were finding National Forest and BLM trails closed.

"I'll tell you what we need to do," one weekend cowboy was holding forth at the campfire. It was part of the atmosphere of the ranch that they kept a fire circle with hot coffee on the most popular days. Sometimes people hung out after their rides or had lunch picnics at the circle. Ramie looked at the dude who was speaking and recognized Rex Wilson, a lawyer from Laramie. He prided himself in having the biggest horse on the ranch so he could look down on everyone else when he rode. The animal had the temperament of an old plow horse, though, and Rex could seldom keep up with other riders on the trail. "We need to send about fifty bulldozers in there and bury that Indian village and the Earth Sister bitch with them. This country runs on oil and industry. You'd think they'd have learned their lesson at Standing Rock."

Ramie seethed, but it only got worse as several of her regular boarders rolled their eyes and said goodbye. Rex wasn't finished and Ramie wondered if he'd been drinking out on the trail.

"We've had too much land tied up by the government for too long. Why are we spending money for people and resources to patrol millions of acres of land that no one uses? If we can make some profit off the land, we should be putting it into the economy. Quit sucking people dry," Rex continued to the two riders remaining at the campfire.

Ramie walked over with a bucket of water and dowsed the fire creating billowing smoke and steam that blew directly onto the blustering dude.

"Hey, bitch! Watch what you're doing. We're having a nice chat here."

"We're closing up for the day. Time to head out, guys." The other two tossed the remains of their coffee and put their tin cups on the table.

"I pay good money for my rights here. If I say I'm staying for a while, I'm staying," Rex said.

"Not anymore," Ramie said. She reached in a shirt pocket and counted out $300 in twenties. "Your horse costs too much to feed. Can't make a profit on him. Not to mention the extra time my hands have to spend grooming him and taking care of his oversize tack. And nobody likes having you around. So, here's a refund on your boarding for the month. If your horse is still here on August 1, he'll be turned out with the rescues. Be happier there anyway."

"You can't do that."

"This is LK Stables. I'm the L. It's mine and I can choose who I want as a boarder. I don't want you."

"Do you know who I am?" he demanded. Ramie could smell the liquor on his breath as he moved into her personal space.

"Another dude who talks out his ass about his own shit. We're through. Get out."

"You can prepare to see me in court, Miss L. I'll own this place when we're done." It looked for a moment like he was going to take a swing at Ramie, but suddenly noticed she was picking her fingernails with a large knife. Kyle was approaching with a rifle laid across his arm.

"Problem, Laramie?" Kyle asked.

"No. Mr. Rex Wilson has violated ranch policy by drinking on the trails and creating a public nuisance. I've terminated his boarding lease and he was just nicely leaving. That big horse of his gets full board for the rest of the month. If he hasn't been moved by then, he goes to pasture with the rescues. Seems an appropriate place for him."

After another scowl at Ramie and Kyle, Rex headed for his Escalade and drove out of the ranch. Kyle pulled out his cell phone.

"I'd like to report an apparent drunk driver," he said. "White Escalade with Wyoming plates headed toward Laramie on 238 from Centennial. Just observed erratic driving. Seemed to be going pretty fast, too. You're welcome. Have a nice day." He grinned at Ramie.

"GOD, CAN THE shit get any deeper?" Ramie said as the family gathered together. "I probably handled that dude all wrong, but when he started talking about burying Mandy and the village, I sort of lost it. He's another one of those assholes that figures that if something doesn't benefit him directly he shouldn't have to pay for it."

"Well, you're probably right about that," Cole said. "Could have been handled better, but so could a lot of things. We're standing at the brink of a war. We might not be able to protect all land everywhere, but we'll protect this land."

"Speaking of which, who the hell is Gold Watch Cattle Company?" Ramie demanded. Cole, Ashley, and Mary Beth laughed.

"We told you about it years ago," Ashley said. "But you were too bent on how your parents had turned crazy to listen to what we were saying."

"Wasn't that about the range war and how much it cost to have 5,000 head of cattle?" Kyle asked.

"Yes, but it was also about how we got the money to support all the ranchers in the county—well, except one—and provide food and security to outwait the market pressure," Cole said.

"You mean when you were time traveling," Kyle continued. "You built up a few million in gold and stuff."

"Yes, but it also had to do with meeting Philemon Morgan the Third when he was time-traveling as the prospector Bill Campbell. We created a partnership back in 1888 and it was symbolized by two gold watches." Cole pointed to the mantel on which a bell jar encompassed a gold watch on display. We told you that belonged to the original Kyle Redtail Wardlaw and was passed down through the Alexander line. The assets are all held in a trust with the stated purpose of protecting the land."

"Pa, did you ever talk to Cait and Phile about time traveling?" Ramie asked.

"No. After the way you and Kyle reacted to it, we decided we'd put it off. Then you and Kyle started time traveling and it never occurred to me that there would be more than the pair of you in this generation."

"If we hadn't been so pig-headed, our siblings might have been warned. They might at least have known that we could share with them. We made so many mistakes!" Ramie moaned.

"Before we read, we should take a look at the recording of what happened today at Yellowstone," Aubrey said. "It was interesting."

Fourth Live Report

"THIS IS EVAN Waitley at the Yellowstone Grizzly Village, filling in for Sarah d'Angelo who is recovering from a vicious wolf attack at this site yesterday. We keep her in our prayers as she recovers from this trauma."

"I bet it was traumatizing to have that big wolf piss on her," Miranda laughed. "I'd hardly call it a vicious attack, though."

"At the end of the broadcast yesterday, Earth Sister promised that today she would darken the skies. As you can see, it is bright and sunny here at Yellowstone. A messenger from the Park Service, who have been the only ones allowed in or out of the camp other than Earth Sister, indicated that she would emerge at noon today. And you can see her as she steps over the earth embankment that surrounds the village. She should be here shortly. The Park Service has been firm about not allowing our crews to get closer."

"Do you get the impression that the government is playing both sides?" Ashley asked. "They're enforcing the leases, but they are also protecting the protestors."

"When Earth Sister promised a darkening of the skies, this reporter did some research. Historically, solar eclipses have been used by the savvy to cow primitive civilizations into believing their mystical powers. However, in our scientific age, we know and can predict solar and lunar eclipses. I was encouraged to note that there are no such predictions for today in any part of the world. As you can see, the sun is bright and the only thing above us is a lone bird circling high overhead. And here is Earth Sister."

The camera shifted as a microphone was quickly clipped to Mandy's dress and the wireless transmitter attached to her belt.

"Earth Sister, we might as well come straight to the point," Evan said. His style was far more brusque than the previous reporter. "You promised darkened skies today. What kind of trick do you have in store?"

"You have witnessed animals of every species native to the Yellowstone over the past three days," Mandy said. "And still you believe in trickery. We have no magic illusions for you. We have only Mother Earth's natural protectors. But you have seen only those who dwell on the surface. I call you to witness the presence of those who dwell in the sky." Mandy raised her hand and the camera panned up to the lone bird continuing its lazy circles. At the same time, the drums in the village began a new rhythm.

"One bird?" Evan asked. Then, as the camera held, another bird appeared and another. From the angle of the camera, the birds appeared to be flying out of the sun as more and more appeared in the sky. In minutes, there were hundreds of birds in the sky, their shadows passing over the village and the reporter. And still more kept pouring through the light.

There was a growing hum on the broadcast and the camera swung from the birds down a level to see swarms of insects launching from the grass into the air, emerging from the woodlands, and coming down from the mountains. Flies, mosquitoes, bees, locusts. Then, from the north came a cloud of bats. The birds, thousands of them now, blocked out the sun as they dove and fed on the insects rising to meet them.

Evan slapped at a mosquito. Earth Sister laughed.

"Don't worry. They have nothing against you personally," she said to the reporter. "Just a demonstration so you know it is not an illusion."

"A mosquito? Not much…" Bird shit hit the microphone in the reporter's hand and dripped onto him. "Nice. Just great," he mumbled.

"It is not only the animals of the earth, but also those of the air that come to protect our Mother. But unseen to you, her creatures of the water and even those who dwell beneath the earth are rising to defend her."

"What next?" Evan asked. "The biblical plagues included boils and frogs, if I remember rightly."

"And even then, it took death before Pharaoh let the people go," Mandy said. So, she was versed in other mythologies than her own. "Sadly, the corporations will not set Mother Earth free until death is rained down on them. You have seen the companies of her warriors. But you have not seen them together. When the battle begins, utter destruction will reign."

"Tomorrow?" Evan asked.

"Tomorrow is a day of prayer and fasting. Just a thousand people in the village have joined their voices in support of Mother Earth and you have seen the response. Tomorrow we ask that people of all faiths—and those of no faith—join their voices with ours as we consider the land. And as we pray, we will also mourn for those warriors whose lives will be lost. Monday will be a good day to die."

Mandy took off her microphone and handed it to the technician standing by. She turned to the village and the drums changed their rhythm. In the time it took her to return to the village, the sky cleared and just one lone bird continued to circle.

The Family

"I THINK I should read this next part," Jason said when the family had found their places. "I have a deep sense of foreboding and I need to be the one to give it voice."

"We love you, Jason," Ramie and Miranda said together. There was an odd timbre to her voice when they both used it at the same time.

"I hope you always will," he answered lifting a batch of papers from the box.

Phile: Building Drums

IT TOOK A while and several dreams to convince Merv that we whites, including two women, could learn to make drums and even then, he withheld certain tasks from us. Ramie and Kyle were still putting in a couple afternoons a week at the gun shop in town, so Caitlin and I acted like responsible adults and took a job with Merv's trading post. The truth was that we sat in his back room, mostly watching him as he prepared the wood and a frame in which to bend it.

"Why are you using plywood for the frame?" I asked. It was certainly different than what we were learning in before-time with Two Sticks.

"It is the way most drums are made today," he said. "It bends and stabilizes. If we used solid wood, it would take much longer and be prone to breaking. It takes a long time to build a drum of dogwood. And you are asking for large drums," Merv explained as if we were babies.

"Grandfather," Mandy spoke softly. "The Wolf Twins are learning from Two Sticks in the sacred mountain. The knowledge is here…" she pointed at our heads, "but our bodies must be trained in the way. Can you do less than Two Sticks?" Merv sighed and scowled at us.

"It is not simply the knowledge, children." I was a little irritated. We were sixteen and functioning with two complete lives beneath our belts. I hardly thought we were children. "The wood curves against its grain to meet itself in the shape of a circle, the symbol sacred to Indian tribes sensitive to the harmony of the universe. The hide stretches across it. The laces pull and bind until it captures within itself the rich roll, the deep thunder, the soft murmur. It becomes a drum. This you can do. The skill can be taught. The drum will look and sound the same. It will even work to move you to your other selves. But it will not be a Cheyenne drum. The Twin Wolves can make Cheyenne drums because they are of the People and White Mouth has brought them to the teacher himself. Even after applying themselves for months with Two Sticks, they will not be skilled. But even if your mind is the same, your body is not Cheyenne. It is not in your blood. You are *Vé'ho'e*."

"*Ma'heónėhetane*, how will we make the thunder drum that White Mouth says we need?" Caitlin asked. "We need to… create. Two Sticks has said no Cheyenne drum that large has ever been made." Merv sat quietly for a few minutes. We didn't disturb him. We needed to make a Cheyenne drum unlike any that had been made before. I understood in an odd way. There was so much cultural appropriation going on that the People were ever more conscientious when it came to keeping their ritual pure. But if we wouldn't have adequate skills even after studying with Two Sticks, how would we ever succeed? At last Merv looked up and searched our eyes. He suddenly looked much older than the 70 years I knew him to be.

"When the time comes, you will take me to *Oxėse* and I will make the thunder drum."

Caitlin: Calluses

AFTER WE'D MADE our first toy drums from plywood following Merv's direction, we did start using dogwood limbs to bend into the correct shape. When we started, Merv only had the plywood in stock. You can't just go down to the lumber yard and buy dogwood. But he had contacts and his contacts had contacts and eventually a bundle of sticks arrived at the trading post. They were three inches thick and six feet long. In case you are slow at math, that will make a drum just under two feet across.

But it doesn't happen all at once.

Merv's workshop included power tools, and as much of a stickler as he was about tradition, he had no difficulty at all using a power saw to rip the sticks in half lengthwise. Nor did he have a hard time using hot water to soak them in so they would absorb more quickly.

"How are we going to split the log for the frame of a big drum?" I moaned. "Are we going to have to build the frame here and transport it to *Oxėse?*"

Merv scowled at me again. He'd been doing a lot of scowling lately. I could tell that he was working on more than the little drums that he was guiding us through.

"I will take some tools. Now you must work on bending the wood," he said. "You will also need a thick, tough hide for the drumhead. For these little drums we will use cowhide. I believe the biggest circle that we could get from an elk or buffalo hide will be about six feet across. We'll make that our target. That means a length of about eighteen feet for the frame board." After I started him talking, he became lost in his own world, just continuing to talk it out. "If I splice pieces together, the frame might collapse. For a hide that large, the frame will need to be at least six inches deep. Better eight. It would take a year to bend a board that size into a circle and a powerful clamp, as well. I have to think about this."

I KNOW THAT we were difficult to live with—always running off and never being where you needed us—but we did work hard on the horse ranch. We loved the horses and especially the rescues. We were used to grabbing hay bales by the strings and slinging them around. We used ropes. Our bodies were pretty hard. Unlike Mandy's. She was soft and beautiful. Oh, I'm not saying I wasn't good looking. There were enough guys at school telling me that. But Mandy wasn't used to hard manual labor.

At Merv's, we used scrapers and sandpaper. We laced rawhide through the skins. It was wet and rough and we had to pull it tight. We got blisters and blisters turned into calluses. For all three of us, our hands became hard.

"Your hands feel more like Wolf Riding Woman's now," Mandy laughed. "So do mine."

"Do they hurt when I touch you?" I asked.

"No, love. Mine don't hurt you, do they? The sensations are different, but we still love and I love your touch."

By the time school was out and our seventeenth birthdays were rolling around, we had each finished a drum and Merv had performed all the rituals to sanctify them. He had painted the frames with earth paint before the hides were applied and smoked cigarettes, blowing the smoke across the skins in the four directions while he chanted blessings. He was still working on technical problems for creating a frame with a big enough diameter.

And in before-time, we reached the time for our departure from Two Sticks and return to *Oxése*.

Phile: Wolfpack

The day we were to leave Two Sticks, our horses arrived at Bear Butte. When we traveled on White Mouth, we'd left everything behind but our wolf robes, knives, and hatchets. We weren't even certain we were going back to the same place, but we'd sent out a call to our horses and they answered.

They were not the only ones who answered. Two Sticks was startled to find Wolf pacing beside them, the horses seeming not to mind at all. Caitlin fingered her hatchet. Wolf owns us. He is our *Nésemoo'o*, spirit guide. We have to follow where he leads. But we don't have to like it.

Two Sticks honored Wolf and then slipped back inside the mountain. I looked back to where he had disappeared and the mountain had closed behind him. There was no trace.

You must return to Oxése and prepare for battle. You will make drums. But you must also gather your armies. This world will soon become a battlefield. Not only here at the Greasy Grass, but following the sun westward. The greedy ones will break apart the People and crush their spirit. Only in Oxése will you have kept them pure. Ride your horses West and see what is becoming of our land. Then return to Oxése and make ready for war.

Creator Wolf's instructions were clear. But what did we know of war?

The pack is war. You will learn from the pack.

AND SO, AS we rode our horses' backs, we rode the mind of the pack and learned.

There is nothing like the hunger of a pack of wolves. As soon as pangs hit the belly, bloodlust fills the soul. If others dare trespass their land, bloodlust fills their hearts. If one is hurt, bloodlust fills their minds. I once heard Mom Ash refer to them as killing machines. This was why the wolves would lead the battle.

As we traveled, we hunted. Gorging and sleeping only works when you are in a single territory and have a den. Our pack was miles from home and intent on returning. Therefore, we killed, ate, and moved on. The wolves were frustrated at the slower pace of our horses, pulling travois filled with drums and pots of the earth paint and glue Two Sticks had given us. And because we never gorged, we were always hungry and looking for a kill.

THE WOLVES THAT constantly paced us had become nervous. They ranged out farther and circled us. We could feel the bloodlust in them. They wanted to hunt. To kill. It is hard to say if they were feeding us this message or if our unrest fueled their desire. I was ready to take a herd of elk and tear them with my teeth. And then we saw them.

The yellow-haired soldier rode with an Indian guide. We'd learned in school that Custer eschewed the blues and had taken to wearing buckskins. His long blond hair flowed out behind him. It took one snarl and the wolves attacked. We attacked with them, arrows on our bows. As the soldier raised his rifle, our two arrows struck home and he looked into our eyes. Above, a Wolf Bird cawed out the death cry.

I looked and did not see the Indian. The wolves were tearing apart the two horses.

Wolf Riding Woman had killed a soldier scout at Horse Creek. She had completed her transition to wolf warrior by tearing his throat out with her teeth. I had never killed a man. I felt the horror and the sadness as he looked into my eyes and the light fled from them. I turned my pony and galloped westward, ignoring the rattle and pain of the travois and the lust of the wolves. It took two days before Wolf Riding Woman caught up with me, bringing the travois.

Somehow in that mad flight, we crossed into *Oxèse*.

"Caitlin, I'm sick," I cried. "How could I do that? He was just a guy. It wasn't the general. I just killed a guy who was riding along minding his own business. He didn't even point his rifle at us."

"He was the one," Caitlin said. "I saw it in his eyes. He knew us. He knew he'd killed our mother. And just like the elk lays down his life when his time has come, he died willingly. He died because he knew what he'd done and welcomed the reward."

Mandy was less sympathetic. We met her at the Bear Claw on Saturday night and she came to our room with us. She'd just returned from Lame Deer where she'd gone in June to continue her education as a medicine woman. She comforted us, but insisted that she talk with Wolf Rising and Wolf Riding Woman as well. It was like slipping on a second skin these days. Her mind flowed into ours.

"You are a warrior, Wolf Rising. You are a warrior, Phile," she said. "You have drunk the blood of your enemies. It is not the last death. When our time comes, others will die. If we are to save Earth Mother from the scorpion, people will die. Later, we will mourn for them. But when the time comes, we will raise our hands in defense of the Mother."

"He was innocent."

"The deer are innocent. Even the wolves are innocent. Humans are not innocent. Let us take our little drums and join together. I want all my lovers tonight," she said.

Wolf Rising and Wolf Riding Woman joined with us, drumming us together. We opened a passage and enjoyed each other. Even though the drumming stopped, our heartbeats seemed to keep the passage open. I had enjoyed all my lovers and we lay together in exhaustion when Yelloweye appeared before us. He looked at us and I realized all five of us were here in now-time. Until this moment, we had always met in *Oxèse*. He turned his head almost all the way around and spread his wings.

It was confusing to look at this world with two sets of eyes. We needed to practice living in one world with two bodies in more ways than just making love. It was confusing enough to be in two worlds at the same time. Wolf Riding Woman and Wolf Rising went to the owl and he sheltered them in his wings.

You have much work to do before the time has ripened. Earth Sister, you are the bridge. You will pass between and help meld the two into one. Be certain you are prepared when you step into Oxèse.

He folded his wings and our two other selves disappeared an instant before Yelloweye did.

Caitlin: Getting Through

WE ALMOST DIDN'T go back to school. I wanted to quit and run away with Mandy, maybe to Lame Deer, and just get on with it. Mom Mar convinced me otherwise. Mom Ash just laid down the law. I was seventeen and I was going to school.

Part time.

Phile and I got on that work/study program and only had to attend classes in the morning. The rest of the time we worked on the ranch. And the work was good. We pretty much took over care of the rescues. They were our herd as much as Ramie's. They had winter pasture with shelters where they could get out of the worst of the weather. We hauled hay down to the shelters two or three times a week and went down every day to make sure the water tanks stayed open.

There weren't as many antelope mingling with the herd as there had been during the wolf attacks, but they still knew a free meal when they saw one. They brought us word of what was happening farther out on the range. Many times, we took the opportunity to cross from now-time to *Oxèse* to be with our other selves. We tried to time our visits so Mandy wasn't in school and could join us in the mud hut we'd made near White Mouth's cave. It never seemed to work to bring Wolf Rising and Wolf Riding Woman to now-time for long.

"I think the magic in now-time is too weak to sustain for long periods," Mandy said. "We can stay together in now-time as long as we are beating our drums but once we stop the time separates again. When we go to *Oxèse*, the magic is strong and we can sustain ourselves there."

It made as much sense as anything, but I did want to have Wolf Riding Woman in a nice soft bed instead of among the furs sometime. We managed it once by having Wolf Rising and Phile continue to drum softly while Mandy, Wolf Riding Woman, and I made love in our room.

We finally graduated from high school. It seemed a lot had changed this winter. Kyle, Ramie, and Aubrey celebrated their first anniversary. They looked pretty damned happy.

Being out of school meant that we could work full time on the ranch. But it also meant that we had a lot more freedom to move around. That could have got us in a world of trouble if Merv hadn't fixed up a little apartment for his granddaughter behind the trading post. Nobody seemed to notice if we went into town and didn't come back at night. And on those occasions, we continued to work in Merv's shop, learning to shape the saplings into flexible strips using draw knives and sandpaper.

Merv made a four-foot drum. I liked the sound of it. It made my whole body vibrate.

"Plywood," Merv said. "It is how we will make the thunder drum. We will scrape many limbs to this thinness and glue them together as they are bent. This way we can make a large frame that is strong enough to take the tension of the straps. Soon you must make the kill that will provide the hide so it can cure. We need a thick hide."

We were just eighteen and Mandy had picked up her horse for a ride along the ridge. We planned to take a little trip to *Oxèse* and had our saddlebags packed. Before we took off for a couple days, though, we had to show Kyle and Ramie the work we'd done on the fences. Kyle had never shown so much interest in our horses. Bells and Bows had definitely become *ours*. They were a perfect match for our horses in *Oxèse*. We knew they shared the same bond that Cait and I had with Wolf Rising and Wolf Riding Woman. We wandered over to them and Kyle looked at us.

"It was you," Kyle said. Only it wasn't Kyle. I knew for sure someone else was talking through him. "Riding down from the hills with a pack of wolves. I thought I recognized those horses from Kyle's memories."

"I killed you," I said.

"Just as I killed your mother. I am so sorry. I hold you no ill will."

"Kyle will hate us."

"I'll keep this knowledge from him. I can do that. I should thank you. You built the bridge that brought us into this world with Kyle and Ramie."

"Her too?"

"My wife, Miranda, lives in her. One day you'll need to tell all… five of us… the story."

"We have to go, Caitlin," Phile said. He looked at Kyle and whoever it was that was in him. "We bear you no ill will," he said. "Thank you for the life you gave to sustain us and make us stronger. I think I can live now."

"We'll be back in a few weeks," I said.

We swung up on our horses and rode for the mountains.

The Family

"YOU KNEW! YOU knew and didn't tell us!" Miranda shouted at Jason. "Kyle, did you know this?" Kyle shook his head.

"How could you?" Mary Beth asked. "How could you not tell us?"

"That's the question," Jason said using Kyle's voice. "How could I tell you that your children had killed me? How could I ever call your brother and sister murderers? And what right did I have? I killed their mother. There was no more just payment."

"You're still carrying the guilt around for that," Ramie sighed. "You were a kid. You didn't know you'd been tricked into killing unarmed people."

"I was older than Wolf Riding Woman and Wolf Rising were when they killed me. They were no more to blame than I was. And you both still carry around the guilt for killing rapists and kidnappers. If we didn't have that guilt, that burden on our souls, we would be something less than human," Jason said.

"How'd you keep it from me?" Kyle asked. "I thought we shared everything."

"I don't know. I just locked it up tight and didn't think about it."

"It's good to know that we can keep secrets from each other. Not that I want to, but that the possibility is there."

"Well, now the box is open. Now you know. They thought I was Custer," Jason said. "But they couldn't have changed it anyway."

"How do you figure that?" Ashley asked.

"You all made a big deal out of the fact that when Kyle and I rode into that village for the massacre, those kids had already lived through it. Years before," Jason said. "According to the way I understand things, it was something that couldn't be altered. It had already happened for them when I fired the first shot. Well, if that's true, then the same is true of them. Miranda and I had been dead for over a year and living with Ramie and Kyle for eight months before those kids rode back from the Bear Butte. They couldn't stop it. It was already an open box."

"You got to admit, that's the one thing that's been consistent for all of us," Ramie said. "Once the box is open, you can't change it. I'd say having a living person who held the experience was the same as having the written record."

"This makes even *my* head hurt," Cole said.

"We'd better get some sleep," Aubrey said. "Don't know about you, but from what I heard, we need Earth Sister's day of prayer tomorrow to consider the land."

10
Day of Prayer

The Family

"**D**ELTA OH Niner, this is base," Cole said into the radio.

"This is Delta Oh Niner, base. Come in."

"What's the status?"

"No way to keep them from knowing we're here and still keep them away from scattering the cattle. It seems that was their intent all along."

"What's the plan?" Cole asked.

"We had a parlay," the voice on the radio said. "We explained the terms simply. They could run around their base with the ATVs all they wanted and we wouldn't say a thing if they ran west. But we would stop them from approaching where the wranglers were rounding up the cattle they'd scattered."

"How'd they take that?"

"About how you'd expect. A lot of shouting and waving their guns around. It's all quiet now. We simply showed them that we had bigger guns. And more of them."

"I don't want any firefights," Cole said. "I just want my cattle rounded up."

"They're sure to call in reinforcements," the voice said, "but not right away. At the moment, they're busy discovering their cell phones don't work up here. By the time they send someone out on the west side of the mountain because the FS Road has been washed out, it will probably be nightfall before they can call for reinforcements. We figure they'll have to go all the way to Rawlins to make a phone call."

"The Forest Service Road was washed out? We haven't had any rain," Cole said.

"Local storm," the voice chuckled. "I figure it was about fifty feet wide."

"You guys know your business. I've asked too much already. Take care and be safe."

"Roger that. Delta Oh Niner out."

"RAMIE, COULD WE ask about our ride?" a young woman leading a chestnut mare said.

"Sure, Dawn. Everything is open except the trails up to the ridge. With the cattle getting ready to move down and the oil company acting aggressive, we don't want anybody risking that ride," Ramie said.

"That's just it," Dawn said. She'd been boarding her horse here for three years and a dozen of the regular riders were tacked up by ten on this Sunday morning. Another dozen had trailered in and all twenty-four or twenty-five horses and riders were gathered together. "We'd like to go someplace to… um… meditate with our horses. Sort of… consider the land," she said sheepishly. Ramie couldn't help herself. She hugged the young rider.

"Yes," she said. "The land needs you."

"Where would you recommend?"

"Take the south trail around the pond. Then bear east a little and you'll hit the river. There's a nice trail there and about two miles along the river, you'll come to an open meadow. Not many people go down that direction because it's not a mountain ride, if you know what I mean. It just meanders along the river. We've noticed a lot of pronghorn gathering in that meadow this summer. I think it would be a great place to sit and consider the land."

"Thank you, Ramie. I knew you'd understand. We… we're all concerned about what's happening to the environment. At least this is something we can do."

"Tell everyone to take curry combs, brushes, and blankets to rub their horses down with," Ramie said. "There's nothing that helps meditation like brushing your horse." The girl grinned and went back to her friends. After scrambling to get their tack together, the long line of horses filed out of the yard and hit the trail.

"Let's pause to consider the land," Cole said as the family sat at the table for dinner.

It was a ritual that had been passed down for generations in the Bell family. Before each meal, whether spoken or understood, the family paused to consider the land. For generations, this land had supported the Bell and Alexander families. They weren't religious, but they felt a deep connection. Markers on the hillside, expanded by Cole, Ramie, and Kyle to include people who had never found their way into the family Bible, lay on the hillside above the woodlot. Generations that went back to Laramie Wyoming Bell and Kyle Redtail Wardlaw, Miranda Lewis and Jason Wardlaw, Theresa Ranae Bell and White Horse. Six generations laid to rest. All tied to the land.

On this particular Sunday, people of many faiths and no faith at all paused with them to consider the land. The land that fed them, clothed them, provided the energy for their lives, and the pleasure for their eyes. Whether they were on the side of corporate exploitation of resources or conservation of the land, people paused to consider the land.

Fifth Live Report

"There is a different tone to the drums from Yellowstone Grizzly Village today," said Evan Waitley, the NNN network newscaster. "It is soft. Humming. Even from here, a mile from the Grizzly Lake, we can hear the chants as they rise and fall. But it is not this that has made this moment one of awe. It is what lies in the valley around the village." The camera swept away from the reporter and focused on a valley full of animals.

"'The wolf also shall dwell with the lamb, and the leopard shall lie down with the kid; and the calf and the young lion and the fatling together; and a little child shall lead them. And the cow and the bear shall feed; their young ones shall lie down together: and the lion shall eat straw like the ox. And the sucking child shall play on the hole of the asp, and the weaned child shall put his hand on the cockatrice' den. They shall not hurt nor destroy in all my holy mountain: for the earth shall be full of the knowledge of the LORD, as the waters cover the sea.' Those words from the prophet Isaiah have never been more fully realized. As you can see, the animals in this basin—thousands of them—lie at peace with each other and at odds with man. All men except the two we have come to know as the White Wolf Twins wandering among them. We can see buffalo, elk, wolves, mountain goats, rabbits, and mountain lions all lying together, staring at the site of the Shale Oil Company well." The camera picked up Earth Sister coming from the village, approaching the reporter.

"A Park Ranger was led by this couple to walk among the beasts a short time ago. The man and woman are different from those around them, both being fair-skinned and light-haired. Yet they wear only loin cloths and a robe made of wolfskin. When he returned, the Ranger said only, 'It is all real. They are really here.' Now Earth Sister approaches."

Mandy had been clipped with a microphone as the camera watched, but no one noticed the technical maneuvering. Tears ran down Mandy's cheeks.

"You called this a day of prayer to consider the land, Earth Sister. Is this what you had in mind?" Evan asked.

"I've lived in their heads for five years and never imagined they would do this," she said. "In all that time, they have prepared for a war they did not want. Look at them. Prey and predator, all knowing their place in the cycle and accepting it. Except man. Except the corporations that hold man captive. This is what *Néške'emāne* wants for her children. My beloved Wolf Twins do not want this war, but they will not relent if the injury to Grandmother Earth continues."

"The Wolf Twins are the two we see wandering among the animals and who led the inspection of the animals with the Park Ranger?" Evan asked.

"They are one aspect. The Twins span time, race, and species, I think. But this is sure. Tomorrow, Shale Oil Company has declared it will begin the pseudo-fracking operation that will force Earth Mother to give up her life blood for their greed. If they proceed, all those animals you see lying peacefully in the valley, and millions more than you can imagine, will rise to fight for their mother. Today, we mourn, for tomorrow, when the thunder echoes from the mountains, those who remain there—or at any other site where the corporation would harm Earth Mother—will die."

The Family

"Radio Rafe," Ashley said. "They need to start the cattle down from the ridge now." Cole ran to the office and made the call to his surprised foreman.

"We won't know for sure if we have them all," Rafe said over the radio. "We could lose ten percent or more."

"We've got two hours of daylight left. We'll lose them all if you wait until tomorrow," Cole shot back. "Don't stampede them, but get them moving. Everyone gets a twenty percent bonus if we have four hundred head when you arrive here tomorrow."

"We'll move them, boss," Rafe said. "I don't think we can break and move the camp, though."

"Leave it. Abandon everything and put every person on the drive."

Cole switched bands on the radio.

"Delta Oh Niner, this is base."

"Come in base."

"We're moving the cattle. Fall back as they move and get away from the ridge. Maintain a defensive position behind the herd. Do not leave anyone on the ridge."

"Understood, base. Delta Oh Niner out."

"If these wild ones get to be too much, I'll take them to the kitchen," Aubrey said as the family settled in to read. "It will be bedtime before long."

"There's six adults," Mary Beth laughed. "Eight if we count you two," she pointed at Kyle and Ramie hosting Jason and Miranda in their heads. "We ought to be able to ride herd on two little ones." She flopped down on the floor with a bit of a groan and Theresa toddled over to her grandma. "When did the floor get so low?" she asked. "Never used to be that far down."

"I think I'd better read today," Ramie said. "It's the only way I'll be able to sit still. I want to ride up to the ridge just to see what happens."

Ramie lifted the pages from the box.

Phile: Leaving Mandy

The battle at Greasy Grass didn't all happen at once. It was four years from the time that we visited until Custer led his army into Crazy Horse's trap. In the same way, we weren't ready to march off to war, either. We didn't even know yet who we were doing battle with.

Once Caitlin and I left Kyle's spirit walker, we just turned and headed toward the mountains. We'd planned to take more with us, but the revelation of what we'd done hit us hard. I didn't know who he was beyond his name, Jason, but we'd both done our deeds and he seemed to be at peace with Kyle. It was news, though, that Kyle and Ramie were spirit walkers and they had been inhabited by people from the past. There were more bridges being built than just our simple drumming.

Caitlin and I just needed to get to Mandy. We met at the thermal spring up on the ridge. We'd been coming here, it seemed, for centuries. It gave us a focus on the land. We could feel it in our bones.

We waved at the hands watching over the cattle in the summer pasture, but we didn't stop to talk. We rode on up over the ridge and Mandy was waiting for us. Cait and I jumped from our horses and wrapped that girl in our arms. We linked and projected every soft touch and kiss to Wolf Rising and Wolf Riding Woman. Caitlin got herself naked before she helped me pull Mandy's dress over her head. I was still working on getting Mandy's brassiere unfastened when Caitlin hauled my pants down my legs and sucked my cock into her mouth. I felt Wolf Rising gasp and knew Wolf Riding Woman was giving him the same treatment. I kissed Mandy and caressed those beautiful breasts that we all loved so much. I guess we were all desperate because in fifteen minutes we'd come in every combination we could and rode in the heads of our partners while they came. I don't think I'll ever tire of experiencing a woman come. It's so different than the way I spurt. Well, maybe it's partly because it always makes me spurt at the same time.

We ate cold rations from Mandy's saddlebag. We didn't want to start a fire that night because we didn't know how long we'd be there. If everything worked like we expected, we'd all be gone by morning. We stayed naked, but stowed all our clothing in bundles on our horses. We cleaned the site and made sure our waste was buried deep.

We'd taken to carrying prayer drums attached to our rifle scabbards wherever we went. They were flat and about ten inches across. They looked like decorations, but we took them off and began a steady rhythm. Mandy had a slightly bigger one that she tapped at. Wolf Rising and Wolf Riding Woman had a bigger drum and we could feel it setting the rhythm over the centuries as we fell into a dance and made the thunder that would let us open the gate.

We were going visiting.

IT WAS AN hour before sunrise before we opened the gate. Three people and three horses with all our gear intact stepped into the clearing in front of Wolf Rising and Wolf Riding Woman. The drumming ceased and we collapsed into each other's arms.

Our two other selves, of course, wanted some hands-on time with Mandy. I could feel and remember everything those two had done, but it was still different to be physically in touch. While Wolf Rising, Caitlin, and Mandy got in every position imaginable, Wolf Riding Woman took me in her arms as well. I looked into her eyes.

"It is strange, isn't it?" she said. "I look into your eyes and I see the same spirit as Wolf Rising's looking back at me. Yet the body excites me because this body does not know it well like it knows Wolf Rising. Do I excite you as much in this body as I do in my now-time body?" she asked.

"Caitlin/Wolf Riding Woman, I know you are one person, but you excite me in different ways. I know that as I enter you, it will be as if I have never been there before and it excites me beyond measure. If ever there was meaning to the term soulmate, this is it. No matter what body we occupy, our souls have been mated from birth. Twice," I said.

Our loving lasted most of the day. It was curious as we switched partners and loved in all the combinations. And I mean all of them. I watched Caitlin as she crawled on hands and knees between Wolf Riding Woman's legs to eat her. I found myself stroking Wolf Rising's rising erection as he stroked mine. I guided his cock into Cait's waiting pussy, caressing his balls. It felt good. It was my cock. As he bent over Caitlin's back, pumping into her, he sucked my cock into his mouth. It didn't feel weird. Like most guys, I'd wondered what it would be like to suck my own cock. Some guys I'd heard in the locker room had said if they could suck their own cocks, they'd never bother dating.

Mandy kissed me as she petted Wolf Rising's hair.

"It's a new dimension of masturbations, isn't it?" she asked. When we'd kissed each other thoroughly, she turned and sat on Wolf Riding

Woman's face. When I came in Wolf Rising's mouth, I tasted myself and decided that it was good, but I'd rather have any of the women. Nonetheless, I would never shy from giving myself such a satisfying come.

WE COULDN'T SPEND all our time making love, though most of the day was spent in some stage of undress. We had work to do and five pairs of hands would be better than two pairs. Even living in two times and knowing what life was like in primitive times, our bodies were not accustomed to the level of hardship. We had to hunt. We had to gather. We would need a good shelter before snow flies.

And we needed drums.

Wolf Riding Woman had prepared two skins that we planned to stretch on frames Wolf Rising had prepared. We laced rawhide strips through carefully cut holes in the skins. These were threaded through a rawhide disk in the back. The skins were stretched wet. That way they would tighten after we had laced them tight. Wolf Rising tested the head by tapping it lightly when it had been stretched. We tightened the braided rawhide by twisting a stick in the disk to tune the drum. Then we set it aside to dry. We would not be able to use it for at least a week as it dried. To beat a drum too soon would stretch the skin and it would lose its timbre.

As Merv had indicated, we would need more rawhide. We needed a big drum that Merv would make, but we needed drums for the whole *Oxêse* village. Fortunately, with five of us to feed and winter supplies to put in, we had no difficulty using all the meat we killed. We had bows and spears, but Cait's and my Remington 700s had come through the portal with no trouble. We didn't use them until the day we saw a moose. Wolf Riding Woman backed us away.

"There are certain animals that we cannot take. Moose hide is very tough. Piercing it with a spear would only make him mad, and a rampaging moose would most certainly kill at least one of us." I nodded, pulled my Remington from its scabbard and drew a bead. In the best of all worlds, I'd prefer something a little more powerful, but I was confident that I could bring him down. The bolt on the rifle drew the big bull's attention and he looked straight at me.

"So, you have come across time for my hide!" he screamed in my mind. I was so startled by his contact with me that I lowered the gun. He pawed at the ground. "Let us see who dies!" he challenged, and began his charge. I was not more than fifty feet away and barely got the gun to my shoulder. He was lowering his head and the round went into his skull. He didn't stop and I sent the second round into his chest. He stumbled forward, still trying to reach me as I jumped back and he fell. His heavy antlers hit my leg and pain lanced up into me.

"You are mighty, *Popóhpoévésémo'éhe*. It has taken the weapon of the future to bring you down," I said. "I praise your might and your bravery. I thank you for the life that will feed my family and will help us to sound the call to defend Mother Earth." He looked at me with the light fading from his eyes. I felt much as I had when Wolf Rising shot the yellow-haired soldier. There was acceptance and sadness.

"You will eat my heart and my liver," he said in my mind. "And when we defend the Mother, you will ride my spirit into battle. Be strong in battle." And with that he died. It took all four of my companions to shift his head so I could pull my leg from under him. Mandy examined it and I screamed in pain. If my leg was broken, I knew that we would have to drum ourselves back to now-time so I could get a cast on it. If it healed in *Oxése*, I would bear the limp for the rest of my life.

"You're an idiot," Mandy declared, scowling at me. "You didn't even know if your stupid gun would work in this time!" In fact, it had never occurred to me. All I had seen was the opportunity to have a very large, thick hide for our drums. "I don't think your leg is broken. But you are going to have trouble walking for a while."

That was the short of it. When we opened the guts, and I found the liver and heart, my companions refused to share them. Eating the warm organs was a task. The heart alone was almost as big as my head. The first shot had hit the pedicle, the point from which the antler grows. It had stunned the big bull, but did not penetrate the skull. It was the second shot that hit the heart and as I ate the huge organ, I found where the bullet had hit and expanded. I pocketed the slug.

Despite their reluctance to share in the organs, my companions immediately fell to work dressing and gutting the kill. The moose weighed close to three-quarters of a ton and it took all day to cart the carcass back to camp. The hide alone weighed more than I did. Even with travois, it was difficult to transport. I was not much help as I could barely walk.

I had fevered dreams that night. I had gorged on the heart and liver, but I did as the moose had commanded and during the night I felt his spirit enter into me. I was not big enough to contain the spirit of the moose and thought I would explode. I had visions of riding into battle with my head lowered as I charged my enemies.

IT TOOK SEVERAL days to cure the meat and stretch the hide. But it was during this time that we discovered that just having the hide stretched on a drying frame made for a resounding thud when it was struck. We were going to need a huge drum frame to use this hide.

We worked for nearly six weeks, preparing the camp for winter and the hides for drumheads. We made use of every part of the animals, including mixing dried and roasted meat into pemmican and stuffing it into cleaned intestines.

"I'm staying with Wolf Rising and Wolf Riding Woman," Mandy said as we made love the night before we would return to now-time. Even with our link, I was surprised. Caitlin rolled to us to embrace our lover from the other side. Our other selves held us together. I could not fault her for her decision and the joy I felt from Wolf Rising fought with the sorrow I felt in my now-time heart. "You must return and prepare for our coming task," she said. "But there is much I need to learn here before you take me to Lame Deer. Come for me at midwinter. Love me with your other time selves."

Caitlin, too, was conflicted as our halves seemed torn apart. We held each other through the night. In the daylight, Mandy, Wolf Rising, and Wolf Riding Woman pounded on the drums, calling thunder echoing from the mountain as we joined their rhythm on our prayer drums and rode into now-time.

Caitlin: Moving the herds

PA AND MOMS never questioned our decision not to go to college. I think they were happy we made it through high school. We're not dumb. We just had so much other stuff to do.

154

We got hit with a bunch of questions about where we'd been for six weeks, but when we said we had to get our heads on now that school was done, we just got the usual big sigh. Mom Mar inspected our clothes and couldn't believe we'd been gone for six weeks and they didn't look worn at all. I guess they hadn't been worn much. We all wore loin cloths and moccasins when we were together in *Oxèse*. Of course, Mandy had been prepared with clothes for a few weeks, but she didn't have stuff for winter. We'd spent part of our time making sure all three of them had warm skins to dress in with deep furry boots to keep their feet warm. Those bighorn sheep piled on a lot of wool as they headed toward winter. Their hide was too soft to make a decent drum out of, but it felt good against our skin. Phile and Wolf Rising talked a whole bunch of them into standing still while the others of us used our knives to shear them. The hut was packed full of wool and it kept them warm when snow flew as well as giving them something to do as they carded it and turned it into yarn.

WE STILL DIDN'T know what our lives were supposed to be like, but Mandy insisted that we start writing things down so there would be a record. We bought an old silverware chest with a lock and key at a flea market and as we wrote stuff down, we put it in the box.

Ramie turned twenty-two and was happy as all get-out with that new stud she got. The five of us linked together and agreed that we should give the box to Ramie. Ramie's got a lot of patience. We were afraid that if we gave the box to Pa, he'd open it and read it all right away. Ramie agreed to just keep the key and we kept the box. I think Phile scared her when he told her she couldn't open the box until she was ready to accept that there could be a dead cat in it. See, Pa? We did listen to some of your stories. We just kept writing pages and putting them in the box as things developed.

WE WENT TO talk to Merv Longsteer early in December to tell him the moose hide was eight feet across. It would have to be a really big drum and we didn't know how to make a frame that big. We'd been down several times to let him know how Mandy was doing and tell him that she loved him. He listened to everything. And then he told us that it sounded to him like Yelloweye expected us to move a lot more than just a couple horses and ourselves through time. We needed to start practicing moving bigger groups. Finally, he said he wanted to go with us.

I tickled at his mind a little and he opened up so I could pop right in. I figured that the whole riding with someone else was part of being able to travel. Once we established that we could make a link with him, we agreed.

It was getting on toward Christmas and Mandy said she was ready for us, so we told everybody we were going to do some winter camping. It wasn't that unusual. We'd all done winter camping for years. We promised we'd be home for Christmas. We set off up the mountain with our horses and two pack mules. We had a bunch more supplies, too, including a few sweets to give to our other selves and the one thing we'd always thought was missing while we were visiting: salt. The last time we'd crossed to *Oxèse*, we'd been naked and led our horses with only the supplies that Mandy had thought to pack.

Merv was waiting for us at the ridge with a string of pack animals and a couple spare horses. It took us all working together to link up with Merv, the horses, and the mules. Then the Twin Wolves started beating on drums. They had a bigger sound than I remembered from before. We started riding and went straight from our little hot spring on the ridge into the clearing where their camp was. Moving all our gear and stock and Merv wasn't a problem once we managed to make the link.

I found the difference in the drums was that they'd moved them to the entrance of White Mouth's cave. The big bear hadn't shown up this fall, but we didn't move into his cave. You just don't want to be in a bear's home when he shows up. I learned that from Goldilocks.

Mandy was thrilled to see Merv and the old man held his grand-daughter for a long time whispering to her. We took care of the live-stock and unpacked all we'd brought across with us. The big thing, of course, was steel hardware. Axes, saws, drawknives, and hammers would make our jobs easier. And Merv had a plan for building the huge thun-der drum. The moose hide was still stretched on its frame and Merv was pleased with the size. We'd all had our work cut out for us when we stripped all the meat, fat, and fur from the skin and stretched it to dry.

The big difference between this and the sheepskin coats we all wore was that the moose hide was raw and not leather. It was stiff and even on the drying frame it made a satisfying boom when we thumped it.

After Merv got used to seeing us in two places at once, he took over the task of building the drum frame. He sent Phile and me to go find a herd and move them someplace. He was vague about that, but we got the idea. It was almost as if Merv had become the voice of Yelloweye.

Whatever Yelloweye had in mind for us to do, it was going to involve moving a lot of animals from one time and place to another. I thought about the number of animals in now-time that were rare or near extinction and wondered if our task would be moving those that remained into a time and place where they could multiply and thrive. It was sad that they'd disappear from the earth, though.

PHILE AND I headed down off the mountain and started casting about for any herds we could find that were wintering nearby. There was a lot of thermal activity a valley over and it kept the air warmer than up where our camp was. Once we got down there, we saw elk, whitetail, and buffalo browsing on the grass that still pressed through a light covering of snow. Phile and I made camp and settled in to watch them for a while. We'd ridden herds as Wolf Rising and Wolf Riding Woman, but even then, we hadn't actually moved them from place to place.

We probed around and found it was easy to enter individual minds that were intent on grazing. Spreading into a small herd was almost as easy. We could give them a nudge and they'd move to some new ground. We managed to get a couple dozen elk to just lie down for a nap, but we got them up and ready to meet trouble when we saw a pack of coyotes headed their way. Coyotes don't usually hunt big animals like wolves do, but they are opportunists. They slunk off when the elk stirred and stood up.

"Where are we going to move them to?" Phile asked.

"Or when?" I answered. "Let's try just moving them to the other valley and back."

And so we began. We took a surprised herd of whitetail deer to the valley with Wolf Rising beating a drum to match our own. Then we flashed the herd back to the thermal valley where it was warmer and had more forage. We split and picked up a herd of pronghorns and a couple dozen buffalo on the next trip.

Things worked well and before long we were moving several dozen elk back and forth. We discovered that if we weren't moving between *Oxése* and now-time, we only needed one set of drums. Wolf Rising and Wolf Riding Woman could stay focused on helping Merv Longsteer.

An old bull looked up at us where we watched the valley and bellowed in disgust. But we were still missing something. I could enter the minds of a herd of one species, and Phile could move a herd of another species, but from what Yelloweye had told us, we weren't going to have the luxury of moving a herd at a time. We would need to move all of them at once. Moving an entire herd of buffalo hadn't been too difficult. But the buffalo were all of like mind. Moving a herd of buffalo with a pack of wolves was a little more daunting. We ended up transporting the buffalo back to the valley and leaving the wolves with a couple cows so they could feast.

But it got better. Before long we were moving a hundred animals of various species at a time. We'd discovered that linking our minds together gave us many times more power than what we'd had before. We linked with Mandy, Wolf Riding Woman, and Wolf Rising and the power multiplied. Finally, we moved all the animals in the winter pasture to the summer pasture and back. We were exhausted, but we were ready to head home.

"I WILL STAY," Merv said. "I like this drum making. But it will take me until spring to get a good start at a drum this size."

"I worry about you," I said.

"Do you not trust yourself to take care of me?" Merv laughed, looking at Wolf Riding Woman. I couldn't argue with that. "And I will have my granddaughter here. At least part of the time."

"Part of the time?" Phile asked.

"I need to start making trips between here and the village at Lame Deer," Mandy said. "There are rituals that need to be performed and they need to start seeing me show up unexpectedly from nowhere. Like on Christmas Eve. We can do this, even when we are all in different places.

Can't you feel how strong our link is becoming? It kept getting stronger as you moved the herds. I can feel it inside me all the time now."

"I love you, Mandy. I want you cradled in my arms again tonight," Phile said.

"Well, no one is going to complain about that," she giggled as she kissed him. I turned my head and was met by Wolf Rising's lips.

"I think I have an appointment here," I said.

"Here, there, everywhere," Wolf Riding Woman said. "Sorry, Grandfather Longsteer, but things are likely to get noisy tonight."

Phile: Moving in Time

OUR WORK WASN'T over for the winter, or the next summer for that matter. It took all of us drumming to move Mandy and us back to now-time. It only took Caitlin and me to move Mandy and her horse to Lame Deer. We didn't stick around, though. There were a lot of surprised Elders when we showed up at the mid-winter powwow and appeared out of the mist. Mandy stepped forward with her horse and mule and Cait and I stepped back and disappeared.

We saw the reaction through Mandy's eyes, though, and in five minutes, she was on her way to becoming a spokesperson to the People of now-time.

We were exhausted when we got back to the ranch and slept through most of Christmas.

IT CAME IN a dream.

That was unusual. Yelloweye and Creator Wolf usually spoke to us directly, but for the first time, we saw a vision of what we would have to do. I can only tell it like the dream it was.

I stood in a village. Wolf Rising had visited this village often, but this time I was pale and felt uncomfortable in the wolf skin robe. It was many years after Yelloweye had led them to Oxèse, though time meant nothing to us in this strange place. They called Caitlin and I the 'day wolves' and Wolf Rising and Wolf Riding Woman the 'night wolves'. Now many sacred drummers held a steady beat as Caitlin and I danced around the circle and summoned the animals. As we danced, the village was surrounded by buffalo. The buffalo waited.

Then we danced the elk around our village. The elk joined the buffalo and waited. Then we danced the wolves and the great Creator Wolf answered our call, howling at the moon. And as we danced and all the four-leggeds of the earth waited, the winged ones appeared and Yelloweye landed before us in the village.

'You have summoned your warriors. Now you must lead them into battle. Open the gate from Oxèse and take them to the war.'

And as I watched, and danced, the drums of the village were joined by the drums of the mountain thunder and a pathway opened and war was upon us.

PA HAD NO idea how many times over the next two years, his herd of cattle ate of the fresh grass of *Oxèse*. Nor did our sister Ramie know how often the rescued horses found fresh untamed fields to play in. We had to move the herds as easily between the two realities as we had moved Mandy over distances.

The Family

"OUR LITTLE BROTHER and sister…" Ramie sighed as she closed the lid of the box. "Is it all just a fantasy? Moving herds from one valley to another in a place and time that we can't possibly know is somehow more believable than that they moved 500 head of cattle out of our fields here into some fantasy world and back without us knowing. And a hundred head of horses. How are we supposed to accept this?"

"I don't think we'll be given a choice," Kyle said, holding his sister/wife. "We saw it on television. We saw a million animals of every species appear in that valley and all lie down together. How can we not believe them?"

"Why does it have to be so hard?" Ashley said. "If they said they'd raised a militia and were going to conduct guerilla warfare against Shale Oil, I wouldn't have had a problem. Hell, I'd have joined them. But I don't understand how they are going to win this war with animals. I just don't understand."

"That must be the same thing that the executives are thinking," Cole said. "For thousands of years, men have been developing machinery, fences, weapons—just to keep the animals out. What do they have to be afraid of?"

"They need to be afraid," Mary Beth said, "of our children."

11
It Takes a Village

The Family

A RANCHER FROM Fort Collins arrived with two brood mares for breeding about seven in the morning. Ramie and Kyle had to deal with that just when the family had decided to let others do the work for the day and get back to the final pages in the box. They wouldn't stand the mares to stud until they'd had a chance to settle down, but the rancher wanted to jaw a while over a cup of coffee. Of course, the topic was all about the tensions building at Yellowstone.

He finally left and their two hired hands took over the morning chores while Ramie and Kyle came into the kitchen.

"How much time do we have?" Mary Beth asked.

"Rafe radioed in that they were about three hours out," Cole said.

"I didn't put food on the stove for the hands."

"I've got it, Mom Mar," Aubrey said. "I prepped everything early this morning. It just needs to heat through. I'll make cornbread and tortillas while you continue to read. I can hear you and keep an eye on the television at the same time. Fill yourselves plates if you're hungry. There's still tortillas and makings for a breakfast burrito."

"Anything happening?" Ramie asked her lover.

"She hasn't moved in two hours, but no one is willing to go approach her. They've gone on with regular insipid programming, but have her in a split screen box in the corner with a ribbon crawling across the bottom every five minutes giving the same update." Aubrey scooped a spoonful of mashed carrots into her oldest daughter's mouth. "Don't worry, honey. Even though I'm in the kitchen, I'm right there beside you." Aubrey kissed Ramie and Kyle sidled up to get his share, too. He kissed his daughters on their heads.

"Let's get back at it," Cole said around a mouthful of burrito.

"Wait," Aubrey said. "There's a bulletin and they are expanding the Yellowstone window."

"Turn it up," Cole said. Aubrey unmuted the TV as the picture zoomed back from Earth Sister standing in the distance as a reporter came into focus in the foreground.

Sixth Live Report

"Tʜɪs ɪs Eᴠᴀɴ Waitley with the National News Network at the Yellowstone Grizzly Village protest site. This has been a tense morning as workers at the Shale Oil Company, prepare to activate the pseudo-fracking equipment on the low rise to our left at the foot of Mount Holmes. We're told that high absenteeism has slowed progress which was slated to begin earlier today. The company is operating with a skeleton crew and a squad of security personnel who are reported to be heavily armed." The reporter turned to the silhouette on the rise, nearly a mile distant.

"On each of the past five days, the spokesperson calling herself Earth Sister has approached our broadcast location to deliver her dire warnings. She has provided what many believe to be illusions of animals coming over the rise. On the third day, a trained wolf pushed reporter Sarah d'Angelo to the ground during her broadcast. We are told that Sarah is still suffering from shock, but that she is physically uninjured. Yet this morning, Earth Sister did not come to our location some distance away from both the installation and the protest site. As the sun rose, she was already at the top of that rise. She has simply stood there all morning. For a while, she was joined by two others dressed in wolf skins before they disappeared over the rise."

"Evan," another voice broke into the broadcast, "what about animals this morning? No illusions yet?"

"Nothing. In fact, there is no sign of any animal anywhere in the park." The camera swung far to the right and into the sky as Evan pointed. "Up there, you can see a Park Ranger helicopter. It is the only sound that has been heard this morning. When we asked about why they were deployed today, the comment we got was startling. They are looking for animals. The Forest Service has been unable to locate any of the five thousand bison that live in the park. Nor have they spotted any of the thousands of elk, the hundred wolves, and the wide variety of other species that call Yellowstone home. In fact, we have not seen a bird in the sky, a squirrel in a tree, or even a fly all morning."

"Evan, we are informed there is activity in Cody. Keep an eye on things there at Yellowstone for us, we are switching to a live report from Rhea Matthews in Cody, Wyoming." The image of Earth Sister on the rise receded to a box in the upper right corner of the screen as the main screen shifted to a woman in jeans and a western shirt. Blonde hair fluttered beneath the brim of a cowboy hat.

"This is Rhea Matthews of KWYO in Cody, reporting for NNN. There are startling developments this morning in Cody as National Guard and U.S. Deputy Marshals arrived on the scene overnight with buses and some heavy equipment. They are staging at Stampede Park, home of the Cody Night Rodeo. I'm here with Deputy U.S. Marshal Grant Donahue who has agreed to give us some background information. Marshal, can you tell us what's going on? There's some heavy machinery moving in here. Are you anticipating an assault?"

"Nothing so dramatic as that, Rhea," the deputy said. He smiled the smile of a front person designated to be in front of cameras while the real work went on elsewhere. "We are here to protect U.S. citizens who have come into conflict with each other. On one side, we have a legal drilling site. We've cross-checked all the permits and environmental statements and legally, Shale Oil Company has the high ground. However, peaceful protest is also allowed under the first amendment to the Constitution. The only law that has been broken is fuzzy at best in terms of the protesters occupying government lands. They have broken several park rules with their unauthorized encampment."

"So, both sides have rights?" Rhea asked.

"Certainly," Grant answered. "Unfortunately, the rhetoric of the past few days has increased to the point of threats against the lives and property of Shale Oil Company and its workers. In response, the company has ramped up its security. We are trying to avoid another Standing Rock situation. The loss of life there was a tragedy. We see no other option at this point than to remove the protesters from the site, in as respectful a way as we can, so that violence does not erupt. I have been informed that once the fracking process has actually begun, the protesters have agreed to leave peacefully."

"Mourning Mother Earth and the lives of those that were lost," Rhea read from a statement. "What does that mean, exactly?"

"The protest is highly spiritual in nature," Grant said. "When they have lost the battle to stop SOC, the Native Americans at the site will undoubtedly have a period of ritual mourning."

"So, there you have it. U.S. Marshals supported by National Guard personnel are preparing to move into Yellowstone and evacuate the protest camp so that violence is avoided," Rhea said. "According to the briefing paper we were given, the encampment will be removed and the land restored to its pre-camp condition. Once that has been accomplished, the gates of Yellowstone National Park will reopen to visitors who have already lost nearly half the season's opportunity to enjoy our treasured national resource. This is Rhea Matthews, KWYO in Cody."

"And we will continue to keep you updated as the situation develops," the network announcer said. "Until there is more, we return you to today's broadcast schedule, already in progress."

THE FAMILY BREATHED a big sigh. Cole radioed Rafe.

"Rafe, we may not be in the pens when you get here. You know what to do. We'll be moving them out of the holding pens and over to the old Calhoun place in a few days. I might have to hire a couple more wranglers to make the move," Cole said.

"We wouldn't have to worry about it if those two kids of yours were here. They'd just point and the cattle would go where they said," Rafe laughed. "Sorry, Cole. I didn't mean to make light of the situation, but I damn sure liked those kids."

"Well, we might get them back somehow. That's why the family won't be out to meet you. Once you've got them all corralled, though, get your guys cleaned up a little and come up for lunch. Aubrey and Mary Beth have a kettle of chili on the stove."

"They'll like hearing that. We'll see you in a couple of hours."

"Mommy, I can't do it," Ramie said. She sat with the last few pages in front of her and tears ran from her eyes. She hadn't called Mom Mar 'Mommy' in many years, but she needed the comfort. Mary Beth moved to comfort her daughter, but Ramie inexplicably held up her hand.

"Let me drive," Miranda said from inside her. "Dry your eyes and sit back. I can't help but love your brother and sister the same as you, but I lived in harsher times. I can handle it." Ramie's head nodded.

"Thank you, Miranda," Mary Beth said. She hugged her daughter anyway.

"I didn't mean to hold you off like that," Miranda said. "Please come and cuddle us while we read." Mary Beth sat beside her daughter on the sofa and Ashley took a spot on the opposite side next to Kyle. Cole watched from the big chair and sighed, but Aubrey came into the room and handed him both his granddaughters.

"Y'all need something for comfort," she said as she kissed her father-in-law on top of his head. She retreated to the kitchen and listened as Miranda began.

Caitlin: Time in a Box

Merv was ready to head back to Laramie after about two months in *Oxêse*. He'd accomplished a lot, but it was cold living on the mountain. It was cold in Laramie, too, but apparently, he thought his house would be more comfortable than the mud, stick, and hide wigwam in front of the bear cave. As far as we could tell, there had been no sign of White Mouth returning for the winter. Even when we beat drums in the mouth of the cave, there was no answering rumble within its depths.

"I should probably go have Christmas with Mandy's parents. They always seem to want me around," Merv said. "Time masters, drum me home." We all stared at him.

"Uh, Merv, we can't take you back to Christmas," Phile said.

"Grandfather, I drove from Lame Deer to Laramie on Christmas Day. You weren't there," Mandy said. "I told Mom you'd met up with some men who were going on a spirit quest and would probably be gone for a while."

"I thought…" Merv pondered as he considered what we were saying. "So when is it in now-time?"

"We came through on February 29. Leap day," I said. "We figured we would take you back tomorrow."

"This is very strange. I hope my cousin hasn't sold the trading post," Merv said. "Come and look at what we've managed so far while I think about the problems of travel."

WE'D PAID ATTENTION to Pa when he talked philosophy and history. Might not have seemed like it, but we listened. We'd figured out the whole concept of Schrödinger's Cat. It didn't apply to most things, but we kind of thought it did to time. The principle was that mostly we only know the outcome of history, not the process. Imagine a boy and girl who meet for the first time and fall madly in love. That's the outcome. History. But the process—what brought them to that particular time and place where they met—is an unknown. Did she just happen to need a cup of sugar and had to run to the store? Was he pressured by his parents to attend that university when he wanted to go to a different one?

We knew, I guess instinctually, that we couldn't change outcomes that were already known. It was the process we could affect. We'd tried to drum ourselves into the future with no luck at all. We had no idea what the outcomes were.

And *Oxėse* was a different matter entirely. Caitlin, Phile, Wolf Riding Woman, and Wolf Rising were synchronized when Yelloweye led us through that gateway. We aged at the same rate. Our day and night and seasons were the same. We'd stepped out of *Oxėse* into before-time to study drum making with Two Sticks because he was there then. We jumped back into *Oxėse* and it might have been the next day for all we knew, because time just didn't make a difference there.

But the four of us, plus Merv and Mandy as they related to us, were locked into a synchronization with now-time.

OF COURSE, WE knew what Merv had accomplished in the two and a half months here, but time wasn't the only thing that was confusing. I don't blame him. We'd gotten used to a perpetual state of confusion through our whole lives.

Merv knew in his head that Wolf Rising and Phile were one person in their brains. Each of them experienced everything the other experienced. But his head told him that those two bodies were two different people and since we hadn't been to *Oxése* in two months, he had to catch us up on his progress. Mandy grinned and just listened to her grandfather tell us about drum making.

"Dogwood doesn't grow in this climate," Merv said. "It is more southerly and easterly. Since we are here, I chose a wood that was available. We have a lot of aspen. The wood is flexible and straight-grained." He showed us a stack of wood. It wasn't just logs. After cutting a number of young trees and dragging them to his lodge, Merv had stripped them of bark and split them into thin boards, using his draw knife to shape them. "These will be the outermost ply of our drum frame," he said pointing at a few that were half-round rather than flat. We will build up the frame inside. But it is too cold to begin that work now. I'll come back in June."

We all laughed and began making up stories that could be told about Merv's long absences from Laramie.

I KNOW WE got pretty flaky that winter, because we were doing without sleep a lot of the time. And we did have work to do on the ranch. Our boss at LK Stables, that's you, big sister, seemed to have a thousand projects backed up for us. When the mares started coming in for breeding, they'd be staying in a luxury hotel. Honeymoon suite, I guess.

Phile and I would have dinner with the family and then go to bed. As soon as we figured the rest of you were asleep, we drummed softly and returned to our family. Sometimes Mandy went with us and sometimes she just rode in our heads. We'd spend the night moving bigger and bigger groups of animals from valley to valley. We even moved over a thousand right onto our pasture land here at home, only three hundred years earlier. We didn't dare put a couple thousand bison in Pa's pasture in now-time!

We couldn't do it every night, of course. It was just too exhausting for all of us. Wolf Riding Woman and Wolf Rising had to hunt, even though we brought them flour and fresh FRUIT and vegetables when we crossed to *Oxése*. All the rest of their time was spent making drums for the village. We still hadn't figured how the village would work into our plan, but we knew there was a reason that Yelloweye brought them with us.

That's when Yelloweye came for a visit. He showed up at our campsite on a night we were there with Mandy and just spending our time making love. I can never say exactly what he said, because it just doesn't make words. So, I'll let Mandy speak her version of owl-talk.

Mandy: To Move the People

Beneath *É'omeéše'he*, the Moon When the Horses Get Fat, I lay with my mates to celebrate the flowering around us. As we lay in our furs, *Heove-'éxané* came before us and spoke to our hearts.

You do well, children. If you move a thousand brothers and sisters, you can move ten thousand. Numbers will no longer matter. Only the size of your spirit matters. You must begin moving between what you call Oxése and now-time. As you began with numbers, so begin with time. Small steps and then large steps.

In now-time, the People have become complacent. They are defeated as they were by the blue riders. Their spirit hides beneath their skin. The People you brought to Oxése have not known defeat and have time to grow strong again. But you must not let them grow without guidance. The Wolf Twins must visit the people in their village each year at the summer apex. This will show the people that you are ageless and continue to watch over them. They will listen to you tell of a time to come when they will lead the People of all tribes in the defense of Mother Earth.

You must show the People that you can move them, too. But first, you must win them. Earth Sister will be the Voice of the Twin Wolves. This is why you have three spirits, five bodies. You are one hand. You will move both the animals and the People. You will even move the earth.

Caitlin: Running Fox

It was summer solstice, so we figured we'd make our first visit to the *Oxēse* village that night. We'd been in sync with our other selves since we arrived in *Oxēse* six years ago. That meant it had been six years since we left the village and we expected it to have been six years for the village as well. But that's part of the mystery of time in *Oxēse*. We were in sync with ourselves in now-time. The People had no such ties. It had been twenty years to them when we returned to the village.

We'd decided to send Wolf Rising, Wolf Riding Woman, and Mandy while Phile and I kept a steady drumming beat at the cave to anchor them. We took nearly a dozen drums as gifts with us.

"I was with you when we passed from the world of whiteman to this land of plenty," Running Fox said as we sat before the fire in the village. "I have seen twenty summers since that day and now I sit at the fire as the chief of our people. Yet, I see you as the youth that you were when I was but a double hand of seasons. How is it that we age and die, but you continue to be young?"

"In truth, Running Fox, six years have passed in our time. As you journeyed to a time and place where there were no whites to disturb your peace, we, too, journeyed to a time and place where we must accomplish much in little time."

"Will we see this place you have journeyed to?" he asked, puzzling out what I had said.

"If it is the will of Yelloweye," I said. "It is for this reason that we must make the mountains echo with thunder from the drums. The drums call together the people and give them one mind. With one mind, we can walk the path to this world."

"Running Fox, hear the words of the Twin Wolves and of our guide *Heove-'éxané*," Mandy said. "You are *Méstaa'e-vo'ėstaneme*, the People Who Follow the Owl. Yelloweye has seen your village and blessed it. Around you there are fields and herds. You have plenty and grow soft. But the day comes when you must go to war for Mother Earth. These drums are your arrows. The wolves are your spear. And Yelloweye is your shield. Tonight, Running Fox will accompany the Twin Wolves to the battlefield where the People will live. He will stay a hand of days. When he returns, it will be at the next Sun Dance. Now, join the drums."

We all joined in with the drumming and the Sun Dance. Phile and I maintained the rhythm at the cave. It was a celebration and the People danced and chanted the songs Wolf Rising and Wolf Riding Woman taught them. I noted with pride that the village had grown from the half dozen tipis with which we started, but was not stretching its resources or expanding unreasonably.

Normally, in the excitement of the drumming, Wolf Riding Woman and Wolf Rising could simply slip outside the ring of firelight and disappear. People wouldn't notice until dawn that we were gone. But this night would be a little more spectacular. When the drumming and dancing was at its peak, we stood on either side of Running Fox and led him into his tipi, followed by Mandy. When the flap fell, the drumming was muted and he turned to us.

"What must we do?" he asked looking around at his familiar dwelling.

"It is done," Wolf Riding Woman said.

"But I still hear the drumming at our fire."

"We, too, have drums." I opened the flap of his tipi and led him out into our valley. Running Fox stepped into a dawn for which he was totally unprepared. I think he expected to fly on Yelloweye's wings or something. In his perception, less than a minute had passed between leaving his campfire and entering the valley. As we stood there, we heard the drums fall silent on the mountain. Running Fox collapsed on the ground.

Phile: White Wolves

Caitlin finally got to kill a wolf. Well, me, too.

It took a while to get Running Fox calmed down. He was a true believer, but this was almost more than he could bear. From our perspective, the experiment was a success. Running Fox and all his possessions had been moved to the valley. Even his fire pit had come along. His travois was propped against the tipi and his horse grazed quietly nearby. When he recovered, Mandy began the slow process of teaching him about what would happen in the future. We didn't have a timeline yet, but we could see now what was going to happen more clearly.

Permits had been issued to some big oil company to use a new drilling technique right in Yellowstone National Park. They said work would begin the next summer and would not affect either the beauty of the Park or the ecology. They also claimed the new process was benign and, while based on old fracking techniques, did not pose the dangers of the previous technology nor risk seismic upsets. We'd seen that proven wrong before and had a strong sense that this would be our battlefield. We made our leap to bring Merv to *Oxése* by way of now-time in the same location. We were in the basin near Grizzly Lake in Yellowstone National Park.

Merv had packed more tools and supplies on his mules for this trip, including an air mattress. We laughed at how soft the old Indian was becoming and he fed the teasing right back at us.

"You have three women to cushion you at night. I have only these old bones. Now do you want a drum or not?" he groused. We wanted a drum.

We also wanted to scout the route that the village would need to use in order to migrate to Yellowstone. The wolves had led us over the mountains and through the Tetons to get here, but moving an entire community needed an easier route. We elected to take them north to the Shoshone River and lead them into Yellowstone from the East. Even without the benefit of modern roads, that route was easier. Caitlin and I started jumping along it, thinking of how long a migration it would be to get the People here.

We estimated it would be about 400 miles from where the village currently was to where we wanted it. I didn't figure we'd want to move it more than fifty miles or so at a time because people needed to stay settled and build their lives. So, Moses led Israel about that far and it took him 40 years. We figured at least 80. Not only did we need to move the People, we needed to grow the population to critical mass for the battle. And we needed a generation of people who accepted the task.

Cait and I were looking around an area with hot springs that we thought the People would thrive at for a few years when there was a snarl behind us and we spun to see two white wolves with hackles up. I immediately jumped to the mind of the male.

"We are not here to harm you, brothers," I said.

You smell of wolf, but you are two-legged. You have trespassed on our territory. You must die.

"We come with permission of Creator Wolf," Caitlin said, joining me. She'd linked the female into our conversation.

Show us this Creator Wolf!

"Creator Wolf does not answer our commands. We answer his."

Then die. This is our territory.

The wolves crouched to spring and Cait started tapping on her drum. I joined and could feel the echo from the mountain where we hit the larger drums. The ground shifted and we arrived in the basin not far from where Mandy was giving instruction to Running Fox. Both turned to look at us in surprise.

"Now you are in my territory," Caitlin bellowed. "We will see who dies."

We cheated.

As the wolves circled, taking in their new environment, Cait and I drew our side arms. It was a rule on the ranch that we never went anywhere unarmed. When we were riding, we had our rifles in their scabbards, but since our sixteenth birthdays, we were never without a gun on our hips.

Throwing off their confusion, the pair turned to rush us. We both fired clean shots into the chest. The wolves fell, red blood staining their white coats. Behind them, Creator Wolf stalked toward us. He paused to sniff at the bodies and then continued toward Caitlin and me. It was tempting to just start emptying our guns in the massive creature, but we both knew we would not survive. We dropped to the ground on our bellies.

I felt his massive paw on the back of my neck. I'd felt it as Wolf Rising years ago, but this body pissed itself. The pressure let up and I heard Caitlin whimper. Then we heard his howl echo through the basin.

MINE!

The big wolf turned and stalked toward Mandy and Running Fox. They both fell to the ground but Wolf did not claim them.

This is a sign to you when you return to the People. You have trusted in the black wolves. You must trust in the white. The black wolves led you to safety. The white wolves will lead you to war.

WE HAD DEPENDED on Mandy to let us know when it was time for Caitlin and me to meet Running Fox. The decision had been taken out of our hands. We were standing in front of him, in jeans and t-shirts with our guns still in our hands. Mandy was quickly explaining to Running Fox what had just happened and who we were. Cait and I had a deep kiss and then fell to skinning our opponents. We opened their bodies and consumed the livers. Then we skinned the dead animals. We would wear their pelts.

"The Twin Wolves are both light and dark," Mandy explained. "Today, the light has manifested and been blessed by Creator Wolf. The light will lead you and tell you when it is time for the People to move forward."

HAVING MOVED INSTANTANEOUSLY to a new to a new location left him malleable and receptive.

When he returned to his village at the end of the week, Cait and I, draped in our white wolf skins, went with him. We never spoke. Mandy filled the shocked villagers in after Running Fox's tipi was restored to its position in the village.

CAIT AND I brought Mandy back with us and took her to Lame Deer where she would work on preparing the tribe. She had also told us that she would have a surprise the next time we saw her.

Running Fox built the myths around the appearance of Creator Wolf and the magical slaying of the white wolves. He and Mandy verified that we were the ones who would lead the battle and move the People forward. Yelloweye's tale of the scorpion stinging Mother Earth filled the People with rage. They were dedicated to their one specific purpose: To call the thunder from the mountain.

And the myth began to grow.

WE CLEANED THE wolf skins more thoroughly and got them prepared as we continued to scout the path for the People's migration. When we were ready, we drummed ourselves into the village on their next solstice. For us it had been just a couple of weeks, but to the People, we entered the village exactly a year after the return of Running Fox.

We explained the route and what to look for along the way. The next day, the 135 villagers packed their tents and began the first migration. It continued through the year as we popped in about once a week in now-time but once a year as they perceived it. Our visits were always accompanied by herds of bison, deer, and even small game for the People.

We said a sad farewell when Running Fox passed away just before the fourth migration. It was the thirty-third year of the People in *Oxèse*, but for us, it was just mid-February. The People chose Thunder Hand to be his successor as chief. At one time, the village would have chosen the strongest or the best hunter or even the wisest of the old men to be their chief. But Thunder Hand was the best drummer.

The People were taking this seriously and they followed the White Wolves.

The truth was that we only showed up at the start of each migration and set out the path. It usually took a couple of days to get them moving and then we'd return to our other selves. Mandy always accompanied us to the village and kept the stories alive. There were always enough people in the community who could recognize us from the last time we'd appeared in our white wolf robes that they could verify to the younger ones that it was really us.

It took a total of two years, but by summer solstice just before our 21st birthdays the tribe began the last migration from about fifty miles east of Yellowstone. We were timing their arrival so that we would all be present. When they reached our basin, we would be in complete synchronization with now-time and would all be present.

Caitlin: The Drum

MOVING THE TRIBE wasn't all we did that summer and winter. In now-time, LK Stables was really taking off. The addition of Ramie's black stud,

Midnight, had attracted some of the top mares in the region. The rescue association assisted in the purchase of an additional thousand acres south of our ranch and we had nearly a hundred head of horses to care for. Apparently, we were the only ones who could separate a single horse from the herd that needed attention. Duh. We were the only ones who could talk to them and listen to their needs. We did get funding to hire two additional hands to work in the stable and breeding program, though. Ramie asked us if we could handle the rescues and since that was our love, we gladly agreed.

We even brought half a dozen horny mares up to the ranch to have Harley, Bolt, or Midnight cover them. It would be good to have some foals in the field. If it wouldn't create a problem for the ranch, we'd have just transported all the horses to *Oxèse* where they could live out their lives in contentment. But they were doing okay at the ranch.

MERV WORKED ALL summer on the thunder drum. He built a jig for it in the most practical way possible: he dug a hole. The hole was as perfectly round as the six of us could make it. Inside the smooth rock facing, it was just under eight feet across. Merv had started soaking the boards as soon as the spring thaw started and gently began bending them into the jig. It took longest to bend the first tier as he'd insisted that it be a single piece, over twenty-five feet long and bent in a perfect circle. He shaped and pressed the supple wood, then glued and pegged the ends together. The next ply was easier to shape as the pieces were just six or seven feet long. These were also glued and pegged.

It wasn't a fast process. Wood had to be soaked and bent daily and then had to dry in its new shape before glue could be added. But by the end of September, Merv had laminated the last ply into the jig. Then he buried it.

"Take me home. I'm tired," he said. "This will lie beneath the earth and the soil will leach out the rest of the moisture. Next summer we will set it in the sun and let it dry completely as we smooth the outer shape. I have work to do in my workshop back home."

We took Merv back to Laramie and made a stop in Lame Deer with Mandy to meet with the elders. Everyone was buzzing over what to do about the oil company drilling in the National Park. Mandy required a spectacular entrance and exit so the elders would listen to her. We were all stunned when she dropped her dress and stood naked before them.

It wasn't that she was naked. It was the new tattoo that covered her torso and arms. At her command, we drummed ourselves into the room wearing only our white wolf skins. Our arrival and our appearance stunned the elders to silence. There was some dissent over tricks, but mostly the council listened and nodded. We had tentative agreement that they would support the village, noting that nothing could be traced back to the reservation.

The argument went on for hours, even after Mandy had claimed the name of Earth Sister, speaker for the Twin Wolves, and had put her clothes back on. Phile and I just backed into the shadows. They argued about everything from who should join the encampment to the religious aspects of mixing Christianity and Native myth. It may have been the fact that Mandy called them whiteman in red skins that finally got them to agree.

Then we drummed her back to our apartment and kissed every inch of her Twin Wolves tattoo.

The Family

THE READING WAS interrupted by the sound of the cattle coming into the pens.

"We need to… get lunch out for the men," Aubrey whispered. "It's hard, but we need to do it. We need to do what we *can* do."

The family moved. The familiar routines of getting the traditional chili lunch out for the hired hands was comforting. Cole and Kyle moved the folding picnic table out in front of the porch and the women began loading it with food, bowls and spoons. The men rode into the yard and tied their horses at the watering trough where they used the pump to wash the trail dirt from their hands and faces. Behind them, two ATVs rolled into the yard with four well-armed men.

"How'd it go?" Cole asked Rafe, his foreman.

"The hardest part was keeping them from stampeding. I don't know what they felt, but not one cow or steer wanted to be left on that ridge. I don't think we lost any. Close to five hundred head, including calves and yearlings," Rafe said.

"We'll take census this week and get them ready to move to the Calhoun place. We close there on Friday," Cole said. "Everybody will get a bonus for this drive. Tell all the men they get ten dollars a head each for every head that was delivered."

"They'll like that. Almost makes up for how spooked they were." Rafe paused and looked at Cole. "How'd you know what was going to happen, Cole? You got an inside source?"

"What do you mean?"

Rafe glanced over at the ATV. One of the men broke loose and walked over to join them.

"Tell Cole what your scout found out, Jay," Rafe said.

"That corporation moved fast," Jay said. "At daybreak, they had security with high-powered rifles crawling all over. They looked disappointed that there were no cattle to shoot. Right behind them, six trucks pulled up. One crew started stretching fence, one started assembling a Quonset hut, and one started assembling drilling equipment. We heard them start pounding the drill in about eleven. Echoed something fierce."

"Shit. That means they'll come here, too."

"Should we move the herd over to the Alexander place?" Rafe asked.

"Mmm. Sorry. That wasn't what I meant, but it's a good idea. I hate to put your men under more stress, though. How are they holding together?"

"I have to admit that they're all pretty exhausted. We've been in the saddle for twenty-four hours," Rafe said.

"Give them a rest. Jay? Your guys fresh enough to stand watch?"

"If we can get a bowl of food first, we'll call the guys in the lower field and set pickets," Jay responded.

"Ramie has her hands moving the horses onto her lower fifteen. There's guards down there, too," Cole said.

"I don't think the corporation will let their mercenaries move far from the installation, but those guys looked real disappointed that they didn't get to kill something," Jay said, glancing up toward the ridge.

"I need a couple hours' sleep and a fresh horse. Then I'll be ready to ride," Rafe said.

"Don't plan on anything until after dinner," Cole said. "Rub the horses down and turn them out in the river pasture. Take ATVs to the bunkhouse up the road and get some sleep this afternoon. We'll know better what to expect by then."

"Thanks, boss." Rafe turned to the rest of the men who were finishing up their food.

"Take ATVs to the bunkhouse and give the horses a rest. Boss says to go get some sleep. I agree," Rafe called out. The guys all voiced their thanks and headed out.

12
The Last Days

Seventh Live Report

THE FAMILY cleaned up the lunch spread and headed back into the house. Cole flipped up the volume on the news station as the main picture switched to the scene of the military staging in Cody.

"This is Rhea Matthews of KWYO in Cody, reporting for the National News Network. A new development here in Cody, where a National Guard military police platoon moved in overnight to stage for an action in Yellowstone National Park, has pitted the National Guard against a handful of regular army troops. An hour ago, First Lieutenant David Bass, the ranking military officer in charge, received orders to move out to Yellowstone. Lieutenant Bass has assembled his troops on the parade ground." The camera cut to the assembled troops in formation as the Lieutenant addressed them. To one side, the U.S. Deputy Marshalls were gathered, waiting expectantly in front of their black SUVs. Four regular army personnel stood behind the Lieutenant.

"An hour ago, Captain Rodriguez, behind me, delivered orders from Colorado Springs. I have diligently verified these orders and will read them to you who are assembled and have sworn to uphold the Constitution of the United States and to protect its citizens at home and abroad," the lieutenant said. His voice did not need amplification. It was strong and sure.

"You are hereby ordered to proceed to Yellowstone Grizzly Village with full force. You are to remove the protesters at that camp and transport them to holding cells provided by the U.S. Marshal Service in Jackson, Wyoming. You are further ordered to remove all trace of human occupation from the ground currently designated as Yellowstone Grizzly Village. Resistance may be encountered and the use of deadly force in the defense of U.S. Marshals and military personnel is authorized. Signed,

Colonel Miles Clark, Commander, 10th Special Forces Group, Fort Carson, Colorado." The lieutenant folded the paper and placed it in his pocket, then resumed addressing the assembly.

"Governor Meade's order mobilizing our company of the Wyoming National Guard was to render humanitarian aid and assistance in relocating the residents of Yellowstone Grizzly Village to their respective homes and to stand between them and danger. Since this new order is in stark contrast to that initial mobilization, I took time to verify the authenticity of this order. I have also consulted with National Guard Headquarters in Cheyenne and JAG. None have been notified that the President is calling the Guard into Federal service—his right if he considers that unlawful obstruction, assemblages, or rebellion make it impracticable to enforce the laws of the United States. In good conscience, therefore, noting that Colonel Miles and the 10th Special Forces Group are not in our chain of command, these orders are not binding, and I respectfully submit that I will not obey and order you into this illegal action."

The captain drew his sidearm and pointed at the lieutenant.

"Execute your orders, Lieutenant, or you will be found insubordinate and derelict of duty. You will be summarily executed," the captain snapped. Before the lieutenant could respond, fifty rifles came to ready position aimed at the five people before them.

"Would you really turn these men into murderers and ruin the lives of so many?" the lieutenant asked.

"If I order them to shoot you, it is not murder."

"Funny definition. But their arms are not pointed at me."

The captain looked toward the troops and the realization that they were pointing their rifles at him and his three companions suddenly dawned on him. He lowered his sidearm.

"Very well," the captain blustered. "We'll settle it in courts martial. Sergeant! Place Lieutenant Bass under arrest and escort him to a secure location. As ranking officer here…" He was cut off by the sergeant's loud bark.

"With respect, Captain Rodriguez, I don't answer to you. You're not in my chain of command and I've seen no lawful orders authorizing you to take over. Lieutenant Bass, I assume your orders are to place Captain Rodriguez and his three escorts under 'protective custody'? Detachment!

Disarm Captain Rodriguez and his companions and confine them." There was a rapid movement and the group was surrounded, disarmed, and led away.

The Marshals, seeing which way the wind was blowing, moved quickly to their SUVs, and roared out of the Rodeo Park. They headed west.

The Family

"THAT SPELLS TROUBLE," Cole said. "I'm going to want all resources of Gold Watch made available for the defense of those National Guard men and women."

"Of course," Ashley said. "We just need to see who else we're going to defend."

The family gathered again in the office and the babies settled down on blankets for a nap. Ramie softly caressed the top of the wooden box and looked up at her wife.

"Aubrey, honey, I hate to ask…" She didn't need to finish. Aubrey held out her hand and took the box. She carefully removed the last pages from it.

Caitlin: Knowing

I DON'T KNOW how we survived knowing and not doing anything. It had become obvious that the assault on Mother Earth would happen at Yellowstone, our oldest National Park. But survey crews had already begun marking the location for Shale Oil Company's drilling site. Oh, they were doing it carefully, by the book as they say. There was a big show about how environmental concerns were being met, statements about no work being done that would in any way upset the natural beauty and ecology of this national monument. But we knew.

There had to be a thousand caverns in the Rocky Mountains like the one where we went to meet White Mouth. Yet his cave overlooked the very ridge where in now-time they were staking out the planned site and the road that would lead their crews in and out. The valley below the site, where Grizzly Lake lay, was the largest grazing area for buffalo in the Park. And in *Oxėse*, it was the place we were leading the People to make camp.

MANDY'S HABIT OF walking into the legislative chambers of the Northern Cheyenne without opening doors didn't make her a favorite among the council. When she came into the first session of the new year, they were angry and asked her to leave.

"Brothers, I do not come as a supplicant," Mandy said. "I do not ask you to forsake your Christian religion. I do not ask you to cease the important work you are doing to contest coal leases and help restructure BLM managed lands. I do not ask you to set aside your continued support for other tribes who continue to stand for clean water, clean air, and a protected environment. Earth Mother knows that you are small and weak."

"We are neither small nor weak!" John Lonebear shouted. "We are a stronger nation now than at any time since the reservation was founded."

"And this reservation is not a tenth of the land the People roamed and hunted before whiteman came," Mandy responded. "When we stand against the corporations who would rape Earth Mother, we are small and weak. But Earth Mother is not small nor is she weak. She has chosen the People as her hands and arms."

"Earth Sister, come to the point. What do you want?" Stan BlackBear asked.

"Sweet Medicine gave us the sacred arrow bundle," Mandy said. "He gave us our laws and our tribes and our council. And he prophesied the coming of whiteman, horses, and cattle. But he gave us another thing that would bring us hope through all this. He gave us the Sun Dance and drums. The drums are the voice of Earth Mother. It is only your hands on the drums that I ask."

"This is a simple thing."

"The Wolf Twins cannot talk in the council. Nor can they visit the other tribes of the Native Nations. We will need all the People to drum when that time comes—the Southern Nation, the Navaho, the Lakota, the Salish, the Cherokee, the Seneca. Someone must be an ambassador of the People and enlist the drums."

There was debate in the council and we retreated to Mandy's little house on the edge of Lame Deer. It was a cold January with over a foot of snow in the village. I was glad to get into more clothes than just our buck-skins and wolf robes. We had eaten dinner and were sitting in front of the cabin's fireplace when someone knocked at the door. Mandy answered. A short man dressed in ceremonial robes was ushered in by the fire.

"Welcome to our hearth, honored one," Mandy said. "We have little here, but what we have, we offer for your comfort."

"My cousin insisted that I come in full regalia," the man laughed. "I'm John Little Elk. I've come to talk about becoming your ambassador."

"May we give you refreshment?" I asked.

"I have a weakness for coffee," Little Elk said. "With milk, if I may."

"Come sit with us," Phile said. "It is a cold night, but our fire is warm."

"I have heard much about the white wolves, but never thought I would meet them. Cheyenne spirits in the bodies of whiteman. It is hard to grasp." I gave Little Elk his coffee and settled between Phile and Mandy as we talked. As we offered him coffee, he offered us cigarettes and we did not speak of his purpose until our empty cups and ashes had been put aside.

"My cousin is Stan Black Bear and he came to me asking if I would serve the council by becoming an ambassador to the First Nations. This has fallen to me for two reasons. The first is that I travel a great deal and, in fact, was planning to leave on Monday to visit relatives in Oklahoma. I will not say that it is warm there, but there is less snow. The second reason is because I am a drum maker. I have studied for many years, including a time some years ago with your grandfather, Earth Sister. I am surprised that you did not simply ask him to become your ambassador."

"Grandfather has other tasks to fulfill," Mandy laughed. "He is building a large drum to call thunder from the mountain."

"Ah. So that is what his questions have been about. We have talked about drum making and how to effectively reinforce the body for greater tension. He did not say he was going to call the thunder," Little Elk said.

"Perhaps we can enlist your assistance when the time comes to stretch the skin. Then you could meet the dark wolves, as well," Phile said.

"Your shadows," Little Elk mused. "Your legends are already spread-ing among the People. Secret whispers. Four wolves that share two spirits. One speaker who binds them together. Let us talk of what you need."

We talked most of the night. We explained the prophecy of Yelloweye and the scorpion. We mourned the water protectors who had been injured or lost their lives in the last showdown with the corporations and our desire to protect the People from a similar situation. And we talked about the need to unite the First People of the world with their drums when Earth Mother was ready to show her strength.

"So, it is not really an ambassador you need," Little Elk said. "You need a missionary." We sat in silence, nodding. He stood and we all rose with him. It was near dawn. "A sacred drum maker is always welcome at any dance. I've visited many of the nations and know people who will help. I will leave on Monday for the South and by spring I will have crafted the songs and rhythms. How long do we have?"

"Until the scorpion stings," Mandy said. "We know now that they plan to strike in the Yellowstone. We expect they will start construction of the site or at least the roads necessary after the snow melts. The weather will slow even the machines of the corporation, so perhaps two years or two and a half."

"We will be ready," he said. "May *Ma'heo'o* guide you."

IN THE SPRING, Merv was eager to return to *Oxése* to complete the drum frame. We were eager to unite with Wolf Rising and Wolf Riding Woman. I don't even know how to begin to describe our relationship. That isn't even a good word for it. We didn't have a relationship. We were one and the same, but even after twenty years, we sometimes found ourselves confused about who we were. Only when we were all together did we seem to be truly complete.

I've heard there are two sides of the brain and one side can talk to the other. You know that voice in your head that you talk to? Only the voice in my head that I talk to is really connected to a different body. If I'm arguing with myself over something, I'm arguing with Wolf Riding Woman. My left brain and right brain share all the same knowledge, accumulated through two lifetimes in two different bodies at the same time. And there are times when I think I will explode.

As soon as we arrived in *Oxése*, my first thought was not of Wolf Rising or of Mandy, but of Wolf Riding Woman. And I could see that

Phile felt the same way about Wolf Rising. We rushed to our counterparts and spent the first night just loving them. To embrace myself. To love and touch and taste myself. I felt whole when we were together.

That didn't mean that I wasn't just as hungry for Wolf Rising, nor that Wolf Riding Woman didn't crave the touch of Phile and Mandy. You put five bodies together that all desire each of the others, and you have a few days' worth of sex in every combination you can imagine.

Of course, we couldn't just indulge ourselves. We had Merv with us. And he wanted to get the drum frame out from under ground and into the light and warmth of day. Phile, Mandy, and I had to get the People moving to their next camping area. There were nearly three hundred now and we brought deer, rabbits, and pronghorn to lead them and feed them. Babies we had seen born were now parents and even grandparents. Yet we were just twenty years old.

Speaking of which, we had to be back on the ranch in time for our birthdays at the end of the month.

With the drum frame out of its form and drying in the sun, Merv was preparing and soaking wide strips of rawhide that he would wrap and glue to the frame, reinforcing the thick laminate he had created. The frame would weigh somewhere near 200 pounds when it was fully dry and cured, and the skin would weigh a hundred or more.

OUR BIRTHDAY CELEBRATION was less about us than about little Theresa, who turned one year old. What a cute little girl! I just loved her. And her mom. Aubrey came to see me a week after she was born.

"I tried to keep my legs crossed until the first," she said, "but the little beauty insisted on being born on your birthday."

"She's such a doll," I said. "I'll try to be a good auntie. Can I take her riding?"

"You and Ramie! Let's let her at least crawl before you put her on a horse," Aubrey laughed. She let me hold my niece and I gazed longingly in her eyes. "I know what you're thinking, Caitlin. And in case you are worried about it, no one in the family will have a problem. It might even push Ramie over the edge. I've hardly been able to pry my little girl away from her this week. I... We thought it would be too confusing to name her after you. We chose… other family names. You aren't upset, are you?"

I shook my head. "I don't think she looks like a junior, do you?" I asked. "Aubrey… No matter what happens, take care of my brother and sister, won't you? They'll need you."

THE WORST PART of the next year was knowing. Phile and I went off to Yellowstone and watched them start building the roads. We knelt on Mother Earth and begged her to let us end it immediately. Waiting until they were finished building seemed like such a waste. But we knew we needed time. We needed at least twice the number of villagers that we currently had. We needed scores of drums for them. We needed Little Elk to recruit the other tribes. We needed to move a million or more big animals.

But it was so hard to wait.

You must have a pack to lead a pack.

I turned at the voice in my head to find Creator Wolf between Phile and me. We'd seen him… talked to him often, but every time he still scared me and I raised my hackles to fight. Yelloweye calmed me before I realized the bird was there.

To you, time is important. There is no time in Oxèse. Days pass. Years pass. But all time is now. Do your tasks. Enjoy your lovers. Gather the People. Live now.

Yelloweye finished speaking and hopped away. Creator Wolf did not speak again. Instead he turned and licked my face. I cringed at the nearness of his fangs and the smell of his breath. He chuffed as if he were laughing and loped off into the woods. Yelloweye hoo-hooed and lifted to the branches of a nearby tree. We drummed ourselves back to the ranch.

Phile: The Last Preparation

LITTLE ELK BEGAN spreading the new legends. He had so carefully woven them into the existing stories of our tribes that no one thought twice about it. What they detected was a new sense of urgency and the call to awaken the drums. The styles of drums in each of the tribes were different from our Cheyenne drums. Some were large barrel drums with one end open. Others were closed on both ends. Some were hollowed logs and others were made of bent wood. Some were meant to be beaten by a single drummer and others had as many as six or eight sitting around a single stretched skin.

Over the summer, Little Elk occasionally called on us to step in and reinforce the story. He'd created a little pageant and we would enter his stage from a curtain. Of course, people assumed that we had been hiding behind the curtain and not that we'd actually stepped through it from somewhere else. Earth Sister would step forward and state the prophecy of Yelloweye as the White Wolves stood silently in the background. Then we'd step back through the curtain and disappear.

I wasn't sure about how effective Little Elk's strategy would be. It felt like he was turning it into a show. I was pleased, though, to hear of a rising fervor in the tribes, especially among the very old and the youth. The very old accepted the stories as a return to the old ways, showing that the traditions were relevant and needed today. The youth were rudderless, upset at the world, disillusioned by their parents' acceptance of the whiteman way of doing things, many of them caught up in the enterprise of selling to the whites, either through 'tax-free' outlets on the reservation or through the casinos.

"WE NEED TO enlist the support of the white environmentalists who are opposing the oilmen," said one young woman. We were riding in the head of Little Elk and he quickly identified her as a Seminole from Florida.

"You know how that would work out," said an old man from the Lakota in Minnesota. "Whites have to own and manage everything. They would adapt our stories and we would possibly have a representative at some of their meetings. This is an Indian affair and we should keep it that way."

"We have to be able to do something besides beating a drum!" said a local Arapaho boy. "Why don't we go to Yellowstone now and sabotage their equipment? The longer we wait, the stronger they become."

"Have you ever seen Yellowstone in the winter?" laughed Little Elk. "Why do you think I come to Oklahoma in the winter? The roads through Yellowstone are closed now."

"In the spring then," the angry boy said.

"I agree that we need to do more than beat drums," the Seminole woman said. "That's why we should be writing to the environmental groups and to our congressmen to raise the awareness at the least."

Little Elk had convened the meeting of a dozen representatives from tribes he had visited this year. It was midwinter and he'd set up the meeting near the Cheyenne-Arapaho Tribal headquarters in Concho, Oklahoma. The delegates had flown to Oklahoma City and Little Elk had arranged the loan of a small bus from the casino to transport them out to Concho. Just south of the tribal headquarters on Black Kettle Boulevard were the three remaining buildings of the Concho Indian School that had been closed for forty years. One of the buildings was converted to a fitness center and Little Elk had arranged for the delegation to meet, eat, and sleep in the gym.

When it seemed that everyone had an opportunity to state their opinion on the issue of how to proceed Little Elk turned to one young man who had been silent throughout.

"Ken, you have not yet spoken. Do you wish to share with the delegates?" Little Elk asked. The man nodded.

"I am Ken Klinekole of the Mescalero Apache. Through all history, the war drums of the Apache have been feared. While we dance the peaceful dances and powwow with our brothers, we keep our war drums ready. Before I call our warriors together to waken these drums, I would hear from Earth Sister directly what it is that the White Wolves can do."

Did you put him up to that? Mandy whispered in Little Elk's head. He shook it. *Then tell him we will come when the delegates unite their drums.*

"In front of each of you is a gift from the Twin Wolves," Little Elk said. "These are sacred drums, made in a different time and place. They are different than those used in your tribes and even a little different than those that I make. These drums have come from the heart of the sacred mountain known as Bear Butte. When you find the rhythm, it will be echoed from Grizzly Mountain and Earth Sister will appear among us."

"An illusion?" asked the old man.

"No. She has said she will come and I believe her," Little Elk said. "While you contemplate the gifts and consider what you are asking, I suggest we eat the food that has kindly been prepared for us."

Unlike their northern counterparts at Lame Deer, Montana, the Cheyenne-Arapaho of Oklahoma had no reservation. The 9,000 tribal members who lived in Oklahoma were mostly concentrated in four counties just northwest of Oklahoma City. In 1892, the U.S. Government broke its 1868 treaty, allotting 160 acres per household to the tribe members and opening up the rest of Indian Territory (Oklahoma) to settlement and homesteading. It was an attempt 'normalize' the natives into the Western European style of farming and society.

The tribes had been fighting to regain their identity for 130 years.

But many of the tribes had been reestablished and the Cheyenne and Arapaho had combined. Cherokee, Apache, Comanche, and others had established tribal headquarters, some still had Indian schools, and some had their own broadcast and media outlets. The tribal media, of course, were very interested in what was happening in Concho and had attempted unsuccessfully to get a television camera into the gym where the delegates were meeting. It was for this reason alone that they decided to drum in the gym rather than at an outside fire.

"You want to meet Earth Sister and she's agreed," Little Elk said.

"Is she here?"

"Not yet. She will come when we drum."

"Where is she now?" asked the Arapaho boy, Luke.

"She is in Lame Deer. The winter drums are starting there. We should start our winter drums as well," Little Elk said. There were many puzzled looks, but all the delegates prepared to use their gift drums for the first time. At Little Elk's signal, the beat began.

We were ready. The drums at Lame Deer would continue for many hours. The drums at Concho were also echoed by the mid-winter dance being held at the tribal headquarters a few blocks away. And in *Oxèse*, Wolf Rising and Wolf Riding Woman were using their prayer drums to forge the link. We were going to attempt something we had never tried before.

Mandy raised her arms and we stepped forward from Lame Deer to Concho. This was the first time that we hadn't entered through a curtain or out of the mist. The drummer delegates gasped as we literally stepped into the middle of their circle. Little Elk raised a hand and three beats later, the circle of drummers fell silent.

Ken Klinehole of the Mescalero immediately stood and walked around Mandy, pausing a moment to consider us at the edge of the circle. When he faced Mandy, he reached out a hand slowly and touched her face. She smiled at him.

"The Apache war drums await the call of Mother Earth. We will ride together," he said.

"Thank you, Ken," Mandy said. He returned to his seat in the circle. "I know, however, that you all have many more questions that you want answered or you would not have asked us to attend. Let me introduce the White Wolves. We don't use any other names when referring to them. They are the Twin Wolves that I have dedicated my body and my mind to." She pulled her dress down a little so our faces were visible tattooed on her chest.

"They're not People like us," the Seminole girl, Jae, said.

"No. But weren't you lobbying a little while ago for us to include whites in our planning?" Mandy laughed. "We want to spend some time getting to know each of you. Even though I do all the public speaking for the Wolves, they have voices and if we sit and powwow together, they will also answer questions. Let's relax and get to know each other."

That began a long evening of just sitting and talking. Everyone wanted to touch us to make sure we were real. They also wanted to touch the white wolf robes.

"I have listened to the tales that Little Elk has spun. We have heard the prophecy of Yelloweye and that there are three spirits in five bodies. Yet we see only three spirits in three bodies. Who are these others?" the old Santee asked. He was a medicine man in his own right and had held himself apart from adopting any white religion. He probably had the easiest time believing everything, but the presence of whites still bothered him.

"The 'who' part of your question is me," Caitlin answered. She poked me in the ribs. "And him. We are two spirits who inhabit four bodies. I believe the question you really wanted to ask was, 'Where are the others?' They are in *Oxése*, which in our Cheyenne tongue simply means 'Other

Place'. We would like to visit you in these other bodies if you will drum for us."

"Before we start," Mandy said, 'let me say that we have managed for a short period of time to all be together in what we call now-time. But the Dark Wolves are anchored in *Oxëse* and can only stay here as long as the drums keep beating. It is an odd thing that we can all be together there with no problem. But the path is open and in answer to the drums, we believe we can be together for a little while. Little Elk, if the drums falter, we will depend on you to maintain the beat. Don't worry, though, you will also have conversation with the Dark Wolves."

Of course, Caitlin and I planned to keep our drums going as well, but having the support of the delegates was important to us. We began the drumbeats that matched the drums of Wolf Rising and Wolf Riding Woman. The group joined us and when Mandy pulled us together, they entered the circle. The drums faltered a little, but they soon returned to the steady beat that we marked.

It was Ken Klinehole again who seemed to be delegate designated to verify that we existed. He faced the two Dark Wolves and held out his arm for them to clasp. Nodding he turned and said, "I will ride to battle with these warriors."

He returned to his seat and the old Santee approached us. We don't have a lot of interaction with other tribes, but our languages are all based on Algonquian. When he spoke, it was not difficult to understand that he was asking if we were 'like him'. I answered in Cheyenne.

"We are of the People. We have lived apart and in isolation from the progress of the world that you have known. We have a tribe that we have nurtured for what seems to them to be a hundred years, but for us has been just half a dozen. There are nearly a thousand of our People who have prepared to come to this time and place as an anchor for the thunder. It is on their behalf that we ask you to join on the drums when we lead Mother's children in battle." While Wolf Rising was speaking to the old man, I stepped into the center of the circle and spoke the words in English.

A young Pawnee woman came before us, fascinated mostly by our wolf robes. She spoke very little, but stroked the fur of all four robes. Tears ran down her face as she turned to address the other delegates.

"The Pawnee are the People of the Wolf. The hand sign for our tribe is the same as the hand sign for 'wolf'. These wolves have been blessed by the Great Wolf that many believe created the world. Others believe he brought death into the world. I believe they are the same thing. I can feel his spirit move in the gifts of the robes they wear. They have eaten the flesh of the wolves they slew and have become one with them," the girl said.

Mandy had just one final word for everyone before we stopped drumming.

"The People do not need a new religion. What appears to be a miracle of moving us through time and space is no more than the spirits we have known all our lives and all the lives of our parents and grandparents exercising their rights. They exist beyond our understanding of the physical world. We merely move at the will of the spirits."

With that, the five of us moved back to *Oxése*. We made love in the dawning hours and spent four days before three of us had to be home for Christmas.

Caitlin: Heartbeats

HAVING APPEARED TO our delegates, there was a new life in Little Elk's movement. We'd stressed to them that we didn't want a new religion tied to us in any way, but there was no question that the delegation was now missionaries, not only to their tribes, but to the rest of the Native American community. Everything was focused on a First People's Drum Day that would occur in the summer a year-and-a-half away. We didn't attempt to fix a date. We had no idea when we'd be called into action, but it was obvious that the road to the Yellowstone site had been finished and in the spring, they would start erecting their installation. We'd gone to the Park and walked around the site, looking at the survey posts and flags marking where the construction would commence.

There had been a lot of news reports that showed how carefully Shale Oil Company was approaching the project. The installation would run on green power while it tapped into the fossil fuel substrata. At least there would be no power lines. The compound itself would look like a mountain lodge, so they said. A footnote to one of the reports mentioned that this was the first of a proposed fifty sites on public lands that had been approved for oil exploration. Any alarm that was raised regarding the misuse of public land was passed off as being from tree-hugging liberals who all wanted to prevent progress and make an issue out of everything.

Near the end of April, Phile, Mandy, and I went to *Oxése* to start the seventh migration of the People. They would move to their final staging area on the Shoshone River east of Yellowstone. The migration was always preceded by a substantial herd of animals moving before the People. It would include bison, elk, deer, game birds, small game, and an abundance of fish. But for three days as we started the four-week journey with the tribe, Phile and I sat with the People at their hearth and reinforced the calling of Yelloweye.

And brought them drums. There were close to 600 at the beginning of this migration. We'd estimated that by the time we got them settled in our valley there would be over a thousand. Most of them had heard of the time when white soldiers brought guns against the Indians. But the People had lived three-quarters of a century without ever seeing a whiteman. Other than Phile and me. We stopped by the village every year in their time to reinforce the stories.

We were happy that the occasion of our presence meant drumming and dancing. The People were marching to their own promised land.

Mandy stayed with Wolf Rising and Wolf Riding Woman for a few days while Phile and I went back to the ranch to help with the mares that were coming in for breeding.

WE MADE SLOW gentle love that night. It had been a warm day and the snow was melting. With the number of mares we had coming into season, you could practically smell the estrus in the air. Making love was everything I wanted. Almost everything.

"Phile, I want to have our baby." I heard him laugh as we heard the echoes of Mandy and Wolf Riding Woman chiming "Me too!"

"I've been thinking about that," Phile said. "About the complications and all. I think I have an idea for getting you pregnant. And no matter what you all say, I don't think we want all three of you pregnant at the same time. But we've got another alternative."

"What's that?" I sighed.

"I'm Wolf Rising as well as Phile Bell. We're the same person in every way except genetically, and I know you enjoy it when it's that body instead of this one that makes love to you. But we don't share any genes. If we did, they'd be centuries removed and way past the point of posing a genetic or legal risk. Why don't we get you pregnant the next time Wolf Rising is on your back? Or your front. Or however you want to do it."

"Probably every way we can. I'm nearly in season. Can we really start this week?"

"Let's tell the folks we are going up to check on the condition of the upper pasture this weekend. We'll go get you knocked up in *Oxèse*."

"Me, too," Mandy said. "I want to be next on the breeding schedule, but for now, I just want to be with my lovers as you unite."

Well, we did take a few days and while the family thought we were camping up by the thermal spring, we were in another place. It was hard to contain Mandy and Wolf Riding Woman. They wanted to get big in the belly as soon as they could, but we all abided by what Phile had said. It made sense not to have all our babies at one time. I could just imagine overwhelming Moms and Pa with more grandchildren than they had knees to bounce them on.

Phile did his best to keep Wolf Riding Woman and Mandy satisfied as Wolf Rising rode me repeatedly that weekend, pouring his seed into my body.

I came home from that 'camping' trip knowing I was pregnant.

Caitlin and I were approaching our twenty-first birthdays and we knew we would have to leave the ranch to prepare for the coming battle. It would be hard. We were going to move the village to our valley in *Oxèse* and from that point on, we'd be working with them every day. Our time-lines would be in sync and they needed to see us move the herds so they knew what we could do. And after generations being removed from Wolf Riding Woman and Wolf Rising, they would be reunited as well.

"Will we ever see them again?" I asked as I cuddled Phile in our bunkhouse room. "Ever see these walls again? See our parents and our siblings and our niece?"

"I don't know, precious." Phile placed his hand over my belly. At just two months along, I wasn't showing yet, but I could feel my body changing with the new life within it. "I think we will want to show our parents their new grandbaby."

"Mom Mar looked at me a little strangely yesterday," I said. "I think she suspects. You know she is always the first to know things like that. She knew Aubrey was pregnant before Aubrey did."

"I'm not ready to answer questions about parentage yet. I think we should leave all that sealed in the box."

"I will write a letter just before we leave," I said. "I just want them all to know we love them."

We headed up to the house for the first of the birthday celebrations.

13
The Oil Field War

The Family

"SO THAT'S it?" Ashley said flatly. "The end?"

"Not quite," Aubrey answered. She held up an envelope that was on the bottom of the box. She looked at her parents and her husband. They all nodded. Aubrey handed the envelope to Ramie. Ramie took a deep shuddering breath and opened it, shaking out the contents in her hand. She opened the pages and began to read.

Caitlin: It's Time

My DEAREST LOVING Parents, My Beautiful Sister, My Brave Brother, My Kind Sister-in-law, My Adorable Little Niece.

I've just turned twenty-one. Our contemporaries in now-time consider that to be an occasion for cutting loose, getting drunk, gambling, and otherwise being adults. They're idiots. In our twenty-one years, Phile and I have lived forty-two. Each. In one of our lives, we have functioned fully as independent adults since we were twelve. In the other, we were just weird, I guess. But we have tried to be responsible, even though we were wild and reckless at times. We were learning double and triple the amount normal kids do. It was a little overwhelming.

We always knew our family was a little strange, but wish we had discovered earlier that we weren't the only ones who lived in different times. Miranda and Jason, we are so sorry for what we did when we were young and filled with rage. And we are so glad that you came to join Ramie and Kyle in this life.

Yelloweye visited us last night. I thought we were going to leave right then, but I needed to write this to you first. And yes, here in the bunkhouse, Mandy and Phile are holding me and drying my tears as I write. Later tonight, we will tap our drums and take Bells and Bows, Midnight, Mandy, and Merv Longsteer with us as we cross to *Oxése*. We don't know if we will ever be able to return after the coming battle. It was so hard to hug you each tonight after our party and not cry.

So, you need to know that I'm two months pregnant with Wolf Rising's baby. Y'all are going to be grandparents again! Mandy has declared that as soon as we get to *Oxése*, she is going to be working on getting Phile to plant her fertile soil, as she says. The thing is that whether it is Wolf Rising or Phile, it is the same father, just different genes. Just as Wolf Riding Woman and Caitlin are the same person. Perhaps one day, you will meet all of us and we will be one happy family.

We don't know how soon the battle is coming, but with the activity in Yellowstone we all believe it will be soon. Our people have never been violent, but their peaceful ways have been destroyed. They see only that an armed conflict is on the horizon and we are trying to prevent that. We've managed to channel most of the energy into the First People's Drum Day. Most believe it will be like a march on Washington, but we plan a more complete solution. It has to be done in an absolute and final way. I am sorry for the lives that will be lost, but greed rules in the hearts and Mother Earth has had enough.

We love you all so much it hurts, but we serve Mother Earth and she has summoned us. Certainly, we must love her even more. We can see Yelloweye outside the door. Beyond him, Wolf is pacing. Bells and Bows are standing at the fence with Mandy's Wildfire and Merv's pack animals. It's time for us to go.

When you open the box and read the story, it will be history. You can help us write the next chapter.

This land is forever ours. Even when we are dead and buried, we are here to protect our pack and our land. The spirits of this land do not rest. And we are deadly when we hunt.

We love you.

Caitlin, Wolf Riding Woman, Phile, Wolf Rising, Mandy

The Family

THE FAMILY SAT in the office crying. Aubrey wrapped Ramie and Kyle in a hug and Cole held Ashley and Mary Beth. Outside they could hear the sounds of the cattle drive as Rafe and his cowboys herded them into the pens. Inside, there was only the sound of sniffling and sobs occasionally broken by a baby's quiet demand.

"My babies are going to war!" Mary Beth sobbed against Cole's chest. There was nothing he could do to comfort his wives but hold them and join their tears.

Eighth Live Report

"WE INTERRUPT THIS broadcast to bring you a special bulletin," the announcer said on the television. It was two o'clock in the afternoon and the corner window still showed Earth Sister standing motionless on the horizon. This announcer was in a studio somewhere in New York.

"Reports began arriving two hours ago that an unusual crowd of Native Americans had begun filtering in to cities across the country. The Native Americans all seem to be dressed in traditional garb and many carry drums of varying sizes. This scene in Central Park shows an estimated thousand Oneida, Seneca, and Mohawk Indians with a scattering of other tribes preparing a circle of perhaps 100 or more drums. In Jacksonville, Florida, Seminole and Miccosukee Indians have gathered. In Atlanta, the Cherokee Nation has set up camp at Centennial Olympic Park," he said.

"Nor is this invasion of Native Americans limited to the East coast. In Washington State, there are thirty-two Federally recognized tribes and another eight that are not recognized. It appears that all forty, however, are represented at Seattle Center with over 5,000 surrounding the famous Space Needle. Oklahoma City has discovered just how many Native Americans there are still left in what was once known as Indian Territory. Thousands of members from the thirty-three recognized tribes and three non-recognized tribes have gathered in Will Rogers Park at the amphitheater. Reports are flooding the news desk from as far away as Hawaii where Kānaka ʻŌiwi, Kānaka Maoli, and Hawaiʻi Maoli have gathered on every island.

"In each area, the Native Americans have gathered around drums silently, as if awaiting a signal. We have finally established contact with a representative of the Northern Cheyenne, a thousand of whom have moved into the same area as the National Guard troops awaiting deployment in Cody, Wyoming. Rhea?"

The picture switched to the reporter in Cody who had been getting quite a workout today. The camera panned from Stampede Park where the National Guard vehicles had been parked to the reporter. Behind her, hundreds of Indians in traditional and ceremonial garb had camped in open space.

"This is Rhea Matthews of KWYO in Cody, Wyoming, reporting for the National News Network. While we were caught up in the confrontation between the Wyoming National Guard and members of the U.S. Army, a quiet phenomenon occurred behind us. Hundreds of members of the Northern Cheyenne tribe, with a reservation near Lame Deer, Montana, quietly set up a huge powwow on the empty plot of land lying just east of the Stampede. When we began to approach the circle, we were met by a representative asking us to not attempt to enter among the natives. There is no barrier between us, nonetheless he pointed toward the circle where large dogs or perhaps wolves were pacing the perimeter like sentries. I am here now with John Little Elk. John, can you tell us a little about what is going on here and in cities across America?"

"I am John Little Elk, a drum maker and story teller of the Northern Cheyenne. Two years ago, I met a remarkable woman named Earth Sister. She and the White Wolves told me of a great evil that was approaching and that our Earth Mother would not suffer it any longer. They said we must make the thunder of our drums heard in every heart and they asked me to take this message to the 500 tribes of America."

"There are 500 Native American tribes?" Rhea asked.

"The United States Government recognizes 345 tribes plus 240 independent native villages in Alaska. Nearly 200 more are not officially recognized as independent tribes by government treaty, but they exist nonetheless. I will mention that there are another 230 tribes identified in Canada."

"Did you visit them all?"

Little Elk laughed. "I had the privilege of meeting many First Peoples, but I am not magic. I have many helpers who have been carrying sacred drums to the People across the continent."

"And why are they all gathered here today? Is this to join the protest in Yellowstone Park?" Rhea asked.

"Two years ago, we decided that we had been invisible for too long. We established a First People's Drum Day. We awaited the White Wolves to give us the date and the time. We know now that it is today and the drums will cry out on behalf of Mother Earth. I must go to my people now," Little Elk said. He turned and walked past the wolves and into the gathering.

"There you have the story," Rhea said. "This is an event that has been planned for two years and no one outside the Native American community has apparently heard about it. Now back to New York."

Rhea's image was replaced by the network anchorman.

"In terms of major protests, this ranks fairly small," the anchorman said. "Estimates are currently that there are between 100,000 and 150,000 Native Americans gathered in a reported forty-seven states and Canadian provinces. That they have chosen this day cannot be a coincidence and we shift you now to Evan Waitley at Yellowstone's Grizzly Village. Evan?"

The image on screen shifted back to Yellowstone where Evan Waitley held his microphone. In the distance, they could see Mandy still standing at the top of the rise.

"We are now five minutes from the time that Shale Oil Company has indicated they will begin pumping the pressurized gasses into the shale layer, forcing the oil into prepared channels. A company spokesman—not here, but in Houston—has indicated that the only sign there will be of the commencement will be a high-pitched whistle as the gasses and steam begin to flow. He says that while this will undoubtedly disturb wildlife in the area for a few minutes, the whistle will rapidly fade as the pressure equalizes, causing less than ten minutes' disturbance."

"Evan," said the studio voice, "has there been any change in the status of the encampment or a report of arrival of the U.S. Marshals?"

"The encampment, as you can see below us, has shown some sign of life, with people moving about. A large fire has been lit in the center of the camp and appears to be surrounded by drums. We projected earlier that there would be a ritual mourning of some sort and we assume that is what is being prepared. Perhaps this will be echoed by the gatherings you have reported across the country. As to the Marshals that you saw leaving Cody, they did arrive at the Eastern Gate and moved toward Fishing Bridge on the north side of Yellowstone Lake. Their progress, however, was suddenly arrested when what appears to be a large portion of the bison herd here in Yellowstone ambled onto the road and are simply not moving. This occurred before the cutoff that could take traffic around to the south. From what the Park Service is reporting, the herd seems disinclined to move and is just standing in the roadway."

"Thank you, Evan. And we are, in fact, just seconds…" the station reporter's voice was drowned out by a piercing scream and Evan plastered his hands over his ears as he doubled over, ripping his headset away from his ears. The camera swung wildly for a moment and came to rest on Evan with Mandy far in the background.

"That, apparently was the high-pitched whistle we were warned about," Evan said once he had regained his microphone. It has left our ears ringing and continues, though slightly abated in the background. We can assume that the pseudo-fracking has commenced."

"Evan! Behind you! Something is happening with the Earth Sister speaker."

The reporter, of course, did not hear without his headset and continued talking, but apparently, the cameraman either heard or noticed and began zooming in on Mandy on the distant rise. She was raising her hands and as they rose, a distant rumbling grew.

"There is not a cloud in the sky, but we are getting some thunder in the background. Wait!" The cameraman got Waitley's attention and the reporter turned to face Mandy. "It's hard to believe that this thunder could be under her direction, but as Earth Sister raises her hands, there is no question that the volume is increasing. It seems to be coming from the mountain overlooking this basin."

Mandy's hands suddenly dropped and a boom echoed over the valley from mountain to mountain. It completely overrode the scream still issuing from the pseudo-fracking site. And at once, the boom was echoed by the drums in the village. Some fifty or more big drums surrounded the fire with at least three people beating on each one. And their call was answered again from the mountain.

The screen suddenly split into four parts with images labeled, Yellowstone, Seattle, Oklahoma City, and New York. It appeared that the drums in all locations were exactly matched. All but the Yellowstone window scenes and windows were renamed Hilo, Cody, and Ottawa. The three windows were rearranged on one side of the screen as the larger picture of Yellowstone expanded.

"It sounds like more drums with an amplification system were set up on the mountain to completely fill the valley with sound. The ground, itself, is shaking under the reverberation of the drums. And now, Earth Sister is pointing at the drilling site as if she were directing… Oh, my! This is unbelievable. Wildlife that we have not seen all day are suddenly teeming in the valley. If this is an illusion, it is not just visual. We can feel and hear the hoofbeats. And… There are larger animals coming over the rise behind Earth Sister. She'll be trampled!"

The Family

THE FAMILY WATCHED in disbelief as the scene unfolded live on the air. The network announcer kept screaming for Evan to pull back to a safer location, but the newsman had no headset and couldn't be heard over the noise of the herds thundering down around Earth Sister on the rise. The animals parted around her as if she were a rock in the stream and stampeded toward the installation. And then two animals stopped momentarily on either side.

"That is the biggest fucking moose I've ever heard of!" Kyle whispered.

"It's not just a moose. It's Phile," Mary Beth said. "That's my son."

"That's not all," Ramie said. "Caitlin is riding Wolf. I'd recognize that beast anywhere. I've ridden in his head. Oh, please be safe, little sister." After the brief pause, the two animals loped ahead with their riders. It took a moment for everyone to realize that Mandy was no longer with them or on the rise.

"They took her to safety," Cole whispered.

Then the first wave of bison hit the chain link fence. For a moment, it looked like it would hold while the defenders poured gunfire into the herd. But then the fence bowed inward and gave way to the thousands of tons of force stampeding into the installation. Once the fence was down, the stampede picked up momentum again, crashing into buildings like a tidal wave and bringing them to the ground.

The drumming thunder and stampeding animals drowned out the sound of the gunfire from the enclosure. A few animals went down, but the herd continued without noticing. Small animals seemed to move to the side or simply avoid the hooves of the larger beasts. In the center of the massive surge Caitlin and Phile, in their White Wolf robes, rode their spirit animals with drums raised over their heads urging the stampede forward. In the small screen, the drumbeats from other locations across the continent looked to be exactly synchronized with the beat of their drums.

A lone gunman remained, firing from a central tower that was already being rocked by the herds. With a look of determination on his face, he sighted in and squeezed off two rapid bursts of fire. Then the tower toppled.

But it had been enough.

"My babies!" Cole, Mary Beth, and Ashley all screamed at once. Even from the distance of the camera, it was easy to see the two rocked back off their animals. In another flash, three figures appeared in the stampede that parted around them. They picked up the bodies and disappeared again.

There was no slowing of the stampede. As one wave moved past the installation, another appeared on the horizon to rush across the valley. It continued for over an hour, the disconsolate parents and siblings unable to tear their eyes from the screen.

Ninth Live Report

EVAN WAITLEY APPEARED to be transfixed. His microphone dangled loosely from his hand as he stared across the valley at the utter destruction rained down on the installation by thousands of animals. Birds swooped in from a darkened sky and picked remnants from among the rampaging beasts, carrying them off or devouring them on the spot.

The network continued to try to get his attention, finally lending a voiceover for the scene.

"Reports have begun arriving that the ravaging of Shale Oil Company was not limited to this Yellowstone location. The company managed evacuation of only three of the twenty-three sites in the Rocky Mountains where pseudo-fracking operations had begun construction. All twenty-three sites have been reported as destroyed by Forest Service helicopters. The destruction has been so complete that it is as if the operations had never existed."

"In other news, drumming continues at all sites currently occupied by Native Americans in over seventy cities. Reports indicate that the numbers are increasing as non-Indians have approached from every direction, some carrying drums to join the rhythm, others beating on pots and pans, garbage cans, and pipes. There is scarcely a corner of any city of any size that cannot hear the beating drums. Even those who have joined late have picked up the rhythms set by the native drummers and have synchronized with them."

Scenes flashed from around the country as local reporters vied for their moment on national television. Helicopters overflew different sites where Shale Oil Company once had installations. All were gone with no sign but the trampled ground where thousands of hoofs had trod.

EVAN WAITLEY EVENTUALLY looked down at his microphone and discarded headset. He donned the headset and turned to the camera. Tears streamed down his face. Across the valley, only a few animals remained. Even those animals killed during the action had been dragged away by predators and scavengers. No sign of the installation remained.

"I'm overwhelmed," he choked. "I am a seasoned reporter, having served embedded with U.S. troops in war zones of the Middle East. In the most intense bombing raids of those wars, I have never seen such utter destruction. And no one can say we were not warned. Will Shale Oil Company attempt to recoup losses by suing the perpetrators? Who? Mother Nature? Was this, in the final analysis, an act of God?" The reporter faltered and pointed toward the road between him and the protesters' village. The camera swung to cover the area.

"The drums continue in the village, though there is a different tempo now. The thunder drum on the mountain is at a low rumble." The camera picked up the arrival of a dozen black SUVs driving out onto the fields off the road. Two hundred yards from the village, they pulled to a stop and the officers piled out of the cars.

"We can see that the U.S. Marshals have arrived on the scene. It is unclear what they intend to do. They are not being supported by National Guardsmen as intended and the fifty or so deputies seem an unlikely number to confront what we estimate to be a thousand souls in the village. Certainly, they have no buses to begin transporting the people."

The marshals donned their riot gear and armed themselves, making a show of their superior force. Mostly smaller animals continued to roam the installation site where a helicopter camera showed the last of the cement blocks that had been used being smashed to dust.

"What we are seeing now is a team of U.S. Marshals, armed with rifles and shotguns, moving toward Yellowstone Grizzly Village. The rhythm of the drumming has changed. The amplified drums from the mountain are softening. It is as if they have been waiting for this moment all day and the entire destruction of the pseudo-fracking installation has been just a warmup. The only people we can see from this vantage point are the drummers and they are shielded from view of the marshals by the rows of tents. It seems that everyone but the drummers has disappeared."

The drumming changed rhythm again to a drone, echoed by the drum in the mountains. The drone rose in volume as it had earlier in the afternoon. Marshals were taking up positions where they could see and raising their rifles. However the drums were being controlled, though, the three strong beats followed by a pause and a single strike were in perfect sync with the beats that echoed from the mountain.

In cities around the country, there was sudden silence and crowds began to disperse without a word.

Before the echo died, the village was gone.

A single shot rang out from a marshal who was apparently too keyed up. There was nothing for it to hit. In front of the marshals, a prairie stood that appeared undisturbed by human presence. Guns were lowered as the marshals took in the situation.

"We heard earlier that the National Guard was ordered to restore this basin such that no sign of human occupation existed," the newsman reported. "It seems that their job has been done for them. We have broadcast this and we have witnessed it. But I cannot explain it. There is not even a sign of the installation…"

The reporter broke off, interrupted by a boom from the site of the installation. The camera swung to the site and a geyser shot into the air over a hundred feet. It lasted for about ninety seconds and then subsided.

"It appears Old Faithful has a young competitor for attention," the reporter said. "This is Evan Waitley signing off from Yellowstone National Park."

The Family

THE TELEVISION, OF course, continued to broadcast repeats of the day's activities complete with analysis from animal behaviorists, geologists, and politicians. Someone picked out and enhanced the picture that showed Caitlin and Phile, the White Wolves, shot from their animals. The family snapped off the television and held each other in silent tears.

Cole extracted himself from his wives, who clung to each other. He reached for the radio on his desk.

"Delta Oh Niner, base calling," he said into the hand mike.

"This is Delta Oh Niner," came the response. "Everything is golden."

"Send a team up to the ridge to see if there are any survivors," Cole said.

"Survivors, sir?"

"The news has reported the complete destruction of all twenty-three Shale Oil Company sites. If there are survivors, we need to render aid. If they are firing, use your own judgment, but if there are injured, radio for helicopter extraction."

"Affirmative. Delta Oh Niner out." Cole placed the mike back on its clip.

"How can you offer aid to those people?" Ashley screamed. "They killed our children!"

Cole rushed to his wives and caught them in his arms.

"I hate them, too," he said softly. "But if our children left anyone alive, it was for a reason. This is our land and we protect it and those who honor it."

"You have been so good for us today, my love," Ramie said as she kissed Aubrey. It was dark. Cole had settled his wives in their room and 'the kids' went back to their bunkhouse home. The two-bedroom apartment would be too small soon. The two little girls could share a room for a while, but soon they would need more space. Cole had mentioned the possibility of switching houses with them, but Ramie couldn't imagine her parents giving up the ranch house, no matter how many generations were arriving. Kyle had mentioned possibly building something new, maybe on the site where the original cabin had been when the first Laramie Wyoming Bell had homesteaded it. That had a certain symmetry to it.

"Don't give up hope," Aubrey whispered to her wife. She turned and kissed Kyle with as much passion as the exhausted pair could muster. Exhaustion had overflowed on the babies, as well, and they were sound asleep in the other bedroom. "We haven't heard the end of this story yet."

"The box is empty," Ramie said.

"Have you opened it to be sure?" her lover asked. "Don't. Not yet. I just think the box holds many possibilities that it has not revealed yet."

The Family

"I didn't want to be there, but… but…" Cole and Mary Beth looked down at the damaged man in the hospital bed.

"You needed the job?" Cole demanded. The man had been identified as Tom Reynolds. Cole's team had found only one survivor at the installation on the ridge. He wasn't the only survivor of the Oil Field War, as it had been dubbed, but he was the only one hospitalized in Laramie. Cole's team had found no other sign of life or of the installation that had displaced the Alexander Bell Ranch cattle just a few days ago. Even evidence that Cole had leased the National Forest lands had been erased. The animal-proof lock boxes, the chuck wagon, and the tent platforms they used while grazing cattle were all gone without a trace.

"Yes," the man whispered. "I needed a job, but… it was the insurance."

"What do you mean?"

"I believed Earth Sister. I thought I'd be killed. Company insurance pays triple if you are killed on the job. My Sara. She can't get treatment. With the money from my policy, she could get well. I volunteered for the job expecting to die. They should have let me die. Now I have these hospital bills, too." The man turned his head away and Cole could hear his sobs.

"You were committing suicide?" Cole asked softly. That was even more troubling. The man weakly nodded.

"Don't give up hope," Mary Beth said. "We'll help you and your Sara. She needs *you* even more than she needs the treatment."

Cole stopped at the desk as he and Mary Beth left the hospital and arranged to pay any expenses the man had that weren't covered by his insurance.

"ALL THIS TIME—EVEN while reading the kids' story—I thought my part was just a failed experiment. I rode off in Kyle Wardlaw's head and collected all kinds of lost treasure, stole it from Joe Teine, and hid it where we could use it to fight him in the range war," Cole said. "I never really understood why there was still so much left. Why it keeps growing and there's more in the Gold Watch Foundation now than there was when we started."

"Now you know," Ashley said. "I want to hate everyone who had anything to do with my children being killed. I want to destroy them, their families, and every trace that they existed, just like the animals did to the installations." She paced around the office, stopping to look at Cole's guns as if she was ready to strap them on herself. "I can't. We have to… help those people who were caught up in the event without knowing… or understanding what they were doing. The injured. Widows. Orphans. Protesters. Mother Earth gave us this wealth so we could pick up the pieces after her war."

"It was our war, too," Ramie said. "We can't lay it at her feet just because we didn't ride animals into battle. We sat around moaning about how awful what they were doing was. All that time, my little brother and sister were preparing to do something about it. We aren't that far removed from both sides."

"There are few casualties that require medical aid," Mary Beth said. She had spearheaded the effort to discover how many were injured and hospitalized when the installations were destroyed. "We have forty-seven in hospitals, who survived the attack, not including the Alabama police officer who was bitten by a wolf when he tried to wade into a drum circle to disperse them. We'll chalk that one up to stupidity."

"What's the number of casualties that don't require medical aid?" Jason asked. He wondered in the dark recesses of his mind if it had been as bad as when he and Kyle massacred the Twin Wolves' village.

"Shale Oil has not been forthcoming about the number of people who were at the installations when the attack began. They managed to evacuate three of them," Cole said. "It will take us a while to get identities, but the news estimates 240 people died in the attack. That means 240 families that need our assistance."

"Then there's legal defense," Aubrey said as she held baby Katherine to her breast. "It looks like Lieutenant Bass may be charged with dereliction of duty, though analysts have said the case is beyond shaky and lawyers are already demanding an open trial rather than a military tribunal. The only charge that might stick is for unlawful imprisonment of those Special Forces people, a civil rather than military offense, and since they were giving unlawful orders that probably won't go anywhere. It appears the other members of the National Guard are being excused for their part. There was a couple dozen protesters arrested. They weren't Indians. They were people who came late to the party and got mad it was over."

"I think those can defend themselves," Ramie said.

"Yes, I agree," Aubrey said. "But… arrest warrants have been issued for John Little Elk and Amanda Stevens for inciting a riot. They identified Earth Sister as Mandy."

"There was no riot," Cole growled.

"Apparently, inflammatory talk is the same thing. If they get caught, we need to defend them."

"How are we for money, Pa?" Kyle asked.

"We can distribute close to a billion dollars without revealing the extent of our resources," Cole answered. "I think maybe we should buy that company and just grind the rest of it into dust."

14
The Aftermath

Shale Oil Company

IN A closed board meeting of Shale Oil Company, Ron Grisholm, president of the company, had just delivered his statement of intent to rebuild the pseudo-fracking sites and continue prospecting for oil. The board members were heads-down examining the report and proposal.

"I don't see how we can invest like that with the stock in the toilet, Ron. Have you got it all in the proposal here?" one of the board members asked.

"There is no sense even reading the paper. The short of it is that we show these terrorists that they can't stop America. I'll drain every drop of oil on the continent if I have to squeeze the earth's tit with my own hands," Grisholm declared.

There was a low growl. Heads turned to see a giant silver wolf leap to the board table. He stalked down the length of the table while board members scrambled back and Grisholm struggled to get a pistol from his shoulder harness. Pulling it free, he swung toward the wolf in time to meet the claws that ripped out his throat. The body jerked as it landed back in its chair, eyes wide but unseeing.

The wolf shook the blood from his massive paw and turned to stalk back down the length of the table. He paused to look each stricken board member in the eye.

"I vote no," the first said, raising his hand as the wolf stared him down. At each board member where he stopped, the answer was the same. "I vote no." At the end of the table, the wolf sprang and disappeared through the door of the boardroom.

No one knew where the wolf came from, nor where it went.

OVER THE COURSE of the next few months, it was revealed that the former president of the corporation—'acting alone and without the consent of the board', of course—had suppressed environmental studies that revealed the Yellowstone location was not stable and that the operation would have an adverse effect on both the ecology and tourism.

The information was 'shocking' and needed to be 'investigated at the highest levels' according to news reports. The Interior Department and USDA both rescinded all energy exploration permits on Federal lands. Both Forest Service and Park Service funding were increased.

A new company, Native Energy Management, Inc., owned by a consortium of Native American tribes and funded by Gold Watch Energy Foundation, purchased a controlling interest in Shale Oil Company at pennies a share. By the time they took the company over, it was a skeleton of the original company and the new owners began transforming it into a research facility to explore earth-friendly energy solutions. Its work would continue for many years.

ATTACKS WERE NOT limited to Shale Oil, nor even to U.S. soil. Periodically, drums could be heard rumbling like thunder but apparently without source. People paused to listen.

An Arabian prince was killed in a stampede of his own horses. A Japanese magnate was killed by a rare komodo dragon. Two South African mine owners were caught in a freak collapse. Each had recently declared their intentions to expand operations that many termed raping Mother Earth.

Park authorities joined by forensic analysts combed the Yellowstone Grizzly Village site and turned up no evidence of habitation either at the village or at the company installation. Investigation of the installation site was hampered by the unpredictable venting of the new geyser. On some days, it went the entire day without erupting. On others, a burst would follow the one before by only a few minutes. It was dangerous to be too close to the vent when it erupted as the ground shifted and was unstable.

An investigation of the mountainside facing the valley revealed little. There was a cave that had previously been uncharted, but there was no sign that anything had inhabited it for hundreds of years. Researchers did, however, note that the cave had unique acoustic properties.

The Family

THE ALEXANDER BELL Ranch and LK Stables returned to a semblance of normal as well. With the additional acreage made available through Cole's purchase of the Calhoun spread, he balanced the number of cattle that he could maintain without leasing the National Forest property on Centennial Ridge. That also reduced the number of men needed to ride herd, even though it increased the dry food requirement. Kyle and Ramie's horses thrived on their allotted pasturage.

The wounds never quite healed. But the two unusual families sought and received solace in the arms of their lovers. The babies continued to grow and reaffirm everyone's hopes for the future.

"I HOPE IT's twins," Kyle said. Ramie looked at him aghast. "We could use more hands on the ranch," he continued innocently. Ramie slugged him in the shoulder a little harder than she intended to.

"When are we going to tell the family?" Aubrey asked. "Moms and Pa will be so excited to hear they'll be grandparents again."

"I think it's a little early, don't you?" Ramie said. "I only missed one period."

"Yeah, that's true," Aubrey admitted. "I missed eighteen of them." The three laughed.

"Aubs, honey? Is it all right? I never meant to get pregnant," Ramie said, looking at her wife and husband/brother.

"Yeah, right," Aubrey said. "Hmm. Maybe it wasn't you. Miranda?"

"What is it, sweetheart," the bright voice came from Ramie's lips.

"When was my darling wife supposed to have her implant replaced?" Aubrey answered sweetly.

"Uh… I… well… I don't keep track of things like that," Miranda said.

"I forgot all about my implant!" Ramie said. "Demon Miranda, we are going to have a long talk."

"Can we do it while making love to our husband and wife?" the voice of her ancestor said.

"Are you really upset, Laramie?" Jason asked softly through Kyle. Ramie looked into his eyes and saw both her husbands clearly.

"I'm a little scared," she said softly. "But you know I love all four of you and if you can be happy for me, I'll be overjoyed."

ON LABOR DAY, the family trekked to the family burial site and Cole placed two plain white marble slabs, skipping a row where his own would lie with those of his wives. He recited the names for each of the seven rows of stones, starting with Theresa Ranae Bell and White Horse. The family, much to Miranda's embarrassment, had decided to add stones for Miranda and Jason to mark their remembrance. They insisted that they weren't dead, but Cole explained that it was so the family would know their lineage, not to mark their resting place. None of the stones had names on them. Miranda then insisted that they add a stone for her precious Katie.

The second row had the stones of Laramie Wyoming Bell, Kyle Redtail Wardlaw, Kat Tangeman, and Caitlin Forster. Cole had added Caitlin's stone, even though she was buried in the pauper's field at Greenlawn, when he found out she was the daughter of Jason and Katie.

The fifth row had only Cole's father's stone. His mother, her brother and his wife, all lived together now and had asked that they be laid next to Earl Bell as a single family and single generation. Cole and Mary Beth still prayed that time would be far away.

The sixth row was empty. One day, Cole, Mary Beth, and Ashley would lie there.

"And here we mark the passing of our children, Caitlin Forster Bell and Philemon Morgan Bell. Their spirits continue to guard our land as they have protected it with their lives," Cole intoned. He closed the big Bible. "My children, I will love you till the day I die. You were the bravest of us all."

A WOLF HOWLED.

It was joined by the screech of a hawk, the cawing of a raven, and the hooting of an owl.

Ramie jammed her feet into her boots and strapped her Colt to her waist as she ran toward the door of the bunkhouse ignoring the fact that all she wore was a t-shirt. Kyle had his Remington in hand as he followed her out in his boxers. Aubrey snatched up the babies and held them to her breast, wrapping a robe around them all as she followed her family.

Cole, Mary Beth, and Ashley emerged from the big house facing the younger generation across the broad yard. His Smith and Wessons hung from his hips. Ashley held a rifle and Mary Beth a shotgun.

Between the big house and the bunkhouse, in the area where Ramie had once met the wolf pack, a different congregation of animals had gathered. Redtail, Blackfeather, and Yelloweye stood on the ground next to Wolf. Behind them a great grizzly bear stood on his hind legs and bellowed. A moose stood next and beside him an elk whose points could not be counted. Around the yard sat animals of nearly every species of mammal and bird. From among them, two horses stepped forward—paint draft horses—and between them walked three people carrying three little children.

The only one any of them recognized was the tattooed woman with the wolf's heads on her shoulders.

"It's us," the young man said. "We'd like to come home."

Mary Beth and Ashley ran to their children and hugged them.

"Did you think I wouldn't know you?" Mary Beth said. "You might not look like Phile, but I see him in your eyes."

"It's going to take some getting used to you looking like this," Ashley said. "But I am so happy to have you back."

"Is this my grandchild?" Cole asked holding his arms out to Mandy. She presented the little boy to him. Cole took the child and put his arm around Mandy, hugging her to him. "I can never thank you enough for what you did for my children," he said.

"Meet Grandma Mar, Beth Ann," the young man said holding her out to Mary Beth. "This is my... Phile's baby with Mandy."

"And you meet Grandma Ash, Avis," the other young woman said. "She's the youngest of the three. I got started late because there was so much going on. She's my... Wolf Riding Woman's baby with Phile."

"But..." Ashley started.

"Yes," Mandy said as Cole continued to hold his grandson. Colin came from the womb you knew as Caitlin's, fathered by Wolf Rising. He's the oldest."

"I think we have a lot of ground to cover and we don't need to do it all out here," Ashley said. "Let's get you inside and warm and find beds for you all."

Cole turned to the animals that had accompanied them and fixed his eyes on Redtail. "Thank you for bringing my children back to me." The hawk bobbed his head once and lifted into the air. They heard his screech in the distance. It tugged at Cole's heart. The other animals began to retreat and once they were away from the yard lights, they seemed to fade away.

The old one-eyed raven hopped over toward Ramie and Kyle and bobbed his head.

"Thank you, Blackfeather," Ramie whispered. The bird hopped and fluttered until he landed on Aubrey's shoulder and looked down at her babies. Theresa, the oldest, reached up to pet the bird. Kyle thought he looked embarrassed by the child's show of affection. Blackfeather made a few soft calls and then launched himself into the night air.

The owl lifted himself up and the boy—Phile? Wolf Rising?—held an arm out for him to land on.

"When you call, we will be ready," he said. The owl gave a soft hoot and launched into the air.

That left only the family standing in the yard holding each other with Bells and Bows looking on. There was a soft chuffing and everyone turned to face Wolf, the massive silver protowolf. He looked at the young woman and her child then turned his eyes on Ramie. She felt him penetrate her mind and brought her head up to gaze at the full moon.

"My land," she said in a voice that was not her own. "My pack." The wolf threw back his head and howled and then bounded off into the night.

"WE SAW YOU die," Ashley whispered again. Everyone had been in bed when Wolf announced their presence so the family had made the first priority to make sure everyone had a place to sleep, was fed, and was warm. The next day, however, no work was getting done on the ranch. All fourteen gathered in the family room where there were places for everyone to sit and the babies could all get to know each other.

"Yeah. That sucked bigtime," Phile said.

"Trust you to make it succinct," Caitlin laughed. She sobered quickly. "It hurt like hell."

"But this is you in what you called your other time bodies?" Cole said. "I can see you and recognize you, but you are definitely different."

"It's different even to us," Phile said. "Yelloweye wasn't clear about it. As much as we can tell, the old ones didn't want to take a chance that any of us would be recognized again. Somehow when we jumped into the stampede to remove the bodies and jumped back, we got welded together. It was only us when we got back. But we're not the same as either Phile and Caitlin or as Wolf Rising and Wolf Riding Woman. For example, we're a lot taller than in *Oxése*, but not as tall as in now-time."

"These are definitely my now-time boobs," Caitlin said offering one to her daughter. "I didn't have much up top in before-time."

"But it's you? It is you, isn't it Caitlin?" Ashley pled.

"If you mean the crazy brat who didn't become a pain until she was eight, yeah. That would be me," she laughed. "It's different, though. It's like half of me is missing."

"Only it's still sort of there," Phile said. Caitlin nodded. "Things like ham and eggs are familiar to me, but still a new experience for this body." The boy took a deep breath. "Moms. Pa. Phile and Caitlin are dead." He paused and sniffed a little. "I can still feel it. I've got all of Phile's memories. I've got everything he ever felt or said or did in here," he said pointing to his head. "But there's no input coming from him. When I talk to myself, I just get answered by his memories."

"It's like my senses have been cut in half," Caitlin added. "I only have this one body instead of two. Even when I'm holding Colin or Avis to my breast and they suck away, there's a piece of me that longs for her to feel it, but those nerves aren't connected any longer. I feel through these nerves instead." It was hard to explain and Caitlin could feel tears in her eyes. Mandy reached over and stroked her cheek. "It's like having had a part of me amputated and still experiencing phantom feelings."

"It will get better, love," Mandy said.

"Were you changed, too?" Mary Beth asked. She'd scarcely let go of little Beth Ann since breakfast.

"Yeah. Maybe not as much, but I'm different. I lived for a long time in Caitlin and Phile's heads. When they died, I think a little of them seeped into me as well." She took Beth Ann from Mary Beth and pulled her shirt down to give the baby her breast. Above the baby, the wolf head tattoo was somehow different than the parents had seen on TV.

"The faces are gone from your tattoo," Mary Beth said. Mandy nodded.

"It doesn't fully cover my arms, either. My blood type is different. I look pretty much the same as I did, but I don't think my genes would be linked to my tribe any longer." She looked up and seemed to puzzle at something. "There was a time that would have bothered me," she said. "Now, I'm a wanted woman and if I got arrested, they'd have a hard time proving I was the same person that you saw on TV. I figure that as much as the camera focused on my breasts, there will be wolf tattoos on every native girl in the country in a year or two. I'm past caring what body I have or what blood. As long as I have these two we will continue to be three spirits in five bodies. Or perhaps we are now five spirits in three bodies. The old ones can sort out how that works."

BABIES GOT PASSED around a lot. Grandparents were thrilled to meet the new generation and even the cousins were intrigued. Avis and Katherine were only a week different in age with Colin and Beth Ann bracketing them by three months.

"What about the children you are carrying now?" Everyone gasped and looked at Mary Beth. Phile looked at his wives with one eyebrow cocked. "Come on. I knew you were pregnant when you disappeared and I thought the two of you had run away to pretend you were married somewhere. I can see that you are both pregnant."

"Well, that's right," Mandy said. She kissed Phile on the cheek. "We were going to tell you but hadn't told Phile yet. This is the man that got us both knocked up again. Genetically, the three on the ground are unchanged. A DNA test would show that they are closely related and share at least one grandparent. The next batch, though, won't show a relationship that is more than a distant ancestor. I hope that won't make a difference to you. In our hearts—all of our hearts—we are one family."

"And how about you, young woman?" Mary Beth continued. Ramie's head bobbed up when she realized her mother was talking to her.

"Me?" she squeaked.

"Did you think my own daughter could hide her pregnancy from me?" Mary Beth demanded.

"No. We were going to tell you as soon as we confirmed everything. We just figured it out this weekend. Um… I'm pretty sure Miranda is pregnant and Jason is the father." She smiled brightly.

"Oh really?" Miranda's voice cut through Ramie.

"No. Miranda and I are pregnant and Kyle and Jason are the father. And Aubrey is the mother. Other mother." Ramie turned to the kids. "I felt so bad for you guys when I read what you were going through. If we'd known, we might have been able to help. You'd have gotten a ton of advice from Pa, too, if Kyle and I hadn't acted like they were loco when they told us about time travel. Then you'd have had comfort and help instead of feeling like you were weird. Not that you wouldn't have still been weird, but we'd all have understood."

There was a good round of laughter, a sound that had been heard all too seldom in the past year. Ramie went back to playing with Katherine and Avis, letting the two babies touch and explore each other. Cousins.

"How are we going to pass the three of you off here?" Ashley finally joined the conversation. "If we call you Caitlin, Phile, and Mandy, folks will start to question what's up. You two don't look like Bells."

"We've had some time to get new identities," Mandy said. "It was just more work we had to do over the course of the past year plus. All three babies were born in Seattle to Mr. and Mrs. Wolfe. The three of us are second generation Americans with passports and everything. I'm Talia. In Swedish, 'tala' is a speaker. We thought that was appropriate. This is Stig. In most Germanic languages, 'to rise' translates to some variant of 'steigen'. Miss Wolf Riding Woman was the hardest to get something for, but in German, 'riding' translates to 'reiten'. We figured Rita was close enough. Right after the birth of their baby, Rita and Stig got divorced and I married him. Divorced, but never separated. So, if you'll keep us, your new hired hands are Rita, Stig, and Talia Wolfe."

"Okay," Kyle said. "Pa, we need to build another house. Eight adults and five children in the bunkhouse is going to make it crowded. And just wait till it's eight. Or nine," he joked, grinning at Ramie.

Caitlin: The Box

I'M PLACING THIS last batch of pages at the bottom of the batch you've already read, knowing that one day you'll want the rest of the story and you'll open the box again. There is so much left to tell you. Mandy convinced us to keep writing the story, even though we were in *Oxèse*. We'll have to slip these pages into the box when we get back. But there are some things that are just too important to leave out.

The first thing we needed to do when we got to *Oxèse* after we ran away from home—well, the first thing after making love with the five of us together again—was to get the village moving on its last migration. Phile and I had been starting each stage and then leaving. We'd meet up with them in a year or so and congratulate them on the move. Of course, Mandy did most of the talking, but we'd really gotten to know some of these folks and it was fun to be with them.

This time, there were nearly a thousand people moving from west of where Cody now is up into the mountains at Yellowstone. It was a longer trek of nearly 100 miles and some of it going into the mountains was pretty rugged. So Phile, Mandy, and I walked with them. We got up to Grizzly Lake, where they set up their village, around the end of the third week of July. We were completely in sync with now-time, but we were still in *Oxèse*. Of course, the three of us couldn't wait to get up to the cave where our twins were and where Merv was preparing the big moose hide to stretch across the drum.

"Beloveds," Mandy said when she had us all in the furs that night, "I have news. I think I'm pregnant." We totally mobbed her. There wasn't one of our bodies that didn't give her an orgasm or two. Of course, I immediately started comparing the tiny bulge that was beginning at my waist. I love that girl so much. If it wasn't for her, Phile and I would never have survived those hard years and now I was going to have Wolf Rising's baby and it was obvious that Mandy was going to have Phile's. It was the second happiest time of my life up to that point.

But then I got to thinking. And by me, I mean I was head-talking to myself in Wolf Riding Woman. I still wanted Phile's baby. I know he's the same as Wolf Rising, but still… We confronted him.

"Phile, I am not yet in season," Wolf Riding Woman said. "And I know we don't want all the babies born at once. But I want your child in my womb. I think maybe we should start working on it."

Phile was still trying to come to grips with the fact that he'd already planted one in me through Wolf Rising and in Mandy with his own horny balls. But Mandy and I had been with him every night while we moved the tribe. Wolf Riding Woman wanted him.

I wanted him. I wanted to feel a life growing in my belly that came from my beloved brother. Even if it was in my other belly.

Moms, we did it this way because of those stupid laws in Wyoming about incest. The only way anyone can prove incest if they don't catch you in the act is through a child. We considered all the birth defect angles, too. We have a slightly higher risk because Mom Mar and Pa are first cousins and Phile and I are half sibs. Um… second cousins? Somebody smart will figure that all out one day.

But I have to tell you that the very next opportunity I get, my Caitlin body will carry the child of my brother Phile. I love him. I have loved him since the day I was born, in two different lives. If I have to live in *Oxèse* forever, I would do that to have his child.

Getting Wolf Riding Woman pregnant didn't happen right away. Her body was just tuned differently and needed to have the quiet stability of our family together before she finally got knocked up near mid-September.

"I am ready to stretch the skin," Merv announced to us in mid-August. He'd spent a month and a half preparing it. It wasn't just cutting the hide into a circle or reinforcing the lacing holes, but he had to have long strips of hide prepared to lace it in the back of the drum. It would take a couple hundred feet of lacing hide. When he came with us to *Oxèse* this time, he brought a hoop he'd had made in now-time. Unlike any of the other materials we were using, this was not natural to the making of Cheyenne drums. It was made of titanium and was about the size of a hula hoop.

While the hides were soaking for the drum head, he'd been wrapping the titanium hoop in strips of hide until it was about an inch and a half thick. "This was the only way I could create a hoop that would withstand the pressure that will be applied when we tighten the drum head. A normal hide would simply be torn apart."

"I'm glad we can proceed," Wolf Rising said. "Shall we begin the ceremony tomorrow?"

"There is one other thing I would like," Merv said. He scrunched up his face as he looked at the five of us. "I would like John Little Elk to help. It will take all our hands to pull the cords tight enough. Wolf Rising, Wolf Riding Woman and I are trained in the making of a sacred drum. We need the fourth direction. It would take me a long time to prepare one of the villagers to work on this." Merv had been a regular visitor to the village and had several people there building frames and preparing hides for drums. But even those drums, he needed to bless and stretch.

We'd talked about inviting Little Elk to join us, and he had even asked to visit *Oxèse*. But there was so much to do in now-time enlisting the support of the other tribes that it seemed impossible. Of course, when we approached him with Merv's request, he suddenly had a miraculous opening in his schedule as one of his disciples took over the meetings he had planned.

"THIS IS AMAZING!" John Little Elk said. It was the last week of August and he looked down from our cave across the valley where the village was nestled near the lake. In order to keep the herds of buffalo from wandering right through the village, we'd been busy showing them how to build an earthworks wall around the tents and few wigwams so the bison would naturally part around it. We didn't plant the village right at the edge of the lake for the same reason. The People had to walk to get water, but the herds had to have access and would be more likely to trample the village if it blocked their way.

Of course, we had a little talk with the herds as well. They avoided coming right up to the village.

"We are building a very large drum," Merv said after John had a chance to greet each of us and wonder at the world in general. Merv showed Little Elk the frame, the hide, the hoop, and other materials.

"I am your student again, *Ma'heónêhetane*," Little Elk answered. "Teach me."

If you think they finished stretching that hide in a week, you're mistaken. We ended up keeping Little Elk another week after he'd touched base with his disciples and sent them on their way. The intricate patterns they used in bringing the laces from the hide to the hoop on the back of the drum each had names and rituals. I knew them all in my head, but my whiteman body wasn't allowed near the drum while the work was taking place. What we were allowed to do was cut wood and make sure the fire in the back of the cave was kept burning so the skin and lacings would dry at an even temperature, even when the weather got cold and damp outside. The slightest dampness will cause the drum head to stretch and the sound to go flat.

That first tap—even on the wet skin—sent a shiver down my spine.

Phile: Preparing the Village

ALL THROUGH THE fall and early winter, Cait and I spent most of our time in the village. After popping up once every year or two for the past hundred years of their time, we were an accepted part of their heritage. No one left in the village remembered living in before-time with whiteman. We were the only frame of reference they had.

Wolf Riding Woman and Wolf Rising made frequent appearances in the village as well and our union with Earth Sister/Mandy was well known among the People. They proudly watched Cait's belly swell with our child, wanting him to be part of their village.

We knew we had to make a place for him in now-time as well, so we located a midwife in now-time Seattle who would attend the birth and file the appropriate papers. She was a Salish woman and had heard Little Elk speak in her community. She was more than willing to help. She was the one who suggested we create the Wolfe family.

As soon as the big drum was stretched, Merv began visiting the village regularly, too. Wolf Rising and Wolf Riding Woman had taught several of the young people how to make frames and they had a few dozen ready to stretch with the hides they had prepared. Merv was considered a shaman in the village who could bless the drums and make them thunder.

It soon ended up that he was living in the village and only visiting the big drum in the cave.

Little Elk wanted to return to *Oxėse* at midwinter. During his short interaction with the People during the summer, he had become enamored of the simple life. He was in his forties and had always been a little isolated. In the village, he was accepted as simply a member of another band of the People who was welcome at their fire. He and Merv spoke a slightly different dialect of the language, but they adapted quickly. After our midwinter celebration, he reluctantly returned to now-time in order to continue visiting the tribes with his disciples.

"When this is over, I'd like to live here," he confided before we drummed him back to Concho. "This is what my life was meant to be."

"We'll see," I said. "We don't really know when or even if this will be over."

You could not have found five prouder parents when Colin Wolfe was born in January. Wolf Rising and I went hunting and brought back a large elk to butcher and celebrate our son. My son. My sperm came from the body of Wolf Rising, but this was my sister whom I had loved from birth.

Wolf Riding Woman was beginning to show and Earth Sister's bulge was now a prominent feature. We were happy to have so many women in the village who wanted to help care for the children of the Wolf Twins. It was funny how the term had evolved. No one knew if Wolf Rising and Wolf Riding Woman were the twins, dressed in their dark wolf robes, or if Caitlin and I were the twins in our white wolf robes, or if it took a black and a white to make a pair of twins. So the name Wolf Twins came to mean all five of us, for Earth Sister was still the voice of the Wolf Twins.

It was clear by now that the legal channels and appeals in now-time had been exhausted and Shale Oil Company would begin stinging Mother Earth as soon as they could get the equipment operational. The five of us, plus Merv, Little Elk, and baby Colin, sat with the elders of the village and explained that the time had come to prepare for war. We were going to move the village to now-time. We wanted the move done and fully established when the roads in Yellowstone opened in April, so the first week of March, we tested the big drum. We had kept a drying fire going all winter in the cave, keeping the drum warm and protected. It was time to waken the spirits.

Wolf Riding Woman, Wolf Rising, Merv Longsteer, and John Little Elk began warming the drum with light taps in the cave. Even the small strikes echoed. Mandy, Caitlin, and I led the drums in the village. Before long, we could hear the thunder rising from the mountain and we moved. We moved the people, their animals, their homes, tents, fires, possessions, and even the earth wall surrounding the village. Of course, no one in the village understood that they had moved. It was less that we physically moved things than that we created a link between *Oxèse* and now-time that manifested them in now-time.

It was not until the People came to the rise of their earthworks to look outside that they saw the monstrous installation about a mile away and the stinger derrick poised to jab into Earth Mother that they realized the magnitude of their task. Some of the younger men wanted to attack immediately, but we knew this was not Creator Wolf and Yelloweye's intent. They did not want an attack. They wanted utter destruction.

In order to keep things under control, we created a bridge between the two realities so that whenever one of the People left the village, whether to hunt or get water or to go to the cave, they left now-time and reentered *Oxèse*. That way our people would not risk interacting with the now-timers.

A MONTH LATER, Mandy gave birth to our precious little Beth Ann. I kept thinking that I wished her other grandparents could be with us. But you… We could never risk the family and the land by pulling you into what we were doing. You are all simply too precious. We'll come to see you as soon as this is over.

OF COURSE, BY mid-April, we'd been discovered. There were Park Rangers at the wall as soon as they could get a snowmobile to us. We all met them, but Mandy was our spokesperson. The rangers were amazed that a thousand people could have snuck into their Park without being noticed and set up a village that looked like it had been there for years. They were also surprised that only those of us from now-time spoke English. We had carefully not taught the People that language.

Our People were equally intrigued by the rangers in their uniforms, their heavy coats, and their strange horses. We explained that these men and women were not the enemy who created the scorpion, but were the caretakers of Earth Mother in this region. When we explained the same thing to the rangers, they were softened and agreed that we were not harming the Park or the wildlife. They decided to list the village as an experimental campground and simply buried it in a pile of their paperwork.

In the meantime, Little Elk kept up the pressure on Shale Oil Company. The company had received over a hundred letters from tribal headquarters across the country protesting the pseudo-fracking operation. They all declared that they stood with the protesters at Yellowstone Grizzly Village as we'd dubbed it in honor of both White Mouth's cave and nearby Grizzly Lake. The hundred or so official letters were only the tip of what the company received. The disciples, as we called them, organized letter writing campaigns among all the People they visited. These letters all declared that SOC would be drummed out of the Park.

And in the midst of the rising pressure, on the third of June, Wolf Riding Woman gave birth to little Avis.

THE RHETORIC IS heated. The company announced they would initiate the pseudo-fracking within a few days. So many protesters have approached the Park that it's been closed. That's good. We don't want that many people in the way when the destruction comes. It's so sad.

But we felt the box open tonight. I understand. Cait and I are twenty-two years old now. We've been gone a year. I'm thankful Ramie waited so long to open the box. But now that it's open, it's all real and we can see the scorpion poised to sting.

In *Oxèse*, thousands… I guess millions of animals have arrived in Grizzly basin. It's time for us to show them how serious we are. Mother

Earth is. We will do everything in our power to limit the damage, but the Old Ones are set on total destruction.

If I don't get back to this, please always remember to consider the land. And that we love you.

15
The Letter

Stig Wolfe: The Truth About Dying

I REMEMBER DYING.

I guess when I was Phile, I started this by telling you I remembered being born. But there are more important things to remember now. I remember the births of my children. I remember my lovers. I remember living as a wild ranch kid in Wyoming and as a renegade in the nineteenth century. I remember holding my sweet sister in my arms at night and knowing there would never be a more perfect match. I remember Mandy welcoming me in both my bodies into her heart and soul.

And I remember dying.

I've decided to write this little letter and put it in the box with the last pages Caitlin and Phile wrote. I know that someday—maybe a long time from now—one of you will open the box again. Perhaps you simply won't believe what happened and need to hear it again. Perhaps it will be one of our children exploring for the first time and trying to dig out the family secrets.

I need to tell you about dying.

It was fast and brutal and painful and unexpected. I rode into battle thinking Yelloweye would protect me. We were confident in Earth Mother and the Old Ones. They chose us for this task. You'd think they'd take care of us.

Imagine having your arm ripped off your body by a ravening beast and then double it. Triple it. It still wouldn't be adequate.

Phile's last thoughts were of Caitlin. For a moment, he imagined them coming home to the land and the family. Of sharing the grandchildren with Moms and Pa. And then it was gone.

Yelloweye was staring at me. Tears were running down my cheeks, but as Wolf Rising, I had to keep pounding that fucking drum or the herds would be lost. We had to return them to their times and places. Wolf Riding Woman, beating on the other side of the drum looked stricken. It was the first I realized that Caitlin had been killed, too, and that she'd experienced that wrenching severance of her other body.

To deal in death, you must know it. Yelloweye swiveled his head from one to the other of us and then fixed Mandy in his gaze. *You must hold them together.*

And poor Mandy! Weeping between the two of us as we pounded the drum and brought death to so many people. We didn't want to deal in death! Merv and Little Elk held the beat steady when we faltered and reached out for our other bodies—to snatch them from the stampede where they'd fallen. When it was over, and our drums fell silent, we collapsed.

I WALK IN the fields here at the ranch, so familiar in Phile's memories yet so new to this body and my senses, and I am still angry at the Old Ones for their betrayal. What right did they have to take away half our being because we were doing what they asked of us? They made us two souls in four bodies and then ripped away half our senses. I hold my daughters in my arms and weep because the body that planted the seed cannot touch the child that grew from it. Rita cries because the body that gave birth to Colin cannot give suck.

So, we spend a lot of time in the fields, riding in the heads of the horses, jumping to the antelope, sometimes catching the lonely cry of a wolf. And we lose ourselves in our precious Talia when we return. She holds us together.

WHAT THE MEDIA cleverly dubbed 'The Oil Field War' or 'The Indian Uprising' isn't over, nor is it limited to oil. Eventually, maybe people will figure out that it is Mother Earth who has decided to fight back. Aside from a few earthquakes, volcanoes, and hurricanes, she'd been silent for thousands of years. And those 'acts of nature' weren't targeted. They were the result of constant irritation and sometimes growth, but they weren't directed specifically.

That's why the spirit animals got involved. Her children. Mother Earth can't just open a crevasse and swallow all the bad people. But her children can be and are more direct. When Creator Wolf sprang at the chairman of Shale Oil Company, it was a direct and targeted attack. I stood in the shadows, riding the mind of Creator Wolf and I felt the death of that evil man. Rita and Talia have children at their breasts and two more on the way. They would suffer any pain to protect them. They understand Mother Earth better than I do. I would also do anything and suffer any pain to protect my children and to protect my wives and to protect the land. But I experience dying each time I act.

I guess there would be fewer wars if we all had that curse. Or blessing. With two more children on the way—and Ramie pregnant, too—it is more important than ever to make the world a better place.

I guess that's all I can tell you.

We won that battle, but the war isn't over.

This land is forever ours. Even when we are dead and buried, we are here to protect our pack and our land. The spirits of this land do not rest. And we are deadly when we hunt.

Still your loving children, Stig, Rita, and Talia

The  End